Inferis

Chris Delude

Published by Chris Delude, 2025.

INFERIS

First edition. November 29, 2025.

ISBN: 979-8998673603

Written by Chris Delude.

Inferis would not have been possible without the help of so many people. My wife, best friend George, and mom have provided so much substantial feedback on the book itself, but also tireless support when I've received hundreds of rejections, spiraled, burned out, and doubted whether I've ever written a single decent sentence in my feeble existence.

My life is also filled with less literate people who haven't done an ounce of work for *Inferis*, but have enriched my life so much that I feel that I wouldn't be capable of writing this without them. My friends provide me with endless laughs, my dad gifted me with the best sense of humor, and my brother will forever inspire me to do cool stuff with my life.

Words cannot express my gratitude toward you all.

PROLOGUE

Living alone is fantastic. I can't say that it gives me an immense joy to walk through the front door and be greeted by nothing and no one; rather, a sense of safety and relief that things are going to be okay the second that walk in. I tried having a roommate to cut costs in half, but after insisting that he was a neat and quiet person, I was still met by the sounds of weeknight parties and puke splattering while I was cooking breakfast in the morning. Never again. That's exactly why I left home in the first place, and why I continue to work at a dead-end job to afford this luxury.

Well, maybe not luxury. I certainly won't be able to heat the apartment above the landlord's required fifty degrees Fahrenheit any time soon. I do what I can to stay warm, though. I've shrink-wrapped every window and sealed it with packing tape. I arguably insulated the apartment too well, given the stifling, greenhouse-level humidity that traps inside after I take showers. I try to do push-ups and sit-ups every thirty minutes. They're not enough to get me in any kind of good physical shape—just enough that I can maintain feeling in my fingertips. I also wear enough blankets that I begin to feel like a mole person, hunched under the weight of them as I waddle back and forth from the kitchen table, bathroom, and bedroom.

I have neighbors above and below me, which makes me horribly claustrophobic. It's clear that each of them lives very distinct lives, because our paper-thin walls allow them the ease of sharing their daily routines with me. The people below are potheads, whose habit seeps through the air ventilation and into my sealed greenhouse climate. They're pretty chill, and the bass from their trap music only pounds my floor until 1:00 AM. Above me is a career woman, who hurriedly gallops in heels at 6:00 AM every weekday. I think she frequently forgets her keys or bag; usually a minute or two after the door shuts, the clip-clopping suddenly reappears in a manic sprint across the length of

1

her room, followed by a door slam. She gets home thirty minutes after I do, sometimes flinging her heels against the door with a relieved thud to end her evening. Once in a while I get the absurd fantasy of knocking on her door with pizza and a cheap bottle of wine, just to have dinner and ask her how her day went. I think she'd like to have someone to talk to. Obviously I don't have the perfect living setup, but I can't afford more. If I moved somewhere else or got another job, I would risk it all getting even worse. This is safe; it's what I know.

Like it or not, I know exactly what to expect at work, too. It's my job to enter peoples' responses from customer satisfaction surveys for the used car dealership, Finway's Automobiles. For nine hours a day, five days a week, I input the survey data into a computer.

TAB-1-TAB-2-TAB-4-TAB-1-TAB-1

We ask each customer a simple question, like "How was your car-buying experience today?" If they check the box that says "Excellent," I code it in our score report as a "5." A score of "4" is good, "3" is satisfactory, "2" is unsatisfactory, and "1" (gasp!) is unacceptable.

1-TAB-1-TAB-2-TAB-1—

Shit. It's easy for me to make mistakes in the score report. I'm staring at a sheet of thousands of numbers. Glaring lights burn my retinas until they ache from the brightness of my computer monitor. Every number looks the same after a while. I'm constantly glancing between the paper surveys in front of me and the monitor above—back, forth, back, forth—like a spectator in the dullest tennis match that has ever taken place. Every day since I started two years ago, the migraines have emerged sooner and sooner. The Minute-Clinic I went to unhelpfully advised me to limit screen time, despite this screen time being the only thing allowing me to pay for the clinic visit. It is my job to keep going, anyway. If my manager walks by and sees that I'm not working, she'll think I'm some lazy, worthless new hire just because I stopped to rub my eyes that one time.

It is 11:42 AM.

INFERIS

I see no one throughout the day. Occasionally I spot the backs of nameless employees inside their cubicles as I quietly walk to the bathroom. No one turns around to say hello. Either they are too absorbed in their work, or too afraid of being caught in a moment of distraction. The best human interaction I experience is with my cubicle neighbor. I have spoken exactly two words to him at a time. He sneezes a lot throughout the day; I assume allergies, poor guy. So, every so often I get to whisper "bless you" toward the dividing wall. He usually mumbles "thank you" back, which I think is nice. If you put him in a police lineup I wouldn't be able to identify him, but I'll be damned if I couldn't pick out that wet sneeze anywhere. I think his name is either Peter or Sonal.

While it's not ideal here either, I'd still be lost without—

"Tim Fischer?"

I swivel in my chair, shocked to hear someone addressing me. I can't place his name, but I remember the forty-something year-old balding man with the long beard from my initial orientation here. He's from HR and seems miserable here, but I could imagine him being the fun bass player in a dad band on the weekends.

"Tim? Could you follow me to my office for a moment?"

"Of course," I manage, standing up.

He leads me down a maze of unfamiliar hallways, and I pass by several people that give me a puzzled...or possibly a pitying look. When we enter, I see that my manager is in there as well.

I swallow.

"Is everything okay...?" I ask.

Of course it isn't.

CHAPTER 1

I am a closeted Oddhobbler. "Oddhobs" are how I classify the strange, niche hobbies that I've acquired over a lifetime of boredom and isolation. Oddhobs can be difficult to define at times, but I typically include anything that I would be ashamed to tell ninety-eight percent of people. For example, I spent an entire summer teaching myself to juggle seven balls at once. One day, my stepdad heard the tumble of balls from my room and opened the door. When he saw me practicing, he asked if I was gay.

"No, I don't think so," my nine-year-old self responded. "I just saw it on T.V."

"What the fuck," he muttered to himself, leaving the room.

I waited until his footsteps were back downstairs and closed the door. Then I went on practicing.

Not all of my oddhobs are circus-based—that was just a phase. Pickling, folding napkins into swans, knot-tying, knitting, book-binding, photoshopping (mostly taking the ears off of pug photos, because it makes them look cuter), collecting edible mushrooms, shaping bonsai trees, calligraphy. For most of these, I spend some brief season of obsession with them and then move on to the next. It took me an embarrassingly long time to understand that my stepdad's reaction to oddhobs was indicative of the standard. Showing kids at school...didn't usually go well. Especially as I got older. Sharing homemade chocolate (after weeks of perfecting the art) earned me the nickname Betty Cocksucker. Knot-tying invoked the suggestion "next time make a noose."

Eventually, I learned—there are some things you just keep to yourself. Unfortunately, if the vast majority of your time is spent doing things that can't be shared, it results in a closing off of the self. I had nothing else to say, nothing to contribute that wouldn't earn me a new name, a new mess in my locker, a new bruise. My oddhobs allow me to find myself and occupy my inevitable boredom, while also contributing to it by isolating me from everyone. They're repetitive, relaxing, solitary activities that reward me for not having plans on a Friday night. They're...safe.

Since I was fifteen, the only person that I've outed myself to is my best friend, Sophia. She giggles at some of them, sure, but with her it's different. She asks me what oddhob I've been up to lately, usually shaking her head and saying "classic Tim" with a smile. She asks me to show her some, too. For her high school graduation gift, I made her a wood carving of her and her dog, Roxie, who had died at the beginning of the year. She hugged me hard and said it was the best gift that she'd gotten. It's still up in her room now, all these years later. She says I should show some of my hobbies to her sister Grace sometime, but I usually find some excuse not to. I like Grace, she's nice. It's not that I'm scared. I...I just don't need everyone to know everything about me. Sophia is enough.

Right now, staring up at the endless, fathomless night sky, I'm enjoying my most treasured and lasting oddhob. Stargazing and astronomy started as a textbook-learning endeavor: memorizing the seven classifications of celestial bodies, the eighty-eight constellations, and the star magnitudes of brightness. It took the entire summer of my junior year of high school—after grueling ten-hour shifts at a local hardware store—to realize it was so much more than studying charts and basic astrophysics. It was escape. No—more than escape; I had hidden in video game and fantasy book worlds before. Looking up at the night sky feels like I'm looking into all of the depths of myself and the universe in one singular moment. It's the contextualization of me and everything. I don't understand myself or why the hell I feel the way that I do, but somehow, breathing this confusion upwards allows my mind and soul to healthily release itself—to stretch out its legs and roam freely, in a way that would be toxic if left shuddered inward and spiraling.

Tonight is my last night to gaze from this familiar vantage. For a while, at least. My back aches from laying on the bench next to my apartment building. It's a familiar ache, and well worth the cost. Weed smoke wafts by me as the basement dwellers light up. I see a shooting star sail across the sky, fading into the beyond. People think that they're rare to spot, but I've seen dozens, maybe hundreds of shooting stars in the few years I've been doing this. Truthfully, it's just that most people never take the time to look up.

After losing my job at Finway's three weeks ago, I started ravenously applying to everything I could. Things that I had experience doing, and things I absolutely wasn't qualified for. It didn't matter. I need a roof over my head, and for a short while, at least, I've found one. I'm heading to Sommers, New York tomorrow morning for a one-month job as a house-sitter. It's for some rich couple, Scott and Jeanette Marsh, who need me to take care of their cute dog and help around the house while they visit their sick mother in Texas. I don't know them at all except for two lengthy Zoom interviews, and a tentative trust that they aren't lunatics. Beyond this house-sitting stint, I don't have any plan or focus for my future—only a vague fear that everything I've started so far has been wrong. This fear has, for the first time, overcome my other vague fear of stepping into the unknown. I've been realizing more and more that I don't know what's actually good for me. How little I understand about my own happiness.

CHAPTER 2

Scott and Jeanette's winding, uneven dirt driveway reminds me that a 2007 Toyota Camry is not an all-terrain vehicle. The GPS tells me that I've arrived, but I can't see any house. Dark, shadowed pine trees are illuminated in my high beams.

This is a murder place; every true crime podcast, horror movie, and Criminal Minds episode that's seeped into my subconscious convinces me of this. I genuinely consider turning back. Just like every idiot horror movie protagonist that you heckle from your couch...I continue driving forward. My nerves gradually fade as the trees end, and I'm suddenly bathed in the warm glow of surrounding gas lamps. Floodlights shine from an old and well-preserved green Victorian house. The dirt road transitions to a newly paved driveway lined with a thick green lawn, pristinely manicured hedges, and tasteful Autumn decorations adorning a white wrap-around porch with a cozy rocking chair.

I slow to a stop, already worried that I might be blocking in one of their SUV's. As soon as I take the keys out of the ignition, the front door of the home opens and a slender female figure emerges. Jeanette (shorter than I expected) comes trotting breathlessly down the porch steps and hastily wraps a gray cardigan around her shoulders. She smiles and waves energetically, face flushed.

"It's so great to see you, Tim! Thank you again for agreeing to do this on such a short notice...you're really saving us. Things have been so hectic lately with my mother's health, and we've just finished renovations on the living room—it's beautiful, and worth it now—but none of this has been good timing, particularly for Scott who's had a lot of layoffs at work and has had to take on a lot more responsibilities..." Jeanette stress-rambles on, winding herself up like an air raid siren. I smile and nod politely as she leads me up the creaking wood porch and into the front door. I inhale the aroma of a Snickerdoodle-scented candle that welcomes me inside. The interior of the house is beautiful, opening up to—

A sudden jingling.

Jeanette tenses momentarily. "Lulu no!!"

Thirty pounds of smiling Jack Russell Terrier pup rush me. I don't stand a chance. Jeanette hurriedly tries grabbing at her collar to pull her back, but I've already gotten to my knees, making panting, tongue-out faces. The cutest living being on Earth. A goddess amongst mortals. I hit all the best spots: scratching behind the scruff of her floppy ears, rustling at her hips after she spins excitedly, tail wagging. Ten seconds later I remember where I am. I look up sheepishly toward Jeanette and the newly emerged Scott who are both grinning. Scott's broad shoulders and red flannel shirt remind me of the Brawny man from the paper towel rolls.

"I think we made the right choice, hun," Scott says, smiling and wrapping his arm around his wife.

Jeanette nods. "Our flight leaves in about five hours," she says, glancing at a thin, expensive-looking watch on her wrist. "We should head out pretty soon. Do you want to give Tim a quick tour of the house while I check our things one more time?"

"Let's do it," Scott says, ushering me to the right. "Alrighty...living room! I'll say this for every room, but we want you to make yourself at home here. Lulu might scratch at the couch a bit, something might get spilled...that's all fine so long as you're generally respectful of the space and take care of it. Sound good?"

No, it doesn't sound good, Scott. The living room looks like the immaculate "after" photos of an HGTV dream home. Every curtain, piece of furniture, painting, and knickknack is perfectly matching, falling within a green, white, and brown color scheme. Everything is evenly spaced and correctly placed. The coffee table by the couch is arranged to give the appearance of casual use, with a few color-coordinated, blank-looking books fanned out on top of each other next to a rustic candle. Who could be relaxed in a place you're terrified to disturb?

While still perfectly designed, the kitchen luckily looks a little Lulu-worn; I see a few scratches on the stainless-steel fridge, and a cozy beige dog mat with messy food and water bowls on the hardwood floor. Lulu trails after us everywhere we go, supervising the tour. In the kitchen she U-turns toward a white-grated wooden pantry door, swiping at the knobbed handles with her paws and poking at it with her nose.

"We're going to need to lock my chocolate-covered pretzels in a bank vault," Scott says, laughing. "She actually managed to get in one time when we left the door open a crack. If you keep it completely shut there shouldn't be a problem."

"Caught in the act," I say, pointing at the terrier pup. She looks back, smiling and panting, then trots back toward the two of us.

Scott shifts a silently sliding glass door at the back of the kitchen. A motion-censored floodlight reveals a beautiful stone patio in the backyard. Cushioned reclining chairs are surrounded by flowerbeds of orange and maroon mums. A built-in stone firepit and a charcoal grill the size of an oil drum overlook a sea of green lawn...followed by an endless dark forest.

"Not sure if you're very outdoorsy," Scott adds, seeing me transfixed, "but there are a lot of great trails out there. Small beginner loops and longer ones, if you're interested."

"Do you have to worry about, like, bears or anything out there?"

Scott's head pendulums back and forth, considering. "There are some black bears deeper out there, sure. But not too many. They generally avoid humans and dogs, so if you let Lulu out or you go out yourself, you don't need to worry."

"Do you let Lulu out there by herself?"

"Oh yeah, definitely. Usually in the morning I just open the slider door and she goes out for a few hours. She always comes back," he adds, seeing my concern. "Dogs have more sense than any of us do, and she gets along with every hiker out there. That puppy energy can only stay inside for so long or it'll tear the place apart. Usually by nine or ten o'clock she'll come back to eat, relax for a while, then I'll let her out at four."

"Got it," I say.

My guest bedroom is simple and neat enough. It has a full-sized bed, a small night-stand, and a dresser drawer for clothes. All of it nautical-themed, for some reason. I didn't know so many anchor and lighthouse statuettes were produced in the world. What percentage of the garbage that's swirling in the Pacific Ocean is faux nautical décor? I'll probably sleep terribly in this house (because I do everywhere I go), but it seems like a comfortable place to lay awake at 3:00 AM. The connected bathroom has framed inspirational wall-art hung everywhere, which should hopefully encourage regular bowel movements.

Finally, the basement. I immediately cough from the dusty air. Scott pulls a dangling metal chain in the ceiling, and an old, exposed lightbulb illuminates the warped wooden floor planks. He walks forward and pulls two more chains, one of which is a dud; the bulb flickers for a few seconds and dies.

"Basement," Scott says, shrugging. A rickety metal boiler stands in front of us. Far to the left is an old tool bench, as well as a dented metal door that looks like it leads to more storage space. To the left of us is a heap of old boxes, appliances, and junk. "We're thinking about having it re-done soon, but with everything going on right now we just don't have the energy to take on another project."

I nod, smiling. It's objectively the shabbiest part of the home, and probably as bad for my lungs as a pack of cigarettes. Still, it's oddly comforting to see a piece of the house that looks original. This basement is authentically built for the function of being a basement.

INFERIS

As we lumber up the stairs, Jeanette is calling down from somewhere.

"Almost ready, Scott? We need to head out!"

"Coming!" he calls back, chuckling to himself. "I swear we would get to the airport three days early if she had her way."

We emerge back up to the immaculate hallway and are assaulted with a barrage of reminders. "We've said all of this before—and it should be listed in the email I sent you—but we will be visiting my mother from September 29 until October 23 while she recovers from surgery." As Jeanette continues, she folds her fingers together in front of her, clasped like a school administrator. Her lips are as thin as a pencil. "We have a few DIY projects that we were hoping to get to ourselves, but given the circumstances we haven't had the time. There are full written instructions for everything on the chore list in the kitchen. The yard is overwhelmed with leaves to rake, the basement needs to get cleaned out, the..."

With every item she lists, her voice trembles in a higher pitch of frantic exasperation. Scott, noticing the same behavior (and perhaps my uncomfortable reaction), dives in.

"Any of these side projects aren't necessary if you don't have the time or aren't interested. We have plenty to keep you busy with if you want, and we would certainly pay you for any extra you manage to get done. We really just care about keeping Lulu safe and having the place in good shape when we get back. We want you to feel at home here."

I nod vigorously, again ignoring this statement. I hardly feel at home in my own home; there's no way in hell I'm displacing a single thing other than perishable food. I'll be like a museum curator, and no one will know I spent a month of my life here.

My face clearly gives away my hesitation. "Settle in, Tim!" Scott goads me, chuckling. "We want this to be a good experience for you, too. We trust that you will do a wonderful job."

Jeanette chimes in, smiling nervously. "From everything you've sent us and told us, we have absolute faith that you will do this responsibly. You had excellent personal and professional references."

"Plus no psychotic face tattoos," Scott adds, raising his eyebrows. "You laugh now, but the last person we interviewed had some...unseemly images inked on his forehead. He may have been as upstanding as his application described, but I got the hint that his version of good judgement may slightly differ from ours." We all laugh, although it seems painful for Jeanette's face to do so.

"The instructions should cover everything," Jeanette continues, "but if you have any questions at all, just call or text us right away."

"Absolutely, you can count on it," I say.

"Thank you again, Tim. This really means the world to us. I..."

A car horn beeps outside, and Scott peeks out of the window.

"Uber's here. All set, honey?"

The front door closes behind them. Lulu and I stand side-by-side, looking out at the couple dumping their luggage into the trunk of a black sedan. Lulu lets out a whimper, then bounds back to the kitchen. They drive off and the taillights fade, amidst the sounds of scratching claws at the pantry door.

CHAPTER 3

Today is my first full day here, and I intend to make the most of it. After feeding Lulu and letting her outside, I spend hours at the kitchen table on my laptop. I was lucky to get this gig, but it'll only hold me over for a month unless I keep aggressively applying to jobs. I expand my search to even more house-sitting opportunities that I find; if this one goes well, I'll have Scott and Jeanette to vouch for me. Maybe this could be my thing...perching in other people's lives and making sure their stuff doesn't burn down when they're busy. I grab a bag of granola from the pantry, munching on it indiscriminately as I scroll through all the opportunities that I don't deserve.

Without any idea of what I want with my life, I feel like it's inevitable for me to end up right back where I started: some low-paying, dead-end job like Finway's that lets me go as soon as it's convenient. I've spent a lifetime of doing exactly what I was supposed to—getting good grades, working hard, following the rules—but none of it has brought a moment's joy. Rather, this blind compliance has festered into wild fantasies of abandoning it all. Fantasies that are unanimously considered fucking up my life—of my sneakers scraping against the gravel along the tracks of a freight train at two in the morning, sprinting to catch up to it and stepping onto a side foothold. Ducking away as the engineer looks back. I ride it to the neighboring town, or all the way to California. It doesn't matter. I dye my hair with streaks of pink and get a job in a worn-out shack along the beach selling fish tacos. I've never had a fish taco, and I don't even like fish. Yet still, my mind keeps creeping back to it again and again.

I sigh, opening five more Indeed tabs and shoveling another handful of granola in my mouth.

In the early evening, I find the energy to make myself an actual meal. Contrary to the stereotype, Jeanette and Scott did not once mention that they were vegan. I stand here agape, looking at the saddest

13

refrigerator I have ever seen. No meat is manageable enough, but everything is...so green...so soy. Entirely void of cheese. Not a single, lonely egg. If I Google recipes it's possible that I could muster up some sadness of a meal, but I'm already managing enough novelty just by being here. I grab my keys and wallet from my bedside table, a thick maroon sweatshirt from my bag, and head out.

I see Lulu darting in circles in the woods by the driveway. The evening sun is waning. A light breeze creates a few ambient flutters of leaves and creaking of trees, reminding me to deeply inhale the fresh, woodsy air surrounding me. Lulu emerges as I approach my car. Oh god, there's something in her mouth...

"Lulu, no!!" I say.

The puppy stops next to me, dropping a horribly mangled, bleeding squirrel on the paving stones at my feet.

"Lulu, bad! We don't..." I grimace at the sight of the lifeless rodent. There are matted smears of blood on Lulu's muzzle and on the fur around her smiling mouth. Yes, disturbingly enough, she's still smiling and happily panting. Just as happy as she is when I pet her, feed her, or let her out. She looks up excitedly, proud of her work. I suppose I shouldn't be shaming a dog for doing exactly what nature designed it to do. I'm certain that Jeanette doesn't want carcasses littering her driveway, though, so I head to the toolshed in the backyard. I suck in my stomach to squeeze past Scott's riding mower and find a plastic snow shovel hanging on a hook. I scoop up 95% of the mess, scraping the plastic against the bloody paving stones—oh god the texture feels so weird—and catapult it into the trees. Luckily, she doesn't treat it like a game of fetch. Lulu tails me throughout the process, still happily boasting of her kill. I shake my head. Confused, upset, queasy...I decide to walk to the market instead. I need the fresh air.

Sheridan's Market is a mile and a half from the house, and the walk there is absolutely picturesque. The sun is setting through the blazing canopy surrounding me, with yellow and orange leaves drifting...twirling...tumbling by my feet like I'm in an Autumn snow globe. I hear them crinkling against the ground, crunching under my sneakers. In the lowering light, I see an adult and baby deer trotting off to the side of the road. They don't even seem to be in a rush. No hunters nearby to make this a Bambi-moment, either. Only one car passes by me, and the driver waves at me like we're old friends. The homes surrounding the street are as small, colorful, and cute as gingerbread homes. The crisp air smells like chimney smoke. Why haven't I done this every day of my life?

The small brick façade of Sheridan's comes into view. The front looks like every other gas station market I've seen in my life: giant lottery and tobacco posters, neon beer signs, and an industrial white ice machine. There's a very thin man to the side of the door in an oversized flannel rummaging through a trash bin. He places several bottles on the ground next to a black trash bag filled with others, each one emitting a hollow clink against the pavement. I get stressed out every time I walk by a potentially unhoused person. Not because I'm afraid of them, but because I never know what to do. Is it kind or enabling to give money? Should I offer to help or is it insulting to go up and ask? My nervous glances and hyperventilating probably feel more threatening to them than anything they've done to me.

As I'm walking by, there's something that catches me in the man's eyes. He isn't angry or crazy looking. There's a sad resolution there that reminds me of...me. Not me if I were unhoused, just me. I don't know if I look like that too, or if it's just how I feel.

"Do...do you need anything?" I ask. "I'm on my way in. I've got some extra cash."

His sad eyes shift down to the ground. Then he goes back to digging in the trash bin. I've fucked up, again. The jangling of bottles resumes—mixing with the jingling of the market door as I cross the threshold to the clean, temperature-controlled rows of food.

CHAPTER 4

I t would be rude to flirt with her.

I open the cardboard egg carton in my hands to inspect for cracks. They mostly look fine, but I need more time to strategize about the cashier. I'm sure the next carton will look better.

Attractive girls get hit on all the time; shouldn't they just be left alone? Especially at work...I mean she's trapped behind that stupid counter, forced to smile at every toothless creep out there. She's got no way to safely say no, even if she wants to.

A large drip of cold water falls from the refrigerator and runs down the back of my neck, as if nudging me to hurry up and decide. I nod my head at egg carton number four and turn to—

"I'm so sorry!" I say instinctively, bumping into an older woman behind me. Her skin is wrinkled leather, topped with waves of curling bleach blonde hair peeling away from tired gray roots. In my sudden guilt, I don't register that she's smoking a cigarette indoors.

The woman finishes a long drag...staring me down silently...and exhales just to the side of my face. "Bump into me again and I'll cut your fuckin' balls off. Little shit." Her finger taps the ashes off the smoldering butt and onto the white tile floor. She walks away toward the Slim Jims. She's wearing dirty pink flip flops and tight blue booty shorts, despite being at least fifty-five years old and it being forty-five degrees outside. She might try to say something else to me, so I quickly stick my head back in the refrigerator and begin inspecting egg carton number five. I let out a small, pathetic cough into the eggs from her lingering tobacco smoke.

If everyone thinks the cashier is too hot to approach (which she is), then maybe she never has nice guys that talk to her. She might wish someone would for once. I'm lonely, why can't she be? We can just chat. So long as whatever I say is something I'd say to a seventy-year old man, then there's no pressure or sketchy undertones to worry about.

And if she happens to give some subtle hint that she's interested in me—for example, "I am wildly attracted to you, egg-boy. Let's make love."—then I might consider engaging more. We'll see.

Carton number five actually looks much worse than number four, but at this point I've misplaced number four among the other cartons and I've been in here looking for a ludicrous amount of time. I put carton five in my basket with my other groceries and head to the front. From behind the candy aisle I hear a tired voice say, "Mrs. Levin don't start this crap with me again...you know you can't light that in here."

"Girl, I told you last time I'm trying to quit! And if I ever talked to my elders like you're doing, I'd be strung up by my toenails!"

I try to stay a safe distance away.

The girl behind the counter rolls her eyes; the black makeup surrounding them makes the annoyance on her face really pop. "Very proud of you for quitting; however, you still can't take it indoors. You were inside for all of 60 seconds. I am quite certain that you can make it that long without lighting up. Your total is $12.76."

The woman mutters under her breath, but no more trouble comes after. She pulls a few crumpled bills from her tight blue waistband and hands them to cashier. To her credit, the girl seems to have put the incident completely behind her now that the woman has stopped blowing literal and figurative smoke in her face. That's what I'll say. Yeah...something like "Damn, that was crazy." Or maybe "What a psycho. Does she come here a lot?" Questions are good. They invite further conversation. But if she's already putting it behind her, then maybe she doesn't want to talk about it more. It might not be smart to get market girl in a bad mood by—

"I can ring you up now."

I've spaced out. I fumble forward and begin rummaging through my basket, flinging my loaf of bread, several cheeses, frozen meals, and other contents onto the counter.

BEEP.

BEEP.

I feel like I'm airing out my dirty laundry in front of her with every barcode scan. What kind of pathetic guy buys frozen dinners at a gas station? If she mentions anything about how long it took to pick out my eggs, I might die.

BEEP.

BEEP.

"Your total is $42.98."

Again fumbling for my wallet. Somehow I'm always caught off guard when cashiers ask for money. I should know the procedure by now.

"Have a nice day," she says, bored but not unfriendly.

"Thanks," I say, scooping the white plastic bags off the counter. I hurry through the doorway of the gas station door, bell ringing behind me to announce my withering exit. The man rummaging through the trash is gone.

The walk home is darker, and I begin to regret not driving. The sun purples and fades in the growing night, and bugs circle around me. There's a warm glow of light in each of the surrounding gingerbread homes, fending off and insulating them against the dangers of darkness. I see families shuffling in the kitchen, gathering and chatting casually.

"School drop-off might be a problem tomorrow because I have a dentist appointment; could your mother take her?"

"This tastes different...you don't usually put red peppers in the stir fry, do you? I think I like it better the other way...still fine though."

"Honey, don't just leave that on the floor—pick it up! Headphones off at the—yes! Because we're eating and I said so, that's why!"

INFERIS

I smile at the thought of their lives. I often tell myself to celebrate the freedom and independence of going home alone to my apartment every night, and yet still there's this nagging feeling that I'm trapped. Sometimes, somehow, I feel less like myself when I'm by myself. A person who knows you can find a way to make you more like yourself; to extract the you right out of you. Gazing into those glowing homes...I would give up everything I have to feel the dullness of their comforts.

CHAPTER 5

S cott was abundantly clear that tackling any side projects around the house wasn't necessary. Naturally, I plan to complete all of them.

Yes, I could use the extra money and a glowing recommendation from them. It's more than that, though. I feel a strange loyalty to Scott and Jeanette for giving me this opportunity when I need it most, and I don't want them to regret giving me a chance. This is such a cushy job, and just doing the bare minimum for them doesn't seem like enough, especially because they're already worried about a sick family member. So, I peruse the laminated, color-coded chore list (Jeanette's neuroticism is a thing of beauty) and decide to clean out some of the mess in the basement.

Scott and Jeanette decreed that their pile of rusted appliances, boxes of old clothes, and items destroyed by the beloved monster Lulu all must go—whether by donation or by dumpster. The items are haphazardly stacked on top of each other, covering at least a quarter of the basement floor. I stare at the pile, uncertain what to pull at without causing an avalanche. I start with a dusty box of clothes near the top that's labeled "old vacation."

I am deranged enough to thoroughly enjoy the satisfaction of cleaning. There's something about the concoction of rat droppings, pinched fingers, cement dust, and bleach fumes that invokes a focused, grounded sense of aggression. Every pulled muscle becomes a personal fuck you to the mess at hand. I make a "toss" pile for appliances that are obviously broken beyond use, and a second for ones that can likely be donated. I lift each appliance to its new pile, occasionally needing to drag some with a horrible metallic shriek. I need a utility knife to flatten the boxes lying around, but the only one that Scott has on his workbench is unused and still in the sharp plastic packaging. Clearly he's not the Brawny man I had assumed him to be. Unfortunately, opening the packaging to get the utility knife requires a knife, which I don't yet have. I try peeling off the back cardboard, carving at it with my car keys, and eventually devolve into gnawing at it with my teeth. Then I remember that there are scissors in the kitchen.

Eventually I manage to flatten the remaining boxes, fill several extra-strength trash bags with clothes, and toss it all in the trunk of my car like a homicide victim. I take a break, sweat beading on my forehead. I heave, coughing; the stale basement air feels like it's pumping spider webs into my lungs like a bellows. But the job is done! The floor underneath the original boxes is now finally visible, and the biggest appliances are neatly shifted against the back wall. I smile at the thought of Scott and Jeanette coming home, surprised and delighted by the progress. Several hours have passed since I started, and it suddenly dawns on me that my stomach is desperately consuming itself from hunger.

As I stand up, I pass by the dead light bulb that I noticed during Scott's tour. I'll handle it quickly before foraging for a meal. I find a box of light bulbs on a dusty storage shelf and hope that one fits. Still red-faced and out of breath, I drag a heavy, paint-smeared stool and prop it underneath the dastardly dark bulb. Climbing up, the stool feels rickety despite being so heavy. I unscrew the existing bulb and give it a shake to hear the satisfying jingle of the dead filaments inside. I delicately put it in my pocket and screw the new one into the socket. The light bulb suddenly turns on! I feel the satisfaction of being "handy" for all of 0.2 seconds before the step stool suddenly jolts. I drop—flailing for balance—landing on the side of my leg and catching some of the brunt force with my right arm. I wince in pain, my knee and arm both throbbing from the impact. The dead lightbulb falls out of my pocket and rolls back and forth across the floor in crescent shapes. At least it didn't shatter.

Lulu hears the thud and comes plowing down the stairs, barking in panic. She runs straight toward me and wiggles her wet nose across my dirty hand, my knee, and my face.

"All good," I tell her, smiling as I scratch under her chin. "Just took a bit of a tumble."

We both calm down and take turns sniffing at the scene. "Crap," I mutter, seeing the cause of the fall. I thought the old stool had broken underneath me. Instead, the back-left leg of it collapsed through the rotted wooden planks of the floor. It left a hole where the splintered planks caved in.

"Crap crap. No...shoo Lulu! No sniffing at splinters!"

I scoot her away, sighing in frustration. Any joy I had imagined giving to Scott and Jeanette instantly vanishes. Beneath the splintered planks, I see wooden support beams that are severely rotted all the way through. Exposed earth is visible underneath. A wide hole—fuck, I could almost fit through that—bores into the ground. I gingerly reach my hand inside to clear one of the splintered boards. The back of my skin prickles as it feels cool, damp air blowing from below. I don't know how big woodchucks or gophers are, but they must have burrowed directly underneath the house somehow.

I take my phone out of my pocket and undo the Ziplock bag that it's in. Yes, most people agree it's ridiculous and paranoid of me to keep my phone in a Ziplock bag. Most of those people have lost their phones to dust and water damage, so their opinions do not concern me. I shine my phone flashlight into the widened gap, seeing nothing but dirt and deeper tunnel.

Okay...okay. I didn't really make the hole. It was rotted and they knew the basement was in tough shape already. I can just go to the hardware store and pick up a few planks...at least a slab of plywood to cover the hole. I'll let Jeanette and Scott know that it's there. They won't appreciate the extra costs, but they will like being able to get ahead of it and call an exterminator to remove the tunneling bear underneath their house. I rummage through Scott's workbench and find a ratty brown tarp. I resurrect some of the boxes I had just broken up, grab a roll of duct tape, and make a patch over the hole. After a few minutes of labor...it looks horrible. For now, at least, it should be good enough to keep Lulu from spelunking.

CHAPTER 6

I'm too tired to work, but the guilt of breaking their floor forces me to do something productive in penance. The next item on the chore list is: *"Scott noticed an issue with the water pressure in the upstairs bathrooms. Please call plumber. He does weekends. See phone number in the directory under P."*

Within fifteen minutes of calling the doorbell rings, followed immediately by a double knock on the door. I open the door and see a forty-something year old Korean man. He has tangled and knotted black hair down to his shoulders, which hold the strap of a heavy, weathered tan bag full of tools. He reaches out his hand to mine.

"Bobby. Trouble with the water heater?"

I'm standing between the doorframe and the open door, but as he shakes my hand he is already in stride to walk in. The John Wayne of plumbing. "Hi...I'm Tim," I say, realizing that he never asked. "Yes, I think there's an issue with the water pressure in some of the faucets, and maybe the shower? I looked..."

He doesn't stop to listen. Bobby is already in the house, and I fumble with my useless explanation while shutting the door behind us. Bobby's faded blue jeans sag just below his cracked and worn black shoes, which squeak a few times against the shiny hardwood. The obsessive in me considers asking him to take them off at the door, but I'm confident that I would have an easier time stopping a freight train. Also, maybe it's some sort of occupational hazard to have handy-people work without shoes?

Lulu comes over on cue. Her claws scrape and slide along the hardwood floor as she propels herself toward us, her puppy weight bowling around the corner. Lulu worms in between my legs and scoots her way toward Bobby.

"Hello, friend," he says warmly, ruffling behind her ears and breaking into a calm, genuine smile. She circles around and in-between

24

his legs in a figure-eight, tail wagging. I open the white door to the basement, and gesture for him to lead the way. He hardly delays before plunging down. Lulu tails him happily, claws scratching down in off-beats between his heavy footfalls.

Bobby looks like a crime scene detective, already leaning by the water heater and checking the pipes behind it. Lulu's attention is split between Bobby and the bugs scuttering into the cracks of the floor.

"Good girl...such a good girl," he says, absently petting Lulu as he pulls a mini flashlight out of his pocket. I stand there watching him work, contributing only to the consumption of limited oxygen in a dank basement. I don't know if it's standard procedure for me to stay here with him if he needs anything, or to give him space to do his job. I glance at the taped tarp on the floor and grimace.

Just as I'm about to summon the nerve to ask him how long it might take, Bobby rises awkwardly—limping a bit on his right leg, which might have fallen asleep. There's a clattering of tools as he returns everything to his bag.

"I fixed the immediate cause of the leak. T&P valve got loose." He adjusts the shoulder strap on his bag. "The valve looks rusted so you might have more issues with it in the near future. Unless you replace the part. It's an older tank so I'd have to order it. I could come back next Friday, same time. The labor for today is going to run you $70; it was nice and easy. The part will run you about $50 plus the labor for installing it, which should be pretty quick, too."

I nod seriously, as if weighing the diagnosis against my vast plumbing expertise. Truthfully, it's not my money, and I surprisingly trust this guy not to invent problems or inflate the price by 80,000%. After what feels like a convincing amount of time, I say "That would be great, thank you so much."

"Perfect," he says, heading back towards the stairs, hound at heel.

Everyone stand back. I will now attempt small talk. "Do you have to deal with a lot of peoples' pets on the job?" I ask, a little out of breath as we return to the first floor.

He reaches down to eye level with Lulu, tenderly rubbing her around the collar. She looks blissfully hypnotized. "Quite a lot," he replies. "It used to be a drag for me, dealing with all of the barking...biting...shitting. But I got good with them when I understood that we're all animals. If you understand yourself at all..." he turns back to Lulu and smiles again. "...then you understand them, too."

I hand him the cash payment, and he crumples it into his pocket.

"I'll be back on Friday. Same time."

The squeaky black shoes see themselves out.

CHAPTER 7

I was unfortunately correct about not being able to sleep. The peaceful nautical décor mocks me, and by 2:00 AM I give up.

I turn on the light and my laptop. Lulu was on the floor beside me all night, but the light cues her in that I'm welcoming visitors; she jumps onto the bed and scoots next to me, laying down. Scrolling Netflix for a few minutes, I decide to watch *Jackass: The Movie* after seeing it recently added on the home screen. I haven't watched it since I was in the sixth grade, but honestly, I'm too tired to think or process anything else of substance. I press play, leaning back against a propped pillow. Lulu rests her sleepy head on my hip, occasionally glancing up at me.

Thinking back, there's something special about garbage MTV programming in the 2000's. Of course I expected it to be stupid, but some of the things these guys are doing is just unreal. Taking riot bullets to the chest, getting attacked by heavyweight boxers in convenience stores, leaving a live alligator in their parents' kitchen...how does anybody act so wild? I feel like I'm crazy if I take one extra Advil than the back of the bottle recommends, yet I somehow share the same species as these maniacs. I'm stupefied by their physicality, spontaneity, and comradery. I can't help but watch more.

Hours pass, until the sun slowly rises underneath the bedroom curtains. I sigh, officially giving up on sleep in favor for the new day. I'm about to get up to brush my teeth when I feel my phone buzz. I glance down lazily, seeing a message from Sophia.

> "Hey! Lawrence and I are coming up to New York for his med school interview this morning. Want us to stop by after we're done? No problem if you're busy, just figured you might want some company."

I look at the lump of dog on my lap, at the mess of bedsheets after a tough night's sleep, and down the empty hallway of the eerily silent house. Sophia always knows how I'm feeling before I do.

"Yeah, stop by! Scott and Jeanette said I can have guests over too."
"Yaaay, can't wait!"

I smile to myself. Since they started dating almost two years ago, I can't say that I've gotten to know Lawrence on any deep or personal level. I really like him, though, because I've seen how Soph truly acts like herself around him. She's never been this happy with someone before.

In high school, a significant proportion of Sophia's angst revolved around dating. Her time was almost entirely focused on schoolwork and family drama. Because she either had her nose pressed against a book or was racing to her aunt's house, she gave off "not interested" vibes to most guys. So they ignored her, and she buried herself deeper in work and home because it took her mind off feeling ignored. When some asshole finally did cross her path—we no longer speak his name—she was so excited and so terrified that it would end, that she inevitably did whatever he wanted. What dates to go on, what friends of his to hang out with, how she should dress, and worse. Everything a girlfriend should do for her man, should *want* to do. The few times she did stick up for herself, he stereotyped her as the "sassy Latina type." Scared to be a puppet, scared to be strong. Scared to be alone.

It was horrible. The two of us would talk for hours, her crying and beating herself up over all the ways she could have been better. It was easy for me to correct her; I've never known anyone nicer than Sophia. I cherished the time we spent together, even if it was under distressing circumstances. I was there for her when she needed someone to listen, to complain about *him*, to tell her that she was a person who deserved love and respect. I was also there to do impressions of our geometry teacher, Mrs. Levinson, who had such a squawking voice that we couldn't hear the word "isosceles" without choking in laughter. Snotty, teary chuckles muffled on the other end of the line every time I did it. Even when I got sick of the impersonation (the high pitch honestly hurt my throat), I never tired of making her feel better.

It'll be nice to see the two of them later. I can get to know Lawrence better, and the three of us can have a nice relaxing hang.

CHAPTER 8

"I am so sorry, Tim!!!" Sophia pleads, as Lulu and Lawrence run up the staircase with Sophia's bags.

"Be careful with your stuff!" I call up to him. "Lulu can possibly open the pantry door, so she might be able to get in closets, too."

All I hear in response is "Girl, you got thumbs under them paws!?"

I already regret saying yes to this.

"Tim..." Sophia begs.

"It's fine," I say, rubbing my eyes to fend off an impending headache. "Remind me what happened again?"

"Well, I told you we were coming up for his medical school interview. Then on our way over, the admissions office at Weill Cornell—his top choice—called out of nowhere, trying to schedule an interview with him in two days. We don't have to sleep over if it's too much for you; we can head home and then just drive back again for the interview first thing on Wednesday. I told him it might not be a great idea to come but...you know how he gets. Boy's like a puppy."

I smirk despite the stress. "Don't worry. It really is great to see you two. It's just not my house, so I'm a little extra..."

"You're a little extra Tim," she says, rubbing my shoulder and smiling. "But I totally get it. We'll stay here for two days tops, and it'll save us a buttload of driving and gas money. We'll cover pizza tonight if that helps?" She gives me the cheesiest, charming smirk I've ever seen.

"Alriiight," I say. "But have you had *the talk* with him yet?"

"The..."

"Come on, he's been wearing those color-coded jumpsuits for almost a year now! I thought it was driving you nuts, how have you put up with it for this long?"

"Don't hate me."

That's all she says. "Sophia..."

She laughs, wide eyes pleading with me. "Tim, I said don't hate me. Those are very clear instructions."

"Are you telling me that you actually like the jumpsuits now?"

She pokes me in the stomach with a creepy grin. "What if I told you I do...and that I have a *really* cute green one in my suitcase at this very moment?"

I sigh. "Sadness. Loss. Betrayal. These are some of the many complex emotions I am feeling at this time."

"Stop itttt!"

"Jumpsuits are a gateway drug. It starts with a 'cute' green one, and pretty soon you're Mr. and Mrs. Crayola!"

From upstairs, we hear Lawrence say the cryptic words "Gotta be a beehive, goddamn!" Not enough context in the world could explain what comes out of that man's mouth. We're both belly-laughing as we hear uneven, thundering footfalls down the hardwood staircase.

"I'll keep Lawrence in line, don't worry!" Sophia says. "And if anything breaks we would obviously pay for it—"

My eyes widen. "How is that reassuring?!"

As if summoned, Lawrence the maroon blur emerges.

"Soph, we were only packed for one *potential* overnight. Why do you have, like, 20,000 lotions packed?"

"Enough whining, more bringing stuff up!" Sophia slaps Lawrence's butt and he trots back up the staircase toward the second guest bedroom. Lulu scampers after him, thrilled to have someone else to chase around the formerly silent house.

Deep breaths, Tim.

CHAPTER 9

My third slice of warm, pepperoni-mushroom pizza droops over the tips of my fingers as I raise it to my mouth. Sophia and Lawrence are sitting across from me on the stone patio, their faces lit by the orange glow of the bonfire between us. Sophia is combing through her thick, curly dark hair with her hands.

"There are definitely a few leaves making a nest in my hair," she says distractedly.

Lawrence and I both see the leaf in question. I'm about to go pick it out, until I see his face show sudden concern. He puts his Corona down on the patio and rises from the rustic wooden Adirondack chair.

"That's not just a leaf. Babe...hold still." He takes his white Nike shoe off, raising it over his shoulder like an axe.

"If there is a bug and you crush it on my head, I'll tell Margie what a gentleman her son was to me."

Lawrence looks pleading. "She'll kill me!"

"Better her than me," Sophia says, grabbing at his maroon shirt and kissing him. "Get me another drink while you're up!" He picks the leaf out of her hair and blows it in her face. Sophia tries to swat at him, but he manages to dodge it before grabbing her a drink.

Playful romance is beautiful to witness...just not when you're single. I pull out my phone reflexively, doing my best to avoid eye contact. My plan, unfortunately, backfires.

"Oh my god, the bag!!" Sophia giggles, seeing the plastic bag my phone was in. "Somehow I always forget. Tim, I cannot believe you still use—"

"Is anyone going to tell me how your first interview went?" I ask Lawrence abruptly, swigging my beer.

"Ehh..." Lawrence begins. "I know med school is going to be worthwhile when I finally get there, but man this application process is killing me right now. The MMIs are a wild ride."

"Multiple mini-interviews," Sophia quickly clarifies. "Basically, he has to have six back-to-back interviews with uber-important doctors, and they all take turns interrogating him on 'what he would do if...some patient had some specific issue.' As you might guess, Lawrence absolutely nailed most of them because he's an intelligent, knowledgeable, personable—"

"Babe staaaahhp!"

"—*but*," Sophia continues, reaching to put her hand on his maroon-jumpsuited knee, "he does have the habit of saying whatever pops into that gorgeous head of his right away, and sometimes that's a dangerous thing."

I wait for Lawrence to defend himself, but instead he groans like a banshee. "Eeeuuuhhh. I swear I was running so hot on the other five interviews! Like, really vibin' through the whole thing. Then the lady asked, 'how would your friends describe you?' I prepped all of the usual questions a thousand times, but in the moment my head just blanked. At one point I used the phrase 'party-hardy'..."

Oh boy. "It'll be fine," I say, getting up and handing him another drink. What a pep-talk. I have no clue if it will be fine, but somehow his smile bounces back immediately after the minor encouragement.

The three of us sit in companiable silence around the fire. The radiating heat in front of us clashes against the chill night air behind. I turn toward the coolness and see the forest stretching behind. The tittering leaves...the wind...the owl noises...there's so much going on in that void. An entire world of horrifying, endless darkness and unknown—

"TIM!"

I jerk my neck back suddenly, greeted by Lawrence and Sophia laughing.

"We called your name like four times!" Sophia says.

I pretend to laugh. "Sorry. Do those woods give either of you the creeps, too?"

"Maybe I'm just paranoid," Sophia says conspiratorially, "but I feel like he's ignoring me on purpose."

"Ignoring what?" I ask.

"I *asked* if you've been, you know, interested in anyone lately?" She's right, I would have ignored the question if I'd heard.

"None of them lady-folk tickling your fancy, as of late?" Lawrence adds, winking.

"No. No one's...tickling any part of me."

Lawrence pretends to lunge at me, fingers wriggling.

"Oh come on!" Sophia continues. "There's no one at all?"

"No..." My voice falters for a half-second, thinking of the girl at the market yesterday.

That moment costs me dearly. Sophia smiles widely. "You can't keep secrets! Lawrence, tell him he can't keep secrets!"

Lawrence smirks and slaps me on the shoulder. It's supposed to be friendly, but I'm quite delicate so it stings. "Hide while you still can!" he calls out, dodging more playful swats from Sophia. "Also, if you are on the chase, remember it's a marathon not a sprint. Gets real easy to get discouraged out there, but you'll find someone if you keep sticking your neck out. You're a catch, my dude."

I try not to look surprised. Not only was that one of the kindest things someone's said to me in a long time, but also the most sincere moment I've witnessed from Lawrence. He might have noticed my reaction; Lawrence quickly reaches for his beer on the ground and drains it. "The sauce must be kicking in, hot damn!" he shouts.

Sophia sighs. "It's not fair. I get to be mad at him for all of two seconds, and then he acts all sweet and gives great advice."

Lawrence proceeds to sit cross-legged in the Adirondack chair, clasping his hands together. "I'm a goddamn fortune-cookie, woman. You know this!"

"Yeah?" she challenges, her face reddening from the buzz. "What am I thinking right now, oh wise one?"

"PLEASE," I interject. "Do not answer that. Have sympathy for my gag reflex."

"Oh hush!" Sophia says, accidentally knocking her empty beer bottle onto the ground with a clink.

"All hands on deck!" Lawrence shouts, and Sophia giggles picking it up. "To answer your previous question, Tim-OH-thee," Lawrence says, "the trees look super spooky. And we're totally exploring them tomorrow. Bring snacks."

Sophia looks out, deep in thought as she leans back in her patio chair. Her breath steams from the cold air. "Definitely creepy if you're alone out here," she says sympathetically. "But it could be fun to explore a bit? Get you out of the house and avoid some cabin fever?"

"Uhhh, not sure," I say, "As a professional introvert, I think it takes more than a few days for me to get cabin fever."

"Well, we can think about it tomorrow. We'll enjoy the rest of the night here."

"I don't know..." I say.

Of course, I do know. Aubrey Plaza—my psycho celebrity crush—could be in there and I still wouldn't hike in those goddamned woods.

CHAPTER 10

We are hiking in the goddamned woods.

"Soph, jerky me!"

Sophia rolls her eyes. She swings her teal blue drawstring bag to the front of her, shielding the early morning sun from her eyes as she retrieves one of the six bags of sweet and hot beef jerky. She hands it to Lawrence with a flourish. "Anything else, milord?"

"Hell naww! What else could a man need besides processed meat, friendship, and the great outdoors?"

Sophia and I look at each other with disgust. We're all hungover. The difference is that some take this physiological torment as a sign from the divine powers that we should take it easy. Read, Netflix, carbs, repeat. Others in our party, who will remain nameless, rebut this with "we drove all the way to New York, we have our own house in the woods, and it's a gorgeous day outside—why are we not grabbin' snacks and looking for bears and stuff!?" The cruel gods smiled down upon the latter sentiment.

"I still don't understand why you got so much (and exclusively) beef jerky," I say, dipping my hand into the bag as Lawrence holds it out for me. I know that it objectively tastes good, but at 9:30 AM the potent artificial flavoring makes my stomach contort into a question mark. I reach for another handful.

"If you wanted other food you could have grabbed it! You've got money!"

"Fair," I say. The horror of going back to the Sheridan Market with Lawrence and Sophia was unimaginable. If I had to interact with cute market girl—or worse, get interrogated by Sophia about it afterward—I would have melted into some kind of goo. I was so relieved to see that she wasn't there that I sort of blanked on everything else, including snacks.

Lawrence is sporting his finest neon-yellow tracksuit this morning, as if to challenge the sun itself in giving us a worse headache. I'm wearing a dark-gray t-shirt of The Smiths and the same trademark light blue jeans that I always wear. They're ideal for every occasion, and if they're not, it's the occasion's fault. Sophia looks like a mom on vacation: curly hair tied back in a factory-worn Red Sox cap with sun glasses on top, a pale blue tank top, and black leggings. If I asked, she could probably materialize juice boxes for us. I debated letting our trusty hound accompany us, but the hike alone was stressful enough without worrying about losing Lulu. We'll be back soon; and if we aren't, I can use her as leverage to speed this up.

The surrounding forest is breathtaking. I've been walking through woods plenty of times before, but this feels like real wilderness. Somewhere you could plausibly claim to spot a sasquatch. We've only been walking for twenty minutes, but we're already isolated in every direction. No car horns, planes overhead, street signs, or litter. Large boulders pierce through the dewy earth. Scattered leaves intermix with a bed of dry pine needles, cushioning our steps forward. We follow a narrow path that's somewhat worn, but we have the sneaking suspicion that Lawrence will see something shiny and take off over the hills. My phone is fully charged, with GPS and compass apps ready to go.

"LAKE!" Lawrence shouts. "Ten o'clock!"

He points nowhere near ten o'clock, toward a shimmering light emitting through the trees. I squint and cover my eyes, seeing what looks like a sprinkling of blue farther down the hill and to the right. I'm smiling as I follow him toward the landmark, my irritability thawing.

"Alright ladies and gentlemen," Lawrence says. He stumbles up onto a rotten log on the ground, and balance-beam-walks across it clumsily. "What is the likelihood that this is a Loch Ness Monster-type situation?"

I laugh, following uncoordinatedly across the same balance beam and leaping down behind him.

"I can push you in the water to find out?" Sophia suggests. "For research purposes?"

Lawrence flashes a smile. "Love where your head is at, babe! What do you think, Tim-Timmy-Tim?"

Sophia sings "Chim Chim Cher-ee," under her breath, and will likely continue for the remainder of the adventure.

"Uhh..." I say, ignoring his question, "I think I see someone by the water."

By the time the others react, the stranger has already stood up and is looking at us. The person is too far away to see well, but they have a slender frame and are wearing an olive-green hooded sweatshirt, wrapped over a white undershirt and tight blue jeans. She has...oh my god. I start trailing behind. Of course, Sophia notices.

"C'mon Tim, you're not this shy, are you?" She keeps going, and after a few seconds looks back again to see me trailing even more. Up ahead I hear Lawrence echo a loud "Eyoooo!" to our guest. I continue looking off into the wilderness, as if I've always been an avid birdwatcher.

"Sorry to disturb you," I hear Sophia say diplomatically to market girl. "We saw the lake from back there and this one can't always contain himself." She gives Lawrence an exaggerated pat on his head.

"Sweet spot!" he says. "Come here often? We're just gettin' our visit on."

When I emerge from behind Lawrence and stand next to him, I see her shadowed eyes widen a bit. Only for a moment. The briefest smirk plays on the side of her mouth; my neuroticism could write a thesis on the thousands of potential implications of that smirk.

"Actually, yes," she says. "Once a week on my day off, I relax by the lake. I work at Sheridan's full-time, which contributes substantially to the sucking of my time and soul. When I finally get a day off, there's no better place to be. Living in Sommers is pretty fucking cancerous, but I have to admit it's difficult to beat the views." She turns to look back, admiring the beauty. The sun glows on her pale cheek, reflecting off the water behind her. I wonder what she's thinking about, and why a place this stunning is so toxic for her.

"We were just over at the market!" Lawrence says excitedly. "I regret to inform you that you will need to replenish your beef jerky supplies tomorrow."

Another smirk from her. "You're forgiven. It won't kill Lucas to stock a few shelves while I'm away." She leans back against the massive, dried tree trunk behind her. Its bark was stripped and bare, and she seems to be using it as a makeshift table, bench, and bed. A book, tattered and dog-eared, sits bridged across the log. A thick brown wool blanket drapes down it with bits of twig caught messily in its frays.

"Anyway, I think we've satisfied our curiosity," Sophia says, "so we'll leave you to your book. Enjoy your day off!"

"Thanks," she says. "Be mindful of falling in a ditch."

"Wiiill do!" Lawrence calls back, already marching forward.

The best part about the great outdoors is how expansive it feels. We re-discover the path and heave ourselves up a rising hill that likely feeds all of its rainwater down to the lake below. Large crows soar above, weaving their feathery tapestries across the open skies. Out here, all of your wandering thoughts melt away entirely. The trivialities that arrest your attention seem so small, so—

"So she was cute," Sophia says, elbowing me in the ribs.

"Am I allowed to comment?" Lawrence asks. My shoe trips on a rock and I stumble forward.

"You have the floor," Sophia announces.

"So she was cute," Lawrence echoes, walking to my other side and elbowing me. "You had a chance to get out and meet some of the locals, Tim-bo? I hear there's no better way to immerse yourself on a trip."

Sophia nods. "He did seem a little shy about going to the market with us today..."

I keep stomping through the leaves as Sophia and Lawrence skip by my side, ping-ponging jibes back and forth until they tire themselves out.

We've walked about ten minutes past the lake (or maybe it's been thirty minutes; I'm no explorer), and a quick detour off the path leads us to entirely lose it. We trudge through a series of thick brambles and muck—faces whipped by a flurry of bending branches. Sophia's Red Sox hat gets kabobbed on overhanging thorns. I've been slashed, pricked, and stuck enough times to feel an angry immunity to the pain and inconvenience. We try retracing our steps, but end up stumbling across a clearing we've never seen before.

"Be careful," Sophia says. "This looks kind of weird, doesn't it?"

"It's fiiiine," Lawrence says, stomping doggedly ahead of her. "Haaa—ho fuck!" His body tenses in front of me. I instinctually grip the back of his shirt—so suddenly I can hear the threads in the neck popping. His face is beading with sweat and his eyes look like he's seen a ghost. "Hole!" he shouts, regaining his balance and stepping back. "Very big hole."

I peek past him, glancing down to see a massive, narrow canyon in the ground. A cavity in the earth that goes at least one hundred...maybe two hundred feet deep. It looks as if some ancient colossal god had swung an axe and struck directly through the forest, leaving a long, narrow gash to heal on its own and form an ecosystem around it. Ferns stretch around the edges of both sides—making it so you can barely see the drop unless you're standing over it—and there's sheer slate rock all the way down. At the bottom of the canyon, there are glimpses of a stream, more vegetation, and a few indents in the rocks that end in shadows.

Lawrence will not be contained. He gets on all fours, wriggling across the leaves. The top of his torso and head are all suspended over the cliff. I quickly shift forward and lean my weight on the back of his calves, anchoring him.

"That's far enough!" I say.

"That's *too* far," Sophia interjects.

He looks around frantically, grinning ear-to-ear at the landscape. "This is the coolest thing of all time!!"

My arms are still gripping tightly—straining but firmly intact. "Great, now shimmy yourself back before I lose my hold on you!"

He obeys, slowly crawling back as Sophia exhales in relief. He brushes the dirt off his neon yellow pants. "We've got to go down."

"Do we?" I ask.

"We do," he responds.

Well then.

"When have you ever seen something like this before?!" he challenges. "Or even heard of something like this?"

I raise my neck and dare to peek down again. Terrifying, but it is unbelievable. "It's...we probably wouldn't even be able to get down without breaking our necks," I say. "And what if we get stuck part of the way down? I mean this place isn't going anywhere, is it? There isn't a huge rush."

Lawrence looks betrayed but quickly turns to Sophia. "Back me up, pleaaase. You'd go down, right?"

Sophia cranes her neck and looks down at the plummet. Unconvinced.

"There *is* a huge rush," Lawrence continues. "It isn't going anywhere, but we are. There's a reason why we've never seen the Great Pyramids or...or Mardi Gras or Usain Bolt at the Olympics; because we have lives and responsibilities and geography in our way all the time. And it's only going to get worse as we get old. Doing cool shit is never convenient, otherwise everyone would do it. But right now, the coolest thing I've ever seen is directly in front of us and we have the afternoon off. Over there—" Lawrence says, pointing around the rim of the canyon to a gentler slope, "—is an easier way down. If we can't manage it safely then we won't. But it shouldn't be for lack of trying."

Sophia grabs Lawrence's arm and pulls him close. He bends down to kiss her on the forehead. "You're my silly dreamer boy and I love you. I refuse to let you break your neck going down, but we'll safely give it a shot. Alright?"

His eyes light up. "No neck-breaking! This is a neck-break free space!" He looks over at me now.

Crap. I drop my head and exhale.

"YES!!" Lawrence shouts. "Thank you, thank you! Timmy, bubby, for your loyalty you're gunna get all the beef jerky you've ever wanted. I'll build you a jerky throne. I'll pre-chew it for you—"

"That's quite all right, friend," I say. "I won't rob you of your snacks, but I will reiterate no neck-breaking."

"Not one neck!"

I look over to the slope, dreading the miserable thickets we'll be delving through just to get to the place I am terrified to be near. In silent protest, I snatch Sophia's Red Sox hat off her head and follow Lawrence.

CHAPTER 11

We've made it about a quarter of the way down into the canyon, and in that time Lawrence has had two false alarm deaths and announced three "EYOOO's" to hear the echoing sound. It is a cool effect, in fairness. Once Sophia stopped having heart-attacks at every exclamation, she pulled out her phone to video his nonsensicalities. My gut asks, "do we really want to be using up all of our battery out here, before we inevitably get lost?" It pains me to realize that I'm turning into the dweeby sidekick in every action movie.

The cliff walls are even more incredible as we descend. An expanse of solidity, as far as the eye can see, surrounds us like a living, natural cradle. I have never been so content to have my existence shrink to near nothingness. Small, faint streams of water cascade down the gleaming walls. It smells like...green. Like the freshest earth waking up after a long day of storm showers. Dark moss is splotched across the stony landscape, with small patches randomly interspersed among massive sheets of shag.

There is no trail; we are the first known explorers of this bizarre and natural landmark. Undetermined whether this is a good feeling. Chunks of rock, perhaps centuries ago, cracked off the cliff walls and piled onto the edges below. Mounds of dirt have been washed down, caked from rain. Every step is uncertain, but we test them carefully with the old "foot stomp, see if it collapses" technique. We—

"Hellooo?!" A woman's voice. We crane our necks up, looking to find the source. "HELLO?" she repeats.

"Hi!" Sophia calls back up, cupping her hand in a cone around her mouth. Far up, I see the olive-colored sweatshirt nearing closer to the edge.

"He-heeey it's our lake friend!!" Lawrence shouts up. I cover my ears to muffle the yell. "How goes it!?"

43

I stare in horror as market girl looks down across the expanse, entirely ignoring Lawrence's pleasantries.

He will not be deterred. "If you're following us, I must say that I'm flattered! You could have just asked to join in the first place!"

"I..." she struggles for words at the sight of the cliffs. "I suppose I was following you; I heard about a dozen screams and thought that somebody was being murdered. Don't ask me why I thought to follow them."

"So!" Lawrence continues. "You are now aware that no one is dying, but you see the same awesome place that we see. Come on doooown!"

"Only if you're interested!" Sophia adds. "We can show you the safest ways to descend. We tested some of the worst ones ourselves!"

Lawrence turns to look at both of us conspiratorially. Whispering (probably still too loudly), "Do I tell her about the jerky?"

"Oh my god," Sophia says.

"I'm just saying..." he adds, "it might sweeten the deal for her, but at what cost? Do we want someone who's only in it for the meats?"

"All I'm saying," Sophia rebuts, "is that if you say anything more, it'll give off creepy vibes and she'll think we're trapping her down here."

Almost in unison, the two of them turn to me. "You've been awfully quiet, ehh Tim?"

CHAPTER 12

It's a strange thing, really. Two incredible things, when coupled together, can yield so much misery.

Lawrence, Sophia, and I stand at the bottom of the deep canyon. We watch market girl come down in about a third of the time it took us to traverse the landscape. Not from some deep-seated wilderness background or any instructions from us. Sophia begins by shouting some helpful guidance on the paths we took...but this quickly shifts to our stunned silence.

Market girl's sneakers skid down a slope of mud and moss. Rather than tensing and leaning her weight backward, she leans forward—flailing her arms sideways and using her momentum to take her down a second drop. Her descent is not athletic. I can't even say whether it's confidently executed. She makes another leap down a section of cliff that took us five minutes to descend. On her landing, her shoe slips on a slick rock. The weight of her body flies back (in Charlie Brown football-kicking fashion), and she lands on a heap of moss. Her arm slams and scrapes awkwardly on the cliffside in an attempt to break her fall. Before we can move, we hear a loud, cackling laugh followed by a groan. Her body slowly exhumes itself, wiping the dirt off the elbow of her sweatshirt.

"Watch your step!" she calls down to us, still cackling and back to plummeting down the next section.

The three of us smile painfully, looking at each other to make sure we're all equally horrified.

Market girl finally meets us on the ground floor. Her face is flushed from exertion, donning a smile as radiant and wild as if it had beat death in a staring contest. Her sweatshirt, white undershirt, jeans, and green-checkered shoes are caked with dirt. Her slender, pale hands both comb through and tousle her long hair until it flops down and rests behind her shoulders. She says nothing. Of course, that leaves Lawrence to break the silence.

"Watching you flail the entire way down was fun. Care for some victory jerky?"

She smirks, glancing back up the slope and ignoring the offering. "Hope there's an easier way up."

At the bottom of the canyon the ground is uneven with clods of wet earth, fluffs of green moss, and rocks cutting at diagonal angles across each other. We resume exploring as if everything is normal, Lawrence leading. He glances every which way to soak in the surreal scene surrounding us. Sophia is behind him, whispering as if this hidden grove we've found is sacred. Behind Sophia is...

"Jupiter." Market girl stares me down when she tells me her name, as if challenging me to make fun of it. Somehow it seems fitting; the other-worldly experience we're having in this landscape and the out-of-body experience I am enduring, standing behind her. She moves fluidly across the rocks in front of me and I try to avoid looking at her too much.

"Do you see anything up there?" I call ahead to Lawrence. "Near those shadows by the rock wall?"

"We shall see!" he says, doing a heel-click over a splintered log.

"Just a heads-up baby," Sophia reminds him as she cautiously steps over the same log. "If you twist an ankle down here, there is no chance in hell we're dragging you back up that cliff. We will leave you at the bottom for some bear to find."

"Aww that's okay pookie, we had a good run," he says, laughing and leaning in to kiss the side of her forehead.

Sophia freezes, violated to her very core. "Please...if you've ever loved me...never call me that again."

I see his smile widening. "You mean, I can't *ever* call you pook—"

She elbows him in the side, and he leans into it, giggling. Lawrence throws his arm around her shoulders and gives her another kiss on the side forehead, this one much sweeter. The two of them walk forward together, squeezing between the narrowing cliffs.

"Are they always like that?" Jupiter turns back to ask me, slowing her pace so we can walk together.

"Umm..." Why do I have to start every sentence with that? Should I talk to a doctor or something? "Yeah, basically," I manage. "It isn't always the most fun as a perpetually single person, but they're really amazing together and two of my best friends, so it's still nice to see." Her light green eyes glance at me, as if trying to read any ulterior emotions I might feel. I'm not sure that I do have anything to reveal (as far as I'm aware), but I still squirm under the scrutiny. Maybe it's just that the walkway is getting narrower. Our arms are almost touching as they swing back and forth.

"Why?" I finally say, struggling to meet her gaze.

She shrugs, continuing on.

We grow painfully quiet. Every footstep on a twig is stiflingly loud, as if the volume knob on my awkwardness is turned all the way up. I can't do it. "So how was the rest of your shift the other day?" I try. "I don't know if you remember, but I was actually at the market the other day when that smoking lady was inside."

"Yes, I remember," she replies. "You were the egg guy."

Never before have I experienced all of my organs screaming inside of me.

Jupiter must have been able to hear them; she looks at me and shrieks with laughter. "You have nothing to worry about; I've just never seen anyone scrutinize poultry products so thoroughly. I assumed you had some sort of salmonella X-ray vision. In fairness, there aren't more than twenty people who ever walk into Sheridan's. It's hard to forget a new face, whoever it is."

My brain stopped working several seconds ago. All I notice is the reckless teetering of her green-checkered shoes, as she hops carelessly from one rock to the next. "Gotcha," I manage. "And I assume cigarette lady is one of those regulars?"

She sighs, smirking to herself. "Mrs. Levin is one of the many local characters here in charming Sommers. She almost burns down her cabin about once a year, and she's been arrested once or twice for harassing neighbors who take out their garbage too early in the morning. Oh! And she used to have this dog! I swear it must have been a diseased rat. Whatever sick breed it was clearly wasn't suitable for conditions on Earth. I don't know what was more unbearable, Mrs. Levin baby-talking to that dying horror all day and puffing smoke into its poor lungs, or how miserable she is now without it."

I smile at the ugly stories, simply from the joy of Jupiter talking to me. "I'm glad she's a little nutso with other people, too. When I was looking at the back fridge, we actually bumped into each other. She...threatened to cut my balls off if I ever did it again..." Yes, Tim. Please continue talking about your genitals with this gorgeous girl you just met. To everyone's surprise—including Lawrence and Sophia, who look back at us—Jupiter suddenly cackles again. An ugly kind of laugh, which for some reason is even more endearing.

"Yes!" she says, wiping at her eyes, "there's that local flavor! Can you believe we don't have more tourism here? I will say, her bark is definitely worse than her bite, but her bite might still give you rabies. Do not let her bite you."

"I usually have this rule where I don't let people bite me." More laughing, and this time I join her. Excellent discovery, Tim: biting and ball mutilation equals good.

"HEYOOOO!" we hear ahead of us.

Jupiter smirks. "Also, does he do that for everything?"

Lawrence is over by a cliff wall, jumping repeatedly with his knees toward his torso like an oversized yellow frog. His arms are scooping wildly toward himself, in an attempt to signal us over.

"Everything," I say. "Always."

Unable to contain himself a moment longer, Lawrence blurts the punchline moments before our arrival. "Big ol' cave! Are you seein' this?!"

Looking in, there's a small fissure in the rock no bigger than three or four feet tall. The opening makes a turn to the right...and disappears into darkness. I pull out my phone—discreetly in my pocket; Jupiter will never see the bag—and turn the flashlight on. The rocks illuminate in the pale glow, but fade into the narrower, deeper shadows further back.

"Well," I say, pulling back to the group. "It sure is a hole."

"A cave!" Lawrence corrects. "If it were a dinky hole there's no way it would keep going in like that!"

"I mean, we don't know how far it goes in," Sophia adds.

"That's why we need to—"

As we bicker, Jupiter crouches down wordlessly and slips inside the cave-hole. Another exchange of confused glances among the three of us.

"Hey, Jupiter," Sophia hesitates. "Can you see anything?"

No response. An occasional crunch of gravel or scraping stone echoes out.

"Scream once if you get stuck," says Lawrence, "two screams if you're being eaten alive, and three...hmmm...gimme a sec..."

Before he can outline a third torment, Jupiter re-emerges. She squints at the sunlight and straightens her back. "Cave," she confirms.

"So, are we going in?" Her green eyes look at each of us. Her hands sink into the sagging side pockets of her olive sweatshirt.

"Yes we are." Lawrence decrees. He marches toward Sophia, holding out the crook of his arm to her regally. "M'lady?"

"You are such an idiot; I love you." She hooks her arm in his and smiles. "We can't stand like this through the cave, though...there's no way my big ass fits. And we aren't going in too far! We could get lost...or find bears or something!"

I had not thought of bears. Bears live in caves. We can barely fit through the cave ourselves, so there's no way a bear could ever make it through. But slightly smaller, equally vicious bear-like creatures might also live in caves. Or maybe a baby bear was tucked in there when it could fit, and was feeding inside there for years and is now enormous. And has night vision after years of evolution, and—

"Tim?" Jupiter asks. She has never said my name before. The beautiful sound hollows out my insides and fills it with an entirely new set of anxieties...all related to her. "You coming?"

"We don't have to go in if you don't want to," Sophia adds.

"We can go," I say. "Maybe we don't go in too deep, if Sophia isn't up for it. But definitely game for exploring!" Yeah, that's right! I'm a cool guy who's up for anything, and Sophia's the chump holding us back.

"Okay," Jupiter says, smirking before disappearing into the darkness.

CHAPTER 13

"We are the motherfucking Goonies right now!" Lawrence shouts from the front, his voice echoing like a Ping-Pong ball across the surrounding rocks.

I wish he wasn't right. Rather than narrowing and closing, the rocky walls widen around us to form a cavernous hallway. Definitely capable of housing bears. Our three phones (I turn mine off to conserve battery) wave pale flashlights across the blackness. After caveman-hunching for a few minutes, we're all able to stand fully upright. Still, some of the changes around us feel almost imperceptibly small.

"Wait, how long have we been going downhill for?" Sophia asks.

Jupiter looks down, interested. "Hadn't noticed."

Sophia looks back to me, stepping close to aim her flashlight back where we came from. "That is steeper than I thought."

"Have you ever been in any caves like these in New York before?" I ask Jupiter.

"Not at all. I have been on a handful of camping trips and some leisurely woods walks. Secret cliffs and spelunking are well beyond my expertise."

The group stands still for a moment, looking back at the hill. "What do we think?" Sophia asks. "Do we go back in another minute or two?"

I wait as long as I can to shroud my dweebiness. "That sounds fine to me, I guess."

Lawrence shrugs his shoulders, as if to suggest he would be equally fine going home or spending the rest of his life as a mole-person. Woo! Almost liberated! Jupiter continues on for our remaining few minutes, and I follow happily behind.

The decline steepens. Ceiling stalagmites hang above us, growing increasingly longer and sharper. I feel like we're in a great beast's mouth, ready to be clamped shut at any moment. I keep going, patiently waiting for someone else to make the final call of turning around. Any second now. Rubble is scattered along the sides of us. Does this seem like...a path? The air grows chill and damp. A strange purplish vein sparkles on the side of the rock walls, tracing its way across and down the cave as if it's tattooed with some precious mineral. The words "ready to go back?" hang suspended on my tongue, yet every step forward leaves us all collectively enamored by the natural wonder. Small tunneling shafts appear in the ceiling, leading to god knows where. Still we descend down, down.

We reach the end of the tunnel. Straight ahead, for the first time since entering, the phone flashlights reflect their cool glow back against the rock. Satisfaction, accomplishment...relief.

"Damn, I really thought we were gunna find something wild down here," Lawrence sighs. "My yeti-senses were tingling for sure."

I ignore Lawrence. I take a deep breath, now focusing on the dreaded trek back to the surface. How the hell are we supposed to climb back up that canyon?

"Uhh guys?" Sophia says. She's looking to the right, concerned at some nook in the stone.

There's a gap. Not huge, but definitely big enough to fit through. It's a little above my waist, and is so camouflaged that it's only visible from where Sophia's standing. Beyond it we can see nothing. Sophia shines a flashlight inside, but the light is swallowed into a vast space of impossible darkness. She aims the light directly up, and...nothing. Left and right...still nothing. All that's visible is about five feet below; a stony floor that fades in the distance.

The four of us are silently transfixed—breaths collectively held—until Jupiter whispers close to us "...how far do you think it goes?"

No one knows how to answer.

"Do we..." Lawrence begins, "want to check it out? Or should we just go back." Even he sounds uncertain.

"I'm ready to go back, I think," Sophia says.

"Yeah," I agree. "It feels like a bit more than we're ready to take on at the moment. This place could go on forever."

The group nods in agreement. Still transfixed, still staring into vast darkness—

BANG!

Sophia screams. A hand on my shoulder suddenly tenses—every muscle in my body stiffens. We all look back to the slope we came from; a stalagmite crashed to the ground and shattered, echoing with a blast around the cavern.

Bats. Swarms of them appear in the shivering phone flashlights, hideously spotlighted. They dive, swirl, and encircle one another in a cyclone retreating from the same noise that startled us. Hundreds of bats flood toward what they know as the deeper darkness...directly toward us. Pinning us at the back of the tunnel.

"GO!" Lawrence shouts, grabbing Sophia's arm and guiding her into the nook. She ducks in and disappears. Jupiter quickly follows. Lawrence wedges through and calls "Now Tim!!"

From my periphery I can tell the bats are at most ten feet away, and fast approaching. Without a thought, I dive through headfirst. The left side of my stomach shaves against the gritty rock walls—a burning, scraping pain that I barely feel in the commotion—and I flop into a near faceplant on the ground.

The swarm pours through. I lay on my back, looking up in horror as the squashed rat faces and papery wings drain out of the hole like a floodgate bursting. On and on it goes, seemingly endless; a shrieking blur of gray-brown, no more than three feet above me. I'm paralyzed with fear. After at least fifteen seconds of a constant stream, the last straggler flutters by. I exhale, closing my eyes.

Sophia and Jupiter are pressed flat against the left-most wall, standing still. Before my brain can process anything, I feel Lawrence's strong hand clasp in my own, heaving me up.

"Easy does it, bud. Up we go." My mind slowly thaws as I steady myself, brushing the gravel off my shirt.

"Everyone okay?" I ask, looking around at all of the eyes staring back at me.

"Yeah man, all good," Lawrence says, smiling in the pale flashlight. "That dive of yours could end up on an ESPN highlight reel. Goddamn!"

"From my angle it actually looked more like Superman," Jupiter says. "Quite the feat."

Likes ball jokes and guys who do their own stunts. Noted.

"Yes, we all agree Tim is fantastic," Sophia says, "but we have to focus on getting out of this creepy-ass place. Are we safe to go back?"

Jupiter guides her phone light toward the nook entrance leading back to the original tunnel. "I don't see anything...but I can hear a few of them squeaking still. Of course, we didn't see anything on the way down, and there were thousands of them. They were likely hiding in crevices or small off-shoots that we couldn't see." She looks around to us, maybe hoping for a decision to be made.

Finally, Lawrence weighs in. "Okay. How about we just give it a few minutes. We wait for things to settle with any stragglers that might be in there, and then head back? We were on the fence about checking this room out anyway, so we can peek around until the coast is clear."

I look at Sophia. She sighs and nods.

"That works," I say. "So long as we don't go far and can still remember how to get back."

Jupiter walks into the darkness, already faster than the rest of us are comfortable with. We see nothingness—not the ceilings, the walls, nor any other landmark. Nothing in the phone light except for a dim haze of fog that creeps toward us as we inch forward, unsteadily. Our pale lights reflect back at us, useless. I continually glance back to make sure I know which way we came from...I can still tell, although each step feels more disorienting than the next. Jupiter is still striding in front and hasn't looked back once. Thundering anxiety is pounding my chest, and it compounds doubly at the thought of insisting we go back. All I can imagine is her smirking and rolling her eyes at me, saying "Yeah, I guess we can." That shouldn't be so painful to hear, but it feels paralytic to all sense of reason.

Seeing becomes nearly impossible. We cluster closer and closer, the four of us drawn together from the surrounding vagueness we wade through. I see Sophia and Lawrence grab each other's hand. A horrible thought makes me consider doing the same with Jupiter, just so that we won't lose each other. The only reason I don't reach out to her is *because* I like her; the universe clearly has a sense of humor. Slowly, blindly shuffling our feet forward, we continue—SPLOSH.

"Hoo!" Lawrence shouts, bobbing his foot in the air. "Watch out for puddles, ladies and gents." Stooping closer, he walks to the left to circumnavigate the water. "How wide is this thing anyway...?"

Following the puddle for about ten feet, we gradually realize that it isn't a puddle at all.

"Listen," Jupiter says, stopping in her tracks. The slightest, rhythmic *wsshh* can be heard, back and forth.

"Are those tides?" I ask.

"We're not anywhere near an ocean," Sophia says.

"I've heard that some lakes can have waves from underwater currents or temperature changes or something," Lawrence adds. "But only if they're...massive."

A loud splash. Jupiter bends down, cupping the water in her hands and splashing it back down playfully. She raises her eyebrows to me and I smile back, momentarily distracted from my terror. The pale reflection of phone light off the lake has a haunting effect. The water stretches fifteen feet at least until it fades into the fog and darkness. All is silent except the quiet, rhythmic *wsshh* of the water gently slapping the rocky shore, in and out. Like it's breathing.

"So," Sophia says, swallowing, "Do you guys think we should begin..." She trails off, looking across the water. "Does anyone else see..."

"Yes," I say.

Far over the black lake shines the faintest glow. My first thought is that it's some trick of the phone light's reflection, but it quickly grows brighter and more distinct. A pale, luminescent blue pierces through the fog, coming clearer and closer. Directly toward us.

"The hell is that?" I whisper.

"No idea," Jupiter whispers back. I tear my glance away for half a second to see her mouth open, enthralled at the alien sight. The faintest silhouette of a rickety wooden rowboat emerges from the fog. The bow heads in our direction with the light hanging a few feet above it. Nothing breaks the water's sheen surface on the sides of the boat...meaning no one is paddling or steering. Yet still it comes, guided with purpose.

We are frozen...and magnetized. A black silhouette comes into view. We can't see it with any clarity, but whoever or whatever is on that boat does not speak a word or utterance to us. Its eyes are beaded black dots reflecting the light.

CHAPTER 14

We're sprinting, our backs turned to the water.

The last thing we hear is the wooden boat grinding to a halt against the rocky shore. Under less stressful circumstances, we would have re-traced our steps the long way to find the nook where we had entered. Something about ol' beady-eyes, however, convinces us that time is scarce. Lawrence makes a beeline toward where he hopes is the original tunnel, and the rest of us do our best to stay close—Soph, then Jupiter, then me—without losing one another in the fog. The sound of our strides is muffled only by the distant echoes of metal chains dragging across the rocky floor. It sounds slow...laborious...and yet we never seem to get away from it. My chest is heaving; I'm gasping for air but know that I can't slow down—

We jerk to a halt.

We're suddenly engulfed in a ring of torches that burst into blue flame. They form a circle around us, held by stone pillars standing sentry around a black marble altar. The polished reflection of the altar sheens with fiery blue light. The altar is entirely empty aside from a thin, circular disk of some purple gemstone.

Dazed...my head starts to feel heavy. Heavy and light, spinning and spinning with the blue flames. My legs wobble underneath me, and I feel...the strongest desire to collapse to my knees. God, that would be such a sweet relief; to just...let go.

I'm warm. Warm like a blanket straight out of the dryer, as if the surrounding darkness and dampness is drowned out by the glow of this beautiful place. I'm sitting in the light of a cozy campfire. I'm lying on a thick, cozy brown blanket by a lake, legs entangled with Jupiter's. There's nothing to think or worry about because everything we've ever wanted is right here on this blanket. I feel the softness of her fingertips trickle playfully down my chest. She giggles and kisses my neck...my cheek. I feel the heat of her breath rise to my ear and the slightest prickle, as her soft lips lean forward to whisper "I love you." Warmth radiates throughout my entire being, as if every weight and all weariness I have experienced melts away in a euphoric sigh...Jupiter...

Jupiter. Looking up, I see Lawrence and Sophia's heads swirling, shoulders drooping down. But Jupiter has entirely collapsed to the cavern floor. Rather than euphoric, she looks completely comatose: her eyes are bulging, staring vacantly toward the altar. I slap myself hard—fuck—really fucking hard in the face, painfully numb like ice water being thrown at me. The euphoria is gone; life is cold and damp and miserable again. I'm scared shitless, and in a strange way the reality feels comforting.

"Jupiter!" I say, dashing drunkenly to her and slapping her face as well (more gently than I had allowed myself). I tug at her arm and heave her lifeless body back to a standing position. As she gets up—slowly, painfully rising—I see her muscles slowly begin to support her weight again. Her eyes flutter and she goes rigid, panicking at the sudden awareness that her body is not where she had last consciously left it. She looks up at me with understanding, the chains scraping their way closer.

"Help me wake them!!" I yell.

Jupiter nods.

I run to Lawrence and shake him by the shoulders, his rag doll body almost toppling beneath the added strain. "Get up! We need to move!" He stirs, and instinctively looks to find Sophia—she's already up, reaching to grab for his arm. We're still shaking the frost from our consciousness...but we're mobile again, at least. We sprint out of the circle of blue flames and toward the darkness once more.

I still don't have my phone light out, but Jupiter's close behind me with hers. She does her best to guide the route I'm improvising. My mastermind plan is to put the most distance possible between us and the scary chains. We're all too disoriented to know where the exit is, but any alternative to where we are feels like an improvement. Within a minute I reach a wall.

"Left or right?" Jupiter calls.

I don't stop. I turn left, pawing at the stone with my hand and tracing the rough surface with my fingertips to not lose my bearing. I glance back quickly to confirm that the others are still following. After some time, the tips of my fingers suddenly meet air. I wave them up and down to determine the height, and still feel nothing. I continue walking past it and connect with the cavern wall again. An idea materializes.

I lead the group past the hole for another twenty seconds, then quietly call back, "Everyone, shut off your flashlights! Turn them off, and leave your hand on the wall!" Jupiter quickly shuts hers off, followed by Sophia and then Lawrence. I glide my fingers back toward the group until I touch someone else's. The chains continue toward us. Almost inaudibly, I whisper, "I don't know where we are, but about a hundred feet back I felt a gap that we can hide in. Let's quietly retrace our steps; that way, the chains might keep going to where our flashlights ended."

"Okay," I hear Sophia whisper. "Lead the way."

I momentarily leave the wall to go around the others, groping my way back to the hard surface. "Follow me. Grab each other's hands if you need."

We walk back, closer now to the sound of chains rather than farther. Louder and louder they come, and a panic comes to mind that we might collide with them before we make it to the gap. We hear a faint groaning, gurgling sound...

Suddenly my hand falls in the air once more, and I breathe a sigh. "Okay," I whisper back. "We're here. I'll pull the next person in and guide them when I'm—"

A massive torch erupts into blue flame across the lake, dissipating the fog entirely. At first it's just one...and then two additional flames blaze, one on the left and one on the right of it. Another two to the left and right of those, then another two. They're cascading across the expanse of the outer wall of the cavern, outlining its perimeter.

"Go," Sophia whispers, pushing the others forward.

In the light of the flames, a gargantuan fortress is revealed behind the lake. It is meticulously and ornately carved into the cavern walls, with towers that have spiked parapets. In the center is a giant gate crafted of the same black marble that was on the altar. The ground rumbles beneath us, and the gate slowly swings open. How deep into the endless stone recesses could the fortress stretch? The blue flames continue to trace the outline of the cavern, now entirely covering the wall of the palace and making their way across the left and right sides of the lake—heading toward us.

I duck into the hole, maneuvering the jagged, damp stone with my sense of touch. The space is narrow, but I hardly have to lower my head. I reach my hand out to grab Jupiter's, doing my best to whisper every step and overhang. She makes it through without a sound, then turns to help Sophia through. Finally, Lawrence. He snags his sneaker on one small corner of the rock on his way in. To us it sounds like a car backfiring, but it's probably inaudible.

We each grab hands, moving silently into some nondescript sub-tunnel in the back. We move...ever so slightly...shifting together for what feels like hours. Finally, in utter darkness I feel a small alcove within the tunnel.

"Let's rest here," I breathe. "Listen to see if we can hear anything."

Silence.

I slowly shift my weight down, and nestle myself deeper into the corner away from the main tunnel. Together, hands still held in unison, we sit in a quiet void.

CHAPTER 15

"I...I just don't understand what's going on," Sophia quietly cries, "Like what the fuck is all of this? It was such a nice morning hike and now it's some horror movie."

"I don't know," Lawrence says, voice shaking. He shifts his weight towards her, probably putting an arm around her. "None of it feels real. Just some dream we should be waking up from..."

"Hell of a dream," Jupiter says to no one in particular. Her voice seems void of emotion.

"I just don't know why we were this stupid!" Sophia continues. "I mean...we...we just kept going in! Why did we ever think this would be a good idea?"

"Part of it was the bats," Lawrence adds, soberly. "We got stuck. It's like...I don't know, man. I feel crazy for thinking this, but it feels like it's happening to us on purpose. Not in some metaphysical fate kind of way...like a trap."

"What the fuck does that even mean?!" Sophia snaps, not at Lawrence but at the world. Her crying renews, even more than before. "I can't be trapped down here!"

"Soph," Lawrence manages. "We'll get through it. We...we'll stay together, and figure this out. Tim's great at strategizing. He came up with the flashlight idea already, and he kicked my ass like ten times in a row that one night we played drunk chess. Ain't that right, Tim?"

"Tim?" Sophia whispers.

My arms are wrapped around my legs, clasped tightly to myself. I don't know what I look like in this dark cavern, but I know how I feel: like I'm tied up and thrown in the trunk of a car, thrashing and flailing to get out. Every breath I take feels like it's spliced in half—catching in my chest—and I need every desperate gasp more than the last. I can't relax or slow down. I'm almost crying now, and god I want to, but if my muffled sob is what gives away our position and that thing comes to kill us all, it'll be my fault. It already is; I should have stopped us from coming in here. I knew it would all go wrong. I'm too much of a fucking coward to speak my mind to my closest friends, to speak at all, to cry in the darkness when no one can even see me...

I feel a hand rest gently on my knee in the darkness. I close my eyes and exhale...a little more deeply than before. Sophia's been my best friend since the fifth grade. Back when I still wore a SpongeBob backpack, even though everyone else had already received the unspoken social cue that we were supposed to be too old for cartoon school supplies. Back when I still had to be afraid of my stepdad. She knew everything about me, often before I did. It's still a complete mystery to me; I don't how she knows I'm having a classic Tim Fischer panic attack without even needing to see or hear me. I'm also baffled as to why a hand on my kneecap can relieve my tightened lungs.

"It'll be okay, Tim," Sophia whispers. "We'll get out of this somehow." Her voice already sounds steadier, supplied by a deep, internal well of strength and courage reserved for all but herself. Her hand squeezes my knee more firmly.

We've been sitting here for about an hour. I guess that only because it feels like it's been ten hours. In the quiet moments when I'm not spiraling, I notice that the silence in this cave isn't really that silent. When we first crouched down it felt like there was a bass amp going off in my ears; a subwoofer of noiselessness. Normal sound was so loud that its absence felt louder. As I've slowly grown accustomed to it, I realize that there are a symphony of sub-sounds: the faintest echoes...dripping of water...an occasional scurrying. It feels like I have super powers, but in reality my life has just finally shut up. The silence and darkness are far from relaxing; rather, they provide a canvas for my mind to paint aimlessly and infinitely. Every horror I imagine comes to life, bursting from every crack and groping for my ankles. Anything could be in this place, anything could happen to any of us...

I reach my hand out, resting it on top of Sophia's. My eyes close, and I exhale fully for the first time. It'll be okay.

"Ehhm. Hello there, young ones," a strange voice speaks in the darkness.

CHAPTER 16

The four of us tense, remaining silent. The voice seems to be everywhere at once, bouncing and echoing off the tunnel. My eyes are reflexively wide, despite not being able to see a thing.

"I understand that you are afraid, hmm," the voice continues, adding a strange throat clearing after he speaks in a nasally, lifeless voice. "Not from around here, are we?"

Lawrence is the first to speak. "No, we aren't. Who are you?" I can hear the stiff composure as he articulates each word. I also think I hear the faintest sound of a rock being lifted from the ground.

"I am one who calls this place home," the strange voice says. "This is a scary place on your first arrival. Even on your five hundredth arrival, heh." A gargling, throaty laugh escapes the voice like a nervous tick. "But I am here to help you. If you can believe me."

Every word he utters raises a thousand questions. Jupiter, however, asks one that seems more thorough and concise than the scattered debris in my brain.

"If you acknowledge how scary this place is, then how are we supposed to judge whether you are one of the dangers that makes it so scary?"

"Heh. Healthy skepticism is an important survival instinct. Which is good. I will say that if I wanted to do you...ehhm...harm in any form, it would have been quite manageable. I snuck up on you all, certainly. You breathe with a great deal of, ehhm, huffing. Puffing. In comparison to the viciousness existing in the ecosystem down here, including the being with the chains that you encountered, the likes of you are lost lambs to the slaughter. I mean no offense; several decades ago, I lived in the Above as you do. I was once a lost lamb exploring unawares down here. I have not forgotten the feeling, heh."

More questions surface. Jupiter interrogation, round two. "If we were to trust you, what exactly is it that you would 'help' us do?"

"Hmph, well. I suppose I have gotten ahead of myself and been a bit, ehhm, presumptuous. I had thought that you were trapped down here, and may require help getting out safely. I was offering to help in that, I suppose."

"And why do you want to help?" she replies. Somehow Jupiter remains casual throughout the entirety of this conversation, as if she were used to such exchanges. Maybe local treasures like the cigarette lady have trained her.

"As I have said, I understand the feeling of being down here, ehhm, as an outsider. It was not enjoyable. I was in far more danger than I had dared realize at the time. I now consider myself to be a steward of Inferis. The title is far too self-important—such a small fish, I am, heh—but I contribute how I can in maintaining balance. Bringing inhabitants of the Above to where they belong, if that is as they wish, is included under that conception of my self-appointed role."

Stewards, the Above...what the hell is going on?

"I think I trust him," Jupiter turns and says to us. "But we can do whatever you all decide."

Somehow her assessment shocks me more than anything else we've experienced.

"Why?" Sophia asks. "You seem pretty confident."

"I'm not saying I would trust him to file my taxes or care for a newborn, but, given the circumstances, a guide seems necessary. I certainly trust him more than the chain gang behind us. If he sounded like a monster or overly appealing, I would be more skeptical. But, no offense meant," she says, turning back to the voice, "he sounds like a nerd. Straightforward, honest. I can't promise it is the right move. I would just say that my bullshit detector has not picked up on any signals. And we have very few alternatives."

"Couldn't we just try retracing our steps or something?" Lawrence asks. "You know, either continue following the rock wall until we find the original hole we went to, or maybe walk back to the beach and try and go back from there?" Even as Lawrence suggests it, he sounds dubious of his own plan. Getting un-lost before the boat, the torch hypnotism, and the mad-dash would have been tricky, but now it seems impossible.

"I might also posit," the voice adds, "that, regardless of whether you accept my help, I would strongly advise you, ehhm, *not* to go out the way you had come in. You walked in while everyone was sleeping, so it was fairly quiet. Now that things are roused, so to speak...it would likely be the most dangerous way for you to go. You have rung the front doorbell, heh. He will have his servants waiting for you there."

"See, now this is the shit that I don't like," Lawrence says, finally losing his cool. "All of these hints of 'he' and 'servants,' like this guy's either totally insane or we're in goddamn Mordor or something."

The man quiets himself considerably, perhaps to emphasize the importance of keeping our voices down. "I was, heh, a big fan of the Lord of the Rings as a young man. I applaud the reference. I certainly can explain more, but must confess that I...am hesitant..." he pauses, as if looking in the shadows for prying eyes, "to say too much while we stand where we are. Most places in Inferis are not safe, but I would venture that our current location is in the 90th percentile of risk. I will therefore leave you with this: I want to help you, but if you do not wish to be aided I will leave you alone, ehhm, entirely. I will not disturb you again. Now I will speak selfishly...I do not desire to be in these passages any longer, or we will all perish together, and needlessly. So please choose now and we will have our next steps, together or not."

The guy has seemingly answered all questions that he's willing to. Anything we ask beyond this point would only raise the same hesitation: if we don't trust him to tell the truth, then anything he continues to share might be more lies. All options might end up getting us killed, which makes things simpler, at least.

"Tim?" Sophia asks.

"Yeah Tim, whatcha thinking?" Lawrence adds.

I can feel Jupiter's eyes on me as well. Or maybe I just want them to be. Jupiter seems like a clear "Yes" vote, Lawrence is leaning towards a "No." Sophia is probably somewhere in the middle, if I know her. It seems like whatever I pick, we'll ultimately end up choosing.

No one wants to be the one who chose wrong.

"I think we should go with him." I wait for the others to protest, but no one says anything. "I agree with Jupiter's logic. If he wanted to kill us, he would have. More importantly, we can safely assume the chain thing out there is bad news because something weird was definitely happening to our heads at the torches. We also know it would be nearly impossible to retrace our steps on our own, even if we hadn't rung the doorbell. It's four against one with this guy, so in the off-chance that he's leading us to some kind of a trap, we can all walk next to him with a rock in our hand and take him down with us. Mutually assured destruction, which at least makes this potential 'trick' less worthwhile for him to try. If it is trick at all." I exhale deeply. I'm quite used to overthinking, but over-articulating is new to me. "I don't know if any of that made sense," I continue helplessly, "or if others agree. Or if he's willing to have us carry rocks at our sides while he tries to help us. But...yeah. Sorry."

The man seems to be waiting for them to respond first. When they don't, he adds "Rocks would be acceptable. Encouraged, in fact. I believe someone picked one up as I first presented myself, heh. There are dangers everywhere that we will pass through, and I would have cautioned you to have some, ehhm, form of protection. I have my walking staff," he says, tapping a strange-sounding wood against the rock walls with a clank.

"Let's do it," Jupiter says, already standing up.

"Agreed," Lawrence says. "I'm going wherever you three go, and I trust Timmy-Tim. He's the boss."

"Yeah," Sophia says, patting my knee.

In no way have I ever felt like "the boss" of anything or anyone, myself included. Slowly rising—knees cracking painfully from the stiff position we've been folded into—I guide my hand on the wall beside me and begin to paw helplessly for my bearings again.

"What's your name, by the way?" Jupiter asks.

"I am Oliver. Heh."

CHAPTER 17

We walk silently through the cave, anxiously following the pace of our guide by feeling along the rock walls. He could be taking us anywhere in this dark labyrinth, but backing out now would only make us more disoriented than when we started.

After some unknown period of time, Oliver halts us. "We are in a safer region now. Conversation can, ehhm, resume normally, unless told otherwise."

"Can we turn on our flashlights, too?" Sophia asks.

"Hem. Light?" Oliver considers thoughtfully, as if seeing where we're walking is an outlandish suggestion. "Well, I suppose you may. If you are so inclined. My eyes are quite adjusted to darkness, however, so if you would be so kind as to, ehhm, keep it to a minimum and away from my line of sight. That would be most ideal."

Sophia hurriedly turns on her phone light, all of us desperate to see again. Oliver is finally revealed to us, grimacing and turning away like a vampire.

I can't say what I expected Oliver to look like. Maybe a tattered shirt and pants, and grimy from the cave. Something like a long-lost coal miner? What we see is equal parts shocking and terrifying. He's wearing one article of clothing: a strange, scaly type of leather that's been fashioned into a romper, and it is aggressively high up his thighs. The reddish-brown hide is sharply contrasted with his sickly, translucent pale skin. Long, nettled black and gray hairs patch across the entirety of his body, sprouting from his shoulders, chest, ears, and the side of his head. A series of deep scars are carved into his skin, some looking so gruesome that I can't fathom the injury that might have caused them. His body is incredibly lean, except a doughy gut that droops slightly out of his romper due to age—probably in his mid-fifties. He's horribly battered, yet still exudes a great deal of vigor in his slouched posture. He's carrying a walking-stick—clattering as he walks—and most puzzlingly of all...a pair of plastic-looking goggles strapped tightly to his head with a leather band. If I had laid eyes on this slutty, goggled tunnel man before I had spoken to him, I am not sure whether I could have made the call to trust him.

"Umm," Sophia begins, trying to move past the awkwardness, "How do you know your way through this place so well, Oliver?"

He glances back, squinting through the light. "My maps, of course! Would you like to hear about my collection?"

"That would be lovely," Sophia says.

Oliver flashes a manic grin that stretches all the way to his goggles.

Sophia would come to regret her politeness after two consecutive hours of listening to his lecture on cartography.

"After my skills had developed further," he continues, "I began using contour intervals—meaning the maps are, ehhm, colored to differentiate changes in elevation—in addition to form lines, which provide details of the shape of terrain! Scale has always been another major consideration. Drawing scale in areas like this, for example—" he points to a nearby alcove, breathless from his rambling excitement, "is really rather tricky. Difficult to know how wide everything is, and, ehhm, some determinations needed to be made about how to portray their size. Does that make sense?"

The rest of us walk in resolute silence; Lawrence, however, is as excitable as ever. "That totally makes sense! Man, dude, I don't know how you could've managed all of this stuff in the dark, that's insane! I assume you don't have any maps stored in that tight get-up you're sportin' at the moment...do you have a storage locker for them all?"

"Heh—why yes! My house. I do not believe you will have time to see it, as it is quite out of the way from where we're heading. If you would like to come back and visit at some point, ehmm, my wife and I would be beyond pleased to show you our collective works."

Sophia's ears perk up for the first time. She looks sideways at me, pointing to Oliver's back and mouthing the word "WIFE?"

I just shrug. I heard the word as well, but I'm still not over how much thigh he's showing in that scaly outfit.

"Oliver?" she chimes in, interrupting Lawrence's tenth map-related question. "Sorry, did you say you have a wife that lives with you down here?"

"Of course!" he says, glancing back and smiling broadly. Several of his teeth are missing, and the remaining few are crossed awkwardly like old, arthritic fingers. "It would be a terribly lonesome place, beautiful as it is, to not have companionship. Elly and I have been happily together here for the greater part of twenty years, heh."

Sophia's face scrunches. "This may be a silly question," she continues, watching her sneakers closely as we walk around a bend of wet stones, "but did the two of you meet down here?"

"Oh no, we were in the Above together for eight years before descending. Accountants at the same firm. She has always been the adventurous one, heh, and she discovered this blessing when she was searching for Wendigo tracks."

Lawrence, Sophia, I all exchange the same confused look, but Jupiter seems to have come to terms with not understanding half of what Oliver says. I'm glad his wife seems equally...eccentric, at least.

"It was I who took convincing," Oliver continues. "When I first saw Inferis for the first time, I knew it was the most beautiful thing I had ever seen." More confusion; rocks and darkness are rarely considered breathtaking. "It was more than merely the aesthetic value, however. There was a, ehhm, a freeness to it all. An escape from the monotony and civility. A realness that was drained out of us from the Above long ago, that we had never realized was missing until we felt what it was like to be alive again. The veil of, ehhm, falsehood and pretention finally stripped away from humanity's core existence in nature. Then came the transition down: moving things here, gradually holding onto or replacing possessions from the Above, ehhm, et cetera."

"So the goggles," Lawrence asks bluntly, "that's an 'Above' thing? Or are you a goggle-maker too?"

"Heh-heh!" Oliver laughs, wheezily double-snorting. "I like you. No, I have not yet learned the craft of goggle-making—far too busy, you see—but it is on my list. These are one of the few Above possessions that I own, as my vision is too poor to allow me to carry out my daily life here without them. When I first came down I broke four pairs of glasses before determining that I, ehhm, needed them to be durable enough to withstand an Inferis lifestyle."

Lawrence is fan-girling big-time, fascinated with every backstory and tale of adventure that Oliver shares. I'm also—crnnnnch.

My foot steps onto a hard, fragile surface, collapsing it with a shattering crunch. It's stuck on my shoe. The light from the others has left me behind. "Uhh, little help?"

Jupiter turns back. "What are you—" Her eyes widen as she tilts her phone down.

I instantly gag, heaving as I stare at a gray mass of human remains. A mush of flesh, bone, and tattered clothes that has congealed into a blob. My sneaker caved into the decaying, featureless skull. I thrash—violently shaking my leg to release myself, still gagging uncontrollably—but it's stuck.

CRACK.

Oliver hits the skull with his walking stick and it collapses to the ground.

"Euuughh!" I shriek—running forward—wiping at myself like there are spider webs clinging to me. I look down at the gray clay of decay still stuck to my sneaker and pant leg. It feels like it's drying and hardening onto me. My heart rate goes down...and is slowly overcome by a creeping embarrassment from being that freaked out in front of Jupiter.

"Oliver, what the hell is on my shoe, and do we need to be worried? I've never seen or heard of a body looking like that before."

"It is...as you guess," Oliver begins. "Remains may appear, ehhm, different in Inferis than they do Above. Different fates may take them."

I sigh. Lawrence gratefully intervenes. "Like, what the does that mean, though? Now is not the time for riddles; our friend just stepped in some gray dead guy."

Oliver merely nods his head, understandingly. "You do not need to concern yourself with this incident. It will wash off him, certainly, with no harm done. The death and decay of this being is the result of many of the dangers I had, ermm, alluded to earlier. Nothing has changed, except you are now privy to the outcome of these dangers."

Jupiter looks up at me. "That clears it all up."

Somehow I smirk back at her. "It's...as good as it'll get, I guess. Just be on the lookout for a garden hose to spray the corpse off my shoes." She cackles, and I swallow back nausea as I walk next to her.

Our legs ache and stiffen as we continue forward for at least another hour. This certainly isn't the leisurely hike our bodies were prepared for.

"Hey, Oliver?" Sophia calls up to him. "Do you know how much further we have until we get out of here?"

"...sister blue skies..." he mumbles, "he ate the fly, and it was poiiison...poiiisonnn." On Oliver sings, ignoring her with his raspy, cracking tune.

Sophia glances at me with a shrug.

"Hey, where's Mrs. Blues, I could go for tea for two." Oliver is in his own world. It sounds somewhat like the Electric Light Orchestra song "Mr. Blue Sky," but the melody and lyrics are so different at times that I'm convinced it can't be. How many memories of his old life have been twisted and warped in his time down here?

"OLIVER!" Jupiter shouts.

"Hmmhaaa?!" he says, startling. I jump too, in fairness.

"Go for it," Jupiter says, gesturing to Sophia.

"Sorry..." Sophia begins. "Do you have any idea how much further until we get out of here?"

"Hmm. One cannot know for certain. Events never quite occur here as you might hope or anticipate. Part of its, heh, charm. If all goes well and we face very minimal interruption, you should be at the nearest exit tunnel in approximately seven to eight hours of intensive marching."

"Seven to eight hours??" Sophia says. "Are you sure this is the fastest way?"

"Well, it all depends on what you mean by the fastest. There are certainly shorter distances between here and the Above. If we are maimed by a pack of markeet or trampled by the colossum, heh, our deaths would lead to an infinitely lengthy delay to your getting where you would like to go. Factoring in all such considerations...yes."

"Right," Sophia says. "Sorry, I was just expecting it to be shorter."

"We appreciate your prioritization of us not getting trampled," Jupiter says. I laugh to myself, and Jupiter turns and smirks at me. "You watch your step, tough guy."

I had assumed that eight more hours of walking meant more of the same rocky tunnels, but the cave is ever-evolving. Somehow sparse plant growth begins to appear; wild-looking ferns crop up in our path that are flecked with spots of a sickly white-green. Vines tangle their way across the rocks, sometimes wrapping entirely up and around the circumference of the cavern like spider webs. Twisted, ragged fungi sprout from the ground, rooting deep in the cracks of stone.

"Anyone figure out why these plants look so alienish?" Lawrence asks.

"Heh!" Oliver snorts, flashing a toothy grin back to us. "I wonder how you would look if you sprouted down here."

The surrounding wildlife intensifies with every step. A few shrubs occasionally force us to hug the walls of the cave, but soon we're practically bushwhacking through the alien ferns. Mushrooms don't get trampled or crushed underfoot; they are so flexible and rubbery underneath our feet that they spring back after we release our weight. Humidity thickens...pores clog...sweat beads and drops off the tip of my nose. The cave no longer smells like a wet dog; pleasant floral aromas now fill the stifling air, growing warmer with every step. A twittering shriek. The four of us tense as a shrub rattles and then goes still again.

"Arnameeds are not your most pressing concerns where we are. Heh." Oliver continues walking, making us feel quite stupid. Being afraid of "arnameeds" is kid's stuff, apparently...

"And where are we, exactly?" Sophia asks.

"Only a few paces from the Great Plains, of course!"

"Of course," Jupiter repeats. I laugh with her, trying to embrace the anxiety of hearing another made-up underground thing. I swat at a few more white ferns, Jupiter and I taking turns holding them back for each other, until we enter a clearing.

I look up...and the cave opens to a mind-blowing expanse of new world.

The Great Plains.

CHAPTER 18

It's unlike anything I could imagine. The four of us stand speechless, mouths stupidly gaping at the plains ahead of us. A beautiful, dim glow shimmers across its vastness—miles upon miles as far as the eye can see. Sweeping hillsides, thick forests, and...is that a mountain? Our phone flashlights are rendered useless by the size of this place, but luminescent violet lights hover and cascade in the air like a sea of stars you can reach out and touch. These stars are pulsating with life, inhaling and exhaling, up and down like some sort of violet sky jellyfish. Massive, prehistoric birds soar with skeletal wings overhead, then suddenly plummet nose-first toward far-off grasses. Off in the distance, a pack of beasts sprints over the green-white speckled terrain. Almost beyond vision—merely a blur in the distance of speckled violet—is a colossal figure taller than any tree or cliff, striding its gargantuan legs the size of redwood trees. Is that...

"How the hell are we underground?!" Jupiter shouts. Her eyes are wide and wild, breathless with excitement.

Oliver is positively beaming. "As much as I appreciate such excitement at my adopted homeland, heh, we had best trot off. If you have the energy for it still."

"Absolutely," Jupiter says, with an unironic enthusiasm that I haven't seen from her before. She turns to the rest of us, smiling. "Are you all ready?"

"Onward, hyeeeaaah!!' Lawrence announces.

A renewed energy comes over us. This magical world feels like it's ours and ripe for exploration. Lawrence, Jupiter...even Sophia seems to have forgotten the weariness, anxieties, and dangers from hours of stumbling through dark caves. To some extent, I've forgotten, too. Jupiter and I are walking in the back of the group, side-by-side, experiencing this new wonder together.

"Our strategy," Oliver begins, "is to make the straightest path toward the...ehmm..." He clears his throat harsher than before, coughing and gagging up what sounds like a thick bowl of clam chowder. We eye him desperately, hoping this isn't how we lose our precious guide. "...toward the northern tunnel." He finally finishes.

I hadn't noticed before in the poor lighting, but as Oliver speaks his head is constantly shifting to the side, his goggled eyes scanning toward every motion and sound. The twitches remind me of a stray cat, on alert and untrusting of the world. Maybe he's adopted the tick down here...or maybe he's always had it. In the Above he would have been diagnosed with something—PTSD, or maybe just ADHD. He'd likely be heavily medicated, even as a child, and made to focus on one boring task for decades of his life. But evolutionarily it makes all the sense in the world, spreading your attention and concerns to all possible threats. His "disorder" might be the only thing that keeps us alive down here.

"It is, ehhm, a fairly straightforward path to the northern tunnel," Olivers continues. "As mentioned, however, you can never predict the delays in Inferis. Currently the only known threat to us, ehhm, are markeet packs. At the present we are presumably safe, as they prefer to pick off lone travelers rather than groups. Still...have you remembered to gather your makeshift weapons, if necessary?"

Lawrence hurriedly bends down and pulls up the nearest objects he can find: a large, bent stick and a baseball-sized rock. He holds them both out for Sophia to browse. "Can I tempt you, m'lady?"

"Uhh..." she says, wincing a bit at both. "I guess the stick? I'm not carrying a damn boulder in my pocket all day."

Lawrence laughs giddily, clearly believing himself to have gotten the better deal. He hands her the stick and tosses his rock up and down to himself.

Farther ahead—maybe a hundred yards away—a group of animals sprints across the plain at a blurring speed. They look like some kind of wild dog or hyena, with greasy black fur flecked in small patches of brown and white.

"Are those the markeet?" I ask.

Oliver smiles. "Incredibly fast and resourceful, they are. If you are ever in a pinch to, ehhm, find water in the Wastes, you can always look to them to sniff it out."

"And what if they sniff you out first?" asks Sophia.

Oliver turns, goggled eyes bulging at us over a toothy grin. "Anything can happen. Heh."

"Temperature is real weird down here," Lawrence says, ignoring the sinister implication of getting eaten. He takes Sophia's Sox cap off her head and fans himself with it.

She steals the hat back with a scowl and fans herself. "It was a gross, damp cave this whole time," Sophia says, panting, "and now I'm burning up."

"Sounds like textbook menopause to me, honey-buns."

Oh dear.

"Bad!" she says, swatting lazily at him a few times with hat. "Bad! Bad!"

He easily snatches the hat from her tired hand, but this time uses it to fan her for a few minutes. She wraps her arm around his waist appreciatively.

Yes, I am incredibly aware of the profuse sweating under my arms. It's a goddamned swamp down there, but luckily my t-shirt is black. I am not the type of guy to pull his shirt off in these types of situations. Lawrence is, and proceeds to tear off his neon tracksuit revealing the shimmering, shredded abs on his dark skin. Bastard.

"Any reason for the sudden heat, Oliver?" I ask.

"The, ehmm, deviation is the result of geothermal heat sources found on the far quadrants of Inferis, as..."

As Oliver continues what I'm sure is a genuinely fascinating explanation, Jupiter zips off her olive-green sweatshirt and ties it around the waist of her jeans. Her arms and chest are glistening (yes, attractive people "glisten" while I "swamp"), with small beads of sweat dripping from her neck...around her collarbone...and down her white tank top. My neck stiffens as I force my glance to stare at the ground in front of me.

"...so really, the climate cycles are quite, ehhm, interrelated with those of the seasonal changes of the Above. Did that clarify for you?" Oliver finishes.

"Definitely," I mutter.

"Excellent! We should be experiencing some more climate alterations as we proceed forward. I would estimate that we are approximately ten miles from our next checkpoint, the Bramble Bridge."

"Sorry," Sophia cuts in, "did you say *ten* miles?"

"Ehhm, yes," he responds.

"Okay. We may have to stop and rest sometime between now and then, if that's okay with you Oliver. I'm just not in..."

Oliver halts, body tensing.

"I'm sorry," she says, thinking she had said the wrong thing. He glances quickly at Sophia, and then his eyes sweep across the plains like a watchdog. He sniffs, rapidly and deeply, nostrils pointed up and flaring.

"What's with the fog?" Lawrence asks, looking at the drifting air thickening, slowly obscuring our vision. Oliver pauses again, still glancing far off.

"...Precisely," he says finally.

"Uhh, what?"

Oliver does not respond; he's clearly on high alert.

A light haze shifts to a dense cloud among us, sweeping quickly across the plains.

"Should we be getting somewhere safer right now?" I ask. Always the hero.

"Yes," Oliver says. "I have seen this a few times before...very early when I had first arrived with Elly. Heh."

"Where is a safe place to be?" I continue. He ignores me, but not intentionally; his eyes are almost glittering with excitement. His teeth are bearing down on one another, clenched.

"Climb one of these," he says without looking at me, pointing to a few stout trees nearby.

I muster the limited upper body strength I have, arms straining and shaking. The wood feels incredibly soft to my fingertips, porous and rubbery, but it holds and my body contorts sideways among its twisting bends. I find a curved loop of branch for my foot to wedge into to secure myself. I look to the nearby trees to find the others. Lawrence makes it up in seconds, and is already hauling Sophia up behind him for the two of them to share. Oliver clambers into one, and Jupiter makes it up into hers a moment after I do. She's looking down at the growing fog beneath us, as excited as Oliver.

"What is it, Jupiter?" I call over to her. In the thickening fog, a rumbling sensation shakes beneath us.

"I have no idea," she says, smiling. "Don't you feel it though? It's like the whole world is coming alive!"

The rumble spreads closer, intensifying. It is no longer a homogenous sound, but a cacophonous clatter of heavy hooves, a thrashing of teeth and claws, shrills and shrieks of desperation. A sudden onset of stampede and battle, shrouded in fog. It's directly below us now—deafeningly loud, rank with the smell of blood and the brute force impact of an incoming train. None of it is visible aside from the tallest feathers of some bird-like beasts, whose beaks are thrusting violently down onto something. We dangle above it all...helpless, unseeing spectators.

Jupiter shifts herself down slightly. I panic, thinking at first that her arm strength is giving out. The rest of us were able to find loops or Y-shaped branches to perch on, but Jupiter chose to be below hers.

She's creeping down toward fog level, practically dipping her checkered shoe into the chaos. I shift in my tree, trying to get a better look if anything's below her. Not that I could really do anything, but maybe I could guide her to a better branch? What the fuck is she doing?!

Before anything serious can happen to her, the fog begins to dissipate. The commotion below passes to a faint roar and eventually dies down. Oliver wastes no time in descending, implementing a smooth, monkey-in-a-barrel swing to the ground. I attempt a similar grace in front of Jupiter and thud instead. The grass is littered with blood stains and shredded intestines. One furry gray critter disappears into a notch at the root of a tree. I see dozens of notches around, just at quick glance, that likely house thousands of animals. I imagine them taking home the spoils of war, burrowing into them knowing that there are cubs to feed, places to keep them warm, companions to mate with. I suppose everyone in the Above is doing the same thing.

"What was all of this, Oliver?" I ask.

He scratches his head again. "I cannot say for certain. From the few acute incidents I have seen, my understanding is that it is a sort of, ehhm, flurry of predatorial chain reactions, brought about by the fog catalyst. Fog rushes in, allowing one predator to sneak up on its meal. The predator of that predator sees the sudden shift in behavior, and similarly weaponizes the fog. Beautiful. Heh."

I'm left staring at the remnant bloodshed, the others eager to leave the rank fields behind. Without warning, I feel a small hand rest on my shoulder from behind. I twitch with surprise.

"Am I that frightening?" Jupiter says.

Yes, you are.

"No!" I begin, "I was actually wondering, up on the tree it almost looked like you were climbing down it. Maybe I was wrong and mistook..."

She cackles, leading us both across the long grass of the plains. "Your vision is spot-on. While I do appreciate the concern, Timothy whose-last-name-I do-not-know, I will ask you this: wasn't there any part of you that wanted to follow me down there?"

I audibly exhale at the loaded question, making her cackle again. Either I'm killing it, or she's laughing at my expense. The thought of dropping down into that bedlam holds zero appeal for a guy who begs for rainy weekends, fuzzy pajamas, and re-runs of the Great British Bake-Off. But following *her* down there might be different. I would probably follow her just about anywhere. I can't say why...only that I would.

"I thought so," she says with a smirk.

CHAPTER 19

I t's easy to understand why Oliver fell in love with this place; it's as if we've been transported to some combination of the Scottish Highlands, Northern Lights, and Jurassic Park. At every step I'm convinced we're going to be eaten alive, yet still I'm thrilled by the thought of whatever might do the chomping. Jupiter—the bored, unfulfilled cashier at a small-town gas station market—is more alive than I could have imagined. Sophia and Lawrence bounce around like a couple on an exotic honeymoon, pointing and gaping at the wonders around us.

Far in the distance, a herd of large, white animals is running across a hill. We continue walking...and I notice that they're getting much larger, very quickly. Massive beasts the size of small elephants thunder directly toward us. Hairy strands of long, thick white cords jostle on their backs like a janitor's mop swishing up and down, side-to-side, with every stomp. My eyes widen, body tensing slightly.

"Oliver? What do we...?"

Lawrence already has his rock poised above his right shoulder, cocked like a football. I have the feeling it would do as much damage as a ping-pong ball would to me.

Oliver quickly turns to us, back facing the herd. He's waving his pale, hairy arms above his head in a gesture to fend us off. "Stay!" he calls. "These are turin, ehhm. Docile beasts that do not harm humans, unless provoked."

I certainly want to believe him. Lawrence lowers the rock slightly to his side, but I see that he still has it gripped tight, the veins in his forearms bulging. Sophia glances rapidly back and forth, as if calculating how long until they reach us. Jupiter alone looks calm. Her eyes close for a moment, following an inhale that carves the features of her face into heavy stone, unyielding. She feels far, far away.

Looking at the storming turin is like staring down headlights on a highway. Closer they charge—the very ground beneath us beating like drums.

"Perfectly still!" Oliver shouts above the chaos. "No movement whatsoever!"

Twenty feet away...ten feet away. The one heading my way locks eyes with me; a soft, kind white with black pupils holding a void deep enough to fall into. A well of emotion and understanding. He's been here for thousands of years, and probably will be a thousand more. It's massive body rushes...and brushes by me. Its fluff swipes at me like a car wash—drowning me in softness coated with the occasional dead twigs and grasses. A whoosh of sound wave hits me like I'm in a tunnel. Jupiter's calm takes me over and I somehow manage to close my eyes, too. I feel every ounce of the sensation, simultaneously relishing the moment and praying for it to be over.

"HIYEEAAAH!" A high-pitched shriek sounds as the herd rushes by. In response, a chorus of surrounding shouts. We turn to see a tribe of at least a dozen women, some running behind the turin while others are jumping off the beasts and landing in the grass. It's nearly impossible to see them at first—they're all dressed in white tunics made of the same fur as the turin. They're all incredibly fit, with biceps showing on even the sixty- or seventy-year-old women that have sagging arms. Like Oliver, they're ghostly pale. Blue veins show through their skin like spreading tree roots.

The women corral the massive beasts with nothing but their voices and large, curved wooden staves thrust powerfully above their head. The beasts listen. At first they buck at the violence of the shouting and encircling women, herding them closer and closer together. As the circle becomes tighter, though, the women's voices quiet to a murmuring chant, spoken in unison. What they're saying is a complete mystery; every fifth word sounds familiar and the rest is some garbled, guttural sound from deep in their throats. With this chant, the beasts calm to a complete rest.

The eldest looking woman approaches us. She has long, gray hair knotted down to her lower back, and a thin beard of wispy hair braided in front of her. She runs her hand across the bridge of one of the animal's noses, massaging deep in its white fur. The turin closes its large, thoughtful eyes like a dog would, slowly nuzzling her hand. The woman glances to Oliver and begins rapidly speaking. Oliver replies in her native language, albeit slightly more clunky. After a few minutes, she nods and shouts something to the other women.

Oliver turns back to us. "The, ehhm, Narubim have..." He sees the blank looks on our faces and corrects himself. "These women, known as the Narubim, are herdswomen of the turin. They have done so for many generations, and their tribes depend on their roaming because it allows the animals to feed, grow, and produce milk and meat for their survival." He pauses momentarily, looking at us like a professor staring across his lecture hall to gauge exactly how lost we are. "So—ehhm—the Narubim plan to rest and make camp in two miles. They are heading north. That way," he says, pointing. "Which is where we had aspired to go ourselves. They have graciously agreed to host and protect us, as they know me well and I have vouched for you."

The four of us nod. It seems like Oliver was expecting more of a reaction, so I politely add a "Cool!"

"Yeah, thanks Olly!" Lawrence chimes in. "Saving our asses yet again. You da man!"

Oliver doesn't seem to understand what that means, but is flattered nonetheless. He smiles awkwardly, revealing his sparse teeth.

The Narubim gently usher the turin across the Great Plains. They carry long strands of grasses that they wave above the herd, gently cascading it back and forth rhythmically. They do so with ease and routine, chatting and laughing to one another in their own language. I catch one of them stealing a glance back at us and I quickly look away. Instead, I focus on the swaying of the grasses they're controlling. Back...forth...back. I see the floating violet globs drifting toward the turin but never going past the swirl of the grasses, as if they're being shooed away like blood-sucking mosquitos. I pass the weary, two-mile march imagining the violet jellyfish with capes, fangs, and cheesy Transylvanian accents.

Moving on auto-pilot, it takes me a few seconds to notice a long piece of grass swirling above my own head. I turn and see Jupiter behind me, waving it like the herdswomen.

"Just practicing my technique," she says.

"MRRRNNHHHHH" I roar, wriggling my head like the other animals.

I don't know if I've ever had the guts to publicly do an impression of anything before. The exhaustion and panic of the day have worn me down, corroding my ever-present filter...but it works. More Jupiter cackling, followed by her grabbing another long grass strand and using the second to jab and tickle at my neck. The Narubim look back at us again, but this time they're smiling. I smile back, and wave. I hope waving isn't some horrible gesture of warmongering among their culture. They snigger to one another and wave back exaggeratedly, as if it were the first time they had ever performed such a silly gesture.

CHAPTER 20

"**M**y god, those are big titties." Lawrence voices what we're all thinking.

The four of us stare, udderly bewitched as several of the herdswoman make their rounds across the makeshift camp and milk each turin. We're only now noticing the turin udders because their thick heaps of fur overhang them like a shag carpet. The Narubim women expertly pull the heavy fur aside, exposing the twelve teats that are so full they almost drag to the ground. I'm shocked the animals were able to run at all.

Jupiter quickly joins the Narubim around the camp, fearlessly approaching one of the women with jet black hair woven into intricate braids. The language barrier is shockingly easy to overcome. Jupiter smiles and touches her hand to her herself...then points to the turin udder that the woman is working on, mimicking the milking gesture that she watched them perform. The herdswoman nods excitedly and takes her hand, guiding her to crouch on the ground beside her.

"Abs-hukunnug" the Narubim says, pointing to an empty, bladder-like sack on the ground.

Jupiter grabs it and points. "Abs...hookunug?"

The woman nods back excitedly. She guides Jupiter's hand underneath the turin, making sure that her forearm extends wide to prop the cords of white fur out of her way. She then takes Jupiter's free hand in her own calloused one, placing the fingertips across one of the turin's nipples.

"Segattho," she says, and mimics a quick, squeezing motion of her fingers.

"Segattho?" Jupiter says, following the same motion. Warm, gray liquid spurts from the turin. "Segattho! Segattho!!" Jupiter cheers.

The woman looks at her like a proud mother. Some of the surrounding Narubim smile as well, while others giggle a bit. Watching Jupiter's face glow up like that is special. It feels so genuine, so earnest—

—"Han sugen!" A hulking, broad-shouldered Narubim woman standing at about six feet, five inches shouts at me. I freeze and stare. There's an annoyed look in her eyes as she thrusts a heap of long sticks at my chest. She points to a partially completed fence that's surrounding a huddle of turin.

"I..." That's all I manage before she shoves me forward. I stumble toward a group of working Narubim, half of them erecting the fence while the others work to calm the turin being fenced in.

When I arrive, the gargantuan woman shouts "Margenoth!" Maybe she isn't shouting, and the sheer size of her creates a sonic boom in her vocal cords every time she talks. She points to the ground. I don't get it. She points at the fence. I hesitantly step toward the fence, looking at her with a desperate need for clarity. "Margenoth!" She shouts, slapping the bundle of sticks in my hand so hard that they come crashing to the ground. A group of the building Narubim quickly scoop up the wreckage below me and begin constructing with it. My giantess points at a small tangle of brush and short trees that stand about fifty yards away. Then she points back to the stick pile on the ground. "Ennegor, Margenoth."

"Got it!" I say. I'm a wood fetcher!

My legs and arms tire out quickly and sweat pours down the neckline of my t-shirt, but honestly I don't mind; it feels nice to be a part of it all. The camp slowly comes together with every trip I make. They pitch a series of A-frame tents, all made of the same scaly-brown leather material that Oliver has draped over his loins. Fires flicker into view as the Narubim send flint sparks flying over piles of dusty-looking twigs—a dust that I watch them sprinkle on themselves, seemingly to make the fire catch more quickly in this damp atmosphere. Rotating spits slow-cook strips of a strange gray meat and long gourd vegetables.

It's incredible to watch a nondescript patch of field become a small village, bustling with work orders, friendly teasing, and quiet rest from a long day's journey.

The fence is finally finished! I collapse on the ground near Lawrence and Sophia, who are already sitting by one of the fires. The three of us lay completely limp, shattered from roughly fourteen hours of walking, running, climbing, fencing, and hiding in the darkness in fear (still exhausting work). My legs feel like tension wires, and I'm pretty sure Sophia is asleep with a large rock digging into her back.

"I am weaaary!" Lawrence calls out to no one, removing his shoes and socks. He rolls up the pants of his hideous neon-yellow jumpsuit that I will never stop loathing, stretching out his calves.

At the sound of Lawrence's cry, Sophia wakes with a loud snort...then groans and lays back down. "It's crazy," she mutters, looking up at the violet-flecked sky above us.

"Yeah," I say, knowing what she means. I look to the camp and see Jupiter still working, smiling and chatting with the women as if she's already adopted their way of life.

Despite being "weaaary," Lawrence is determined to make new friends. Narubim passersby receive offerings of his ceremonial beef jerky, which I had completely forgotten about.

"He's been sneaking some from my bag this whole time," Sophia says, rolling her eyes. "No idea how he isn't sick of it yet."

One of the younger women pauses at his commotion. She clearly doesn't understand a word he's saying to her, but the aggressive "EAT" he shouts along with the miming of chomping teeth seems to do the trick. She accepts the jerky he extends to her, cautiously taking a bite. We all wait on bated breath. Of all of the modernized, Western gas-station junk food, surely jerky has to be the most culturally translatable? At least more so than a Zebra Cake or Mountain Dew.

She immediately makes a face of disgust, holding out her tongue and waving her hand in front of her mouth. I then remember it's the

Hot and Sweet flavor, which is doused in some sort of nuclear-level seasoning and chemicals. Sophia and I laugh along with the other Narubim women. Deeply offended but undeterred, Lawrence approaches the bison pen that I proudly contributed to. The fence is reasonably far away, but Lawrence's communication technique makes it easy for us to eavesdrop.

"MAY. I. TOUCH. NICE. ANIMAL?" he yells, struggling to charade every word. Oliver quickly shuffles over to him to more adequately translate. The woman looks surprised, but nods and leads Lawrence over to the nearest turin.

"Sophia..." I say, seeing the disaster that's about to unfold.

"Yep," she responds, already rising and brushing off her grass-stained leggings. She heads toward Lawrence, and I resume my well-deserved relaxation. My eyes close, and I relish in the warmth of the fire by my side. My arms feel hollow, but my mind feels light for the first time since we've been trapped down here. Maybe even before then. There's a simplicity to this life; a singular focus on basic needs that is easy to wrap my head around. Find wood, make fence. See scary things, hide. The circumstances I need to worry about will stare right at me, so it's easy to know when I can rest easy. Time passes steadily by, the chatter of camp a soothing backdrop.

"Don't you look comfortable?" Jupiter says with a smirk.

CHAPTER 21

"So you're not even going to look around?"

Jupiter is standing over me. She reaches down her slender arm to lift me up before I can attempt to stammer a response. "I'm tired," I might say. "I have had a traumatic alien experience and would like to go to bed and pray it was a dream," I might confess. But no.

"It's not every day you get to see a world outside of your own," she continues, lifting my weight with surprising ease. She's already walking ahead, talking to me without looking back. I thought I wanted sleep more than anything in the world, but here I am jogging to catch up with her. "I think I saw some revelry over here; some of the women were..."

I miss the rest of her sentence. The Narubim are excitedly moving about the camp: some brusquely finishing their chores, others gleefully running toward one another, laughing and chatting. I'm jostled—disoriented from the small crowd and activity. Most of them are smiling, though. Beautiful smiles that soften the sternest faces, the harshness of the underworld that's carved them. A herdswoman with wild black hair lifts her white tunic and flashes her backside at another, running off and shouting as the other playfully shouts back and chases her. A few young girls, probably only ten or eleven years old, throw tennis-ball sized rocks in unison, one of them shouting in triumph as hers lands much closer to a stick anchored in the ground. Another is drinking a liquid from a sagging waterskin that makes her face contort in disgust. A shorter woman with a wide gap in her teeth grabs it from her and drinks it without flinching.

"Coming?" Jupiter says. She waves for me to follow her and ducks into the flap of a tent, disappearing. I can't say that I feel welcome or wanted in this strange dwelling, but I don't hear shouting at Jupiter's intrusion. I push the flap aside and enter a warm, glowing tent. Inside are piles of beautifully colored weavings hanging and stacked in a corner. Four women sit on small stumps around a fire. One of them—the only one whose hair isn't graying with age—leans toward Jupiter who is sitting on the floor, legs underneath her.

I sit down beside Jupiter, trying not to stand out too much. She glances at me, smirking. She separates a thread pile in her lap, and floats half of it to me before turning her attention back to the instructor.

"Nulayah" the woman says, pointing to herself. Nulayah is draped in a sheen white gown with curling black hair down to her waist.

"Tim" I say, tapping my chest.

"Teem," she says, smiling and returning to her work. Her slender, bony hands dexterously manipulate several threads. I stare in amazement as the dirty fingernails take two strands and swirl a looped knot between them in a fluid, half-second motion. Again and again Nulayah does it, extending the single strands into lengths of three, four, five. After it's several feet long, she adds it to a pile of other extended strands. When she has enough, she lays out about a dozen extended strands on the hide floor and begins the most confusing plaiting I've ever seen. It results in a long, strong coil of rope thread, beautifully entwining itself with waves and curves. She tosses the rope onto a pile of similar ones in the corner. The older women are picking from this pile, turning these individual coils into a half-formed tapestry on their collective laps.

Nulayah turns back to us, nodding excitedly toward the thread piles on our laps. Jupiter and I look at each other, smiling. We get started. Nulayah is leaning over Jupiter, muttering and pointing to her hands. The knotting gives me no trouble at all, although I'm at least four times slower than Nulayah. The thread gets longer and longer, and Nulayah only stops working with Jupiter for a moment to say "Hreet!" She makes a chopping gesture toward my extended thread before I can continue on. I count...ten individual threads with nine knots. Each one needs to be this. I hesitantly place it to the side and start with a new one.

"Yes?" I say.

She nods encouragingly.

"How did you finish one already?!" Jupiter demands, staring at my pile. My face reddens. I keep my head down on my work, trying to think of how to explain myself.

"I've...just done a few things like this before. Like knot tying and things, so it's similar."

"Were you a boy scout?" she asks, glancing up from her work. She's up to 5 knots on her first extended strand, but it looks good. I'm almost finished with my second strand.

"No, not a boy scout. Just...learned it myself. For fun."

A pause. She's scrunching the side of her lip in concentration, then releases as her black nails manage to tie the knot. "That's really cool. Any other secret hobbies I should know about?"

I am sure, to her, this feels like a perfectly normal and innocent line of questioning. My organs shut down.

"A few," is all I manage. My face is probably blue-ish from lack of oxygen.

Jupiter is smirking. "Like what? Anything impressive?"

"Nothing important."

"Well obviously!" she says, not bothering to look up from her work. "You don't do hobbies because they're important; all hobbies are objectively dumb. Football is just twenty-two grown men maneuvering a ball across a lawn. Puzzles are just putting together a picture piece-by-piece and then taking it apart and hiding it in a box. All nonsense. I'm not doing this because it's important for my survival in any way," she says, holding up her now completed strand with a smile. "I do it because it's fun, therapeutic, or expands my mind in some way. It's a luxury that makes the requirements of life worth doing."

I hadn't thought of that. Everyone else's hobbies had always made more sense, or at least were more accepted.

"So," Jupiter adds, now working on her second strand, "care to actually answer my question?"

I smile, thinking of how strange it must be to talk to me. How many times has a simple question like "What do you do for fun?" sent me into a tailspin? "Well," I begin, "I mentioned the knot-tying. Also crocheting, which probably helps. I've done some wood-carving, juggling, some—"

"—You cannot juggle," she interrupts, dropping the thread she was working on.

"Umm...yeah? I spent a summer learning. It's not that...hard..."

I trail off, seeing Jupiter reach toward the fire at the center of the tent. She grabs at the edge of the logs and picks up a few stray sticks that are unburnt, handing three to me. "Go, circus man. I'll believe it when I see it."

I laugh, bouncing them in my hand for a moment to feel their weight. Sticks are a bit harder than balls because they flip, but still very doable. I send them up and across from each other, one at a time. I catch a fluid rhythm, but almost lose it the second I look up at Jupiter's face.

"Tim, when did you get this cool?! What else can you do?"

I let the sticks fall into my hands and do a mock bow. I completely forgot about the Narubim women, who are now pumping their fists in front of their chests and smiling.

"A lot of silly things like that, I guess. I call them...oddhobs."

Sweat drips from my back, possibly from the heat of the fire...or more probably because I've just outed myself as a weirdo. She scrunches her face at me, leaning back.

"As in...odd hobbies?"

"Bingo," I say, trying to be nonchalant. "Things that are weird or niche enough that I don't feel comfortable sharing with the general public. For their protection."

"God, I love introverts," Jupiter says, laughing to herself.

Nulayah quietly sips some mystery liquid from a drooping waterskin, and Jupiter reaches out her hand for it as well. Nulayah shakes her hands, as if imitating her is a bad idea, but Jupiter reaches for it anyway. Jupiter takes a large sip, and her face immediately contorts inward like a black hole filled with lemons. Nulayah laughs, reaching for the pouch back, but somehow Jupiter manages to go back in for seconds, this time shuddering violently in her limbs. She ignores the giggling Nulayah and extends the skin to me with her slender arm.

"Bottoms up, Tim. It's time to get real weird with these oddhobs."

It's the dumbest possible rationale, but hearing her say "oddhobs" is what does it. In one second, she mentions a decade-long shame of mine and shares in it with me. Asks to participate in it. A tension in my chest—a deep knotting that I never knew existed—suddenly releases. I grab the mystery liquid and chug as hard as she did. The taste is nightmarish. My brain and taste buds don't even know what to compare it to. Curdled helicopter fuel? Fermented battery acid? She laughs at my expression and I love it. I'm about to make some joke back to her, and then whatever I just consumed hits me like a ton of bricks. Harder than any alcohol or substance I've ever taken.

My head feels heavy in a great way. Drooping, dipping, and then swirling back down like a rollercoaster. I giggle giddily at the image, and at the sensation itself. Across the fire I see the older Narubim taking swigs as well; gentler, but with a reaction as dulled as if it were tap water.

"You feeling it this much, too?" I ask.

She pats her hand on the knee of my jeans to steady herself. "I sure am, Timmmyyy. Let's see how good your knitting is when you're zonked out of your miiind."

CHAPTER 22

O ur bodies stumble to the ground like fallen leaves. We're back at our section of camp. My head is buzzing from whatever toxin we drank with the weaving women; Inferis dwellers haven't figured out taste, but their substance potency is on-point. It's been a whirl of conversation, of jokes, of us. It could have been an hour or six, I really can't tell. Jupiter's hand is pressing on my shoulder, leg tangled across mine. I've never seen her this relaxed before; even when she acts wild and impulsive there's a kind of spiteful intentionality to it, like she's daring the universe to try and stop her.

The green and white flecked grasses brush against our clothes and bare skin. I rip a handful of grass by the roots and throw it at Jupiter thoughtlessly.

"Ohhh no you DON'T!" she erupts, digging for her own ammunition. She crawls over, straddling me and grabbing at the neckline of my shirt to stuff grass inside. I'm able to grab her wrist, pinning her arms to her side as she strains. Then, I feel her muscles loosen. She drops the patch of grass, still laughing, and collapses her weight onto me.

The sensation of her wakes me up. For the first time our bodies are pressed together, and I feel the heat radiating off her. Her face is hovering above mine, a foot away, maybe less. She's still smiling, but this time it's not playful or devious. There's a kindness...a sadness to her eyes that soften the expression.

"Hey," she says. "I like you."

She leans forward before I can process what's happening. Her eyes close, and her lips press into mine. I press back, realizing how hungry I've been for this, for her. Jupiter's hand is already resting on my shoulder, and I slide mine onto the soft, cotton fabric curving above her hip. I squeeze—desperate to grip and paw at every square inch of her frame—while my right hand reaches gently to caress the side of her cheek. It glides across her skin, sliding back her hair like a curtain. I lean forward more. We press ourselves into one another as if these are the last seconds we'll ever have again. Maybe they are. Her hands scratch through my hair, glide under my shirt. She pulls me closer to her, despite not having any space left for us to bridge. Our breath desperately escapes in the milliseconds our lips spend apart from one another—still too long—steaming the sides of our cheeks, bathing them in our desire to embrace again. We do. Again and again we come together...

I hold her away from me, gently. We're gazing into each other's eyes, hearts slowing but beating in sync with each other. I lower my gaze. She looks confused, hurt.

"I'm sorry," I say. "I...I really like you too. I desperately want this to happen another time, but right now just doesn't seem like a great idea, you know? We're both drunk, or whatever this feeling is."

"Yes," she agrees. "We are." She's smirking at me now, shaking her head.

"Listen, I'm really sorry, I—"

"Tim," she cuts me off, "Don't ever apologize to someone for worrying about sexual consent. If something feels not right to you, that's a good enough reason to stop. A lot of guys could learn a thing from you." As she says this last phrase, she slaps my chest and drops down on her back beside me. "Hell of a kiss, by the way." She's smiling to herself, looking up at the drifting violet flecks above.

"Yeah," I say, already reminiscing about the seconds before. She glances back, her green eyes fixed on me.

"So. Shall we talk? Get to know one another? Young, unrequited lovers must pass the time somehow." What a weird, wonderful woman.

"I'd love that," I say. "Can I start with a question?"

She looks surprised. "You have the floor, Timothy."

"Is...that a tattoo of a stapler on your hip?" I say, pointing to the exposed skin below her tank top.

"It certainly is."

Another moment of silence.

"Why..." I begin, and she already starts cackling.

"Because fuck it. Fuck everything. That's why." She's still smiling, but the wildness has returned; that same look I saw when she was climbing down the tree into a foggy stampede. The light from the campfire flickers across her corneas. At first it's scary to see, but some magnetism within them draws me in. It's infectious—maybe this whole place is.

I reach my hand out to her, clasping our fingers together. "Is this okay?" I ask.

"Very okay." Her slender hand tightens in my own, welcoming it.

"Can I ask you something else?"

"A third question? We seem to be getting quite greedy, but I'll allow it."

I hear a pleasure in her voice, as if excited to be finally asked about herself. We'll see if she still feels that way after I ask. I prop myself on my side, leaning my weight on my elbow so that I can face her.

"What was it that you felt when we were hypnotized by the ring of torches at the altar?"

Her smile falters momentarily. Still there, but with a well of sadness behind her eyes. She picks at the grass by her feet, absently tearing them and tossing them at the fire. "I...I saw my mother's funeral. She was lying there dead. She looked really peaceful."

"I'm so sorry. She's dead, then?"

She shakes her head but resumes picking grass. I do the same, hoping that might make it easier for her to continue. "I don't hide it, but I also don't share it frequently because most people are too absorbed in their own lives to care. I don't blame them for that, either; it's just a fact. Essentially, my mom is an alcoholic psycho because she was assaulted and abused often as a child. My dad left soon after I was born because he couldn't handle caring for her or me, let alone both. She was allegedly more useful when I was young; for as long as I was physically incapable of caring for myself, she managed to hold it together with the shred of maternal instincts she possessed. Things were difficult for a while. Still are," she clarifies with a shrug, "but once I turned fourteen, I could at least fudge a few papers and get a job, help pay rent, work more around the house. Still, at twenty-four years old, I can't make enough income to move out and support her. I likely hate my mother more than anyone else in the world ever has—even more than my dipshit dad who couldn't be bothered to try—but there is no one else to take care of her. The thought of her rotting in some state-run institution feels worse to me. But coming home from a twelve-hour shift knowing she will be there waiting for me..."

Jupiter's fingers unsteadily dissect a blade of coarse grass, jittering as they manage to tear it in half, in half, in half until there's nothing but a speck left. She drops it and picks up another.

"There's a pit in my stomach, every second—even if I'm away—knowing that I have to go back. To clean her up after she's shit herself, or sweep up shattered glass after she tried to throw it at my head, or puked up blood and whatever poison she's drowned herself in again. Unless, by some fucking miracle, she chokes on her Cocoa Puffs one morning and drops dead. I'll probably have to clean that mess up, too, but at least it will be the last time."

I stop pretending to pick at grass and grab her hand tightly. She glances up again, this time with no trace of a smile. Her face stiffens in a painful effort not to cry...and she doesn't.

I listen intently, all while racking my brain as to how the hell anyone should respond. The sharing of "hope my mom dies" goes well beyond my stunted social capacity. I squeeze her hand a little tighter.

"I'm really sorry. That...sucks."

She snorts. "Sucks, huh?"

"I'm sorry! I just...that sounds like it's impossibly hard. Feeling anchored to something toxic like that for so long, and someone that you love."

She nods. "Yes. Fun stuff."

I can imagine why she's so happy down here, where she's able to forget. "I'm sure it doesn't matter to you, but I think it's badass how much you do for your mom and yourself. Not many people would be able to or willing to fill that role, and you do it so...confidently."

She squeezes my hand back. "I won't say it isn't nice to hear, especially from someone so quiet. You can be a bit hard to read at times."

I hesitate for a moment. "Am I?"

She cackles to herself. "Oh, just a bit perhaps. I don't mind," she adds, seeing the look on my face, "but for me it's helpful to open up to others, when I can. You're only as sick as your secrets."

How sick does it make me if I don't share anything with anyone ever? "If I tell you..." I begin, my voice already shaking. "If I tell you what my torch hallucination was, could you promise not to laugh?"

She shakes her head. "I will not promise that. Laughing can happen involuntarily. I can promise that I'll show kindness and respect to you regardless of what you say, in gratitude for your willingness to share."

Ugh, I'm obsessed with her. "Okay," I say, hyping myself up. "Okay. It was...me and you. We were...together."

Another smirk. "Together as in dating? Or as in...what we were just about to do now?"

I swallow. "Closer to option two, although my vision felt a bit more tasteful."

"Are you insinuating that drunkenly wrestling with me in a campsite with strangers isn't 'tasteful?' And on the subject of you not sharing much, admitting that you had hobbies seemed as painful as pulling teeth. Why the coyness?"

"Divulging parts of my hobbies or personality hasn't always gone well. At various parts of my life, including when I was a kid, people have..."

"People suck," she finishes easily.

I snort with laughter. "It's just been easier for me to not share, so I don't. At first I assumed no one cared, so I wouldn't share anything unless I was explicitly asked. I considered it being a 'closed book'—it's really easy to just flip open the cover and learn whatever you want. But then, even when I was directly asked, I would still get harassed. It's like...how many times can I get called a fucking loser or creep? How many times can they hurt me or make me do things before I just stop? Stop engaging. Stop taking the bait. It just..." I didn't mean to ramble like this. Still, she's patiently waiting for me to finish. "It's easier to be the pre-approved versions of myself, rather than risk anything more. At a certain point it just becomes my fault for not learning, for continuing to put myself in that position."

She eyes me closely for a moment. "...I'm guessing there are some deeper parts of that story that you aren't ready to talk about yet. Is that right?"

I swallow. There's always been those few flashing images that find a way of jamming their way into my brain when I'm trying to sleep. No matter how hard I push them away, they come back more persistent. A hand at the throat...unzipping corduroys...stale cigar hovering inches above when I'm almost asleep. Sometimes I hear my own dissociated voice, yelling.

"Can I ask you a favor, Tim?"

I return to reality, slowly registering Jupiter's words. I don't feel well. Either that drink had a horrible side effect, or it's wearing off and I have to feel normal existence again. I feel claustrophobic. I—

"Could you take a few deep breaths with me?" she continues. I watch her chest and stomach rise slowly, swelling with air. Her lips purse, slowly releasing air. It takes me a few seconds to notice that I'm doing the same. Simply watching her breathe puts me at ease.

"I've got a few responses to your sharing, if you'll allow," Jupiter says. I nod in agreement, terrified at what she might say. But I keep breathing.

"I'm sorry you dealt with all of that. That you're still dealing with it. Everything that you've ever shared with me has only made me like you more. Some people might not like your hobbies and personality, but there's so many more who are missing out on a great deal of joy and happiness that your unfiltered self would have brought to them. Me, for example."

"How..." I begin, overwhelmed by the kindness. "Thank you." I feel a breeze come across the sky; the first one I've experienced since we've been down here. I don't know where it's coming from or how it can possibly exist, but I see a clustered cloud of violet lights above us, gently gliding with the air current.

She smiles. "It's truly my pleasure. I could have used some of your undaunted hobbying when my mom was at her worst. On nights when she passed out, I would have to stay up late to make sure I didn't need to drive her to the emergency room. I would play ridiculous games with myself to pass the time. On one occasion I watched *Count of Monte Cristo*, so I spent the entire summer counting and naming each floor tile in my kitchen like they do in the movie."

"Most of my hobby ideas aren't prison-based," I clarify.

"I could have guessed; they don't usually allow knitting needles in the slammer. Part of the tile-naming was that it was hilarious, like an inside joke with myself. I also derive a certain sick pleasure in the notion that my sanity and survival are solely nurtured in my own mind. My outer world could be any prison or torture imaginable, but a sanctum can be crafted internally that I can take with me anywhere. I'm not saying it's emotionally healthy, but...it's fucking rad."

"It is," I say. "I think I'm more the opposite, actually. The external world generally distracts me from the internal spiraling I put myself through. More importantly, are you going to share the names of your prison tiles?"

"Certain stretches of the kitchen had funnier names, so those sections were my favorite to rehearse. For example, Goose Ravenscrofts, Eddie McDoom, Admiral Troutnet—"

"Woah, hold on. You give each tile first *and* last names?!"

"Well, how else was I supposed to differentiate Eddie McDoom from Eddie Heathouse?"

"You're right, how silly of me. I love the fact that Troutnet has worked his way up to the title of Admiral. It shows his depth of character as a floor tile."

"*She* is a floor tile of action, I agree. Any other questions?"

"No, the floor is yours."

"Ha. After Admiral Troutnet was Thunder Stick, then—"

"Thunder Stick!!" I repeat, bursting into laughter to the point of violently coughing.

"Eaaasy, Tim," she says, clapping my back. "You'll never rise to the rank of admiral with such a frail disposition."

"DID YOU SEE THAT?!?" Lawrence shouts, stumbling back to camp.

I fling myself off Jupiter so quickly it's like I've been tased. I land hard on the ground and she cackles louder than I've ever heard. Lawrence practically collapses in front of us, looking pale and out of breath. He lifts his gross sunshine jumpsuit to wipe the sopping sweat on his forehead, revealing a series of scrapes on his chest.

"What the hell, are you okay dude?" I ask.

He looks up at me completely worn, defeated...hurt. "You mean you missed it?"

"I saw it baby," Sophia says, striding into the camp and sitting by him on the ground. She rubs his sweaty back tenderly. Sophia glances momentarily at Jupiter and me, the faintest grin on her lips. I don't like it. "Law, you're an absolute moron but I love you and you're beyond impressive. A true cowboy."

"Cow-MAN!" he shouts dramatically, rolling over.

Sophia looks up at Jupiter and me. "For those of you who aren't dating a wild animal, Lawrence got so excited from petting the bison-things that he wanted to ride one. And they let him."

"WHAT?!" I say.

"Why would they ever let him?" Jupiter asks.

Sophia shrugs. "Frankly, I think he's the most entertaining person these herder ladies have ever seen, on account of living in a dark cave. They seemed surprised that he didn't fall off in the first two seconds. He was actually fairly comfortable up there."

"I was a beautiful cowman and I could have stayed up there for hours."

I look back at the scratches on his side and point them out to Sophia. She rolls her eyes. "The animals aren't used to being ridden. There was some straggly little tree that the animal rode underneath because *it* could fit, but Lawrence on top of it couldn't."

"He forgot about little ol' me," Lawrence whines. "I did great otherwise, Timmy-Tim!"

"Tim Timmy-Tim, Tim-Tim, Cheroo..." Sophia sings to herself, nestling in the grass. I settle myself down next to Jupiter. The four of us went through hell today, but I feel happier in this moment than I can ever remember. With one final effort, I lean my body up and kiss Jupiter on the cheek. She opens her eyes and smiles at me, in a way that warms me to the core.

"Goodnight, Tim," she whispers.

CHAPTER 23

When I finally wake up, I realize we're alone again. All of the Narubim have left.

The camp we had labored on is entirely deserted, vanished in the night like some traveling circus. Scattered branches are piled on the ground, ashes are stomped into the dirt, and all that's left is the sight of Oliver viciously biting at his own arm as if it were a haunch of meat. Maybe he's itchy?

"My baaaack!" Lawrence announces upon waking. The rest of us are slowly stretching, all looking worse for the wear as yesterday's clothes hang on our bodies like dirty rags. Splotches of grass and ground stick to our faces. I hear a loud pop, and turn to see Jupiter twisting herself into knots to crack her joints.

"Ooh, someone do that to me!" Lawrence calls out. "Crack me like a goddamn walnut, papa's tense!"

Sophia presses the palms of her fingertips on each side of her forehead, massaging the headache that won't be cured until we find a Keurig in Inferis. "We ready to get the hell out?" she asks.

"Yee yee!" Lawrence responds, jumping up.

We begin another trek, accompanied by the slow, familiar crunch of grass. The marching order seems to revert to the same routine every time: Oliver guides us in front, Lawrence eagerly follows at his heels, Sophia stays shortly behind to make sure Lawrence doesn't fall in a ditch, Jupiter is watching them like a reality show and enjoying the scenery, and I'm in the back overthinking something. For example, the kiss last night was real. It happened and it has wormed its way through my brain like a virus. Nothing passes the time like obsessiveness.

Twisted, bizarre forests grow steadily nearer. A dragonfly the size of a baseball circles me for about a half hour. Oliver tells me my hearing will improve if I let it lay eggs in my ear, but I'm not ready to donate my body to science just yet. Lawrence practices throwing a stick like a spear, making a loud "hoouuppa!" sound with every toss. He's getting pretty good. Sophia stops to examine wildflowers with horned petals of lime-green and yellow. It feels insane to me, how quickly we've grown accustomed to our new lives as underground explorers. Yesterday this could all have been a dream, but waking up in it reinforces its reality.

"Tell me something I don't know about you," Jupiter says, walking up to me. "This is rapid fire! I require an answer in three, two, one..."

My mind races to the first thing that comes to mind. "I...love your shoes. And sweatshirt, too, actually."

"Love them on me? Or covet them for yourself?"

"Both," I say. "You pull them off wonderfully, but I bet I could give you a run for your money."

Jupiter raises an eyebrow and starts cackling. "Tim, the confidence! I love it! I mean, you're dead wrong and utterly delusional about besting me, but if your main point is that I have great taste, then I accept. Yours is commendable as well; I love The Smiths. Have any other band t-shirts?"

"Umm, two more. A Modern Baseball shirt with a dog that has sunglasses on—"

"—delightful."

"And a Starfucker shirt with the rainbow prism on it."

"That's such a great album."

"I know, right? Any from you?"

"I have one awe-inspiring David Bowie rhinestone sweater," she says, "but not the full repertoire that you have."

"Hey, we love Bowie in this cave. Oliver might even be a fan."

"Ehhm, huhh?" Oliver shouts behind him. Deep in conversation, I failed to notice that Oliver has his pinky finger several inches into his ear canal. His head is bouncing up and down, trying to jostle something out.

"Okay," Jupiter whispers, both of us giggling. "So to recap: once we get out of here, we're agreeing to joint custody of our wardrobes?"

"I would commit to that," I say, "but I don't know if your shoes would even fit me. Or if they're gross or something. My t-shirts are way more versatile."

"I'll first address your statement by saying that you injure me deeply, Tim. I have beautiful, giant lady-feet that are probably the same size as yours. To your second point, unless we've grown some feral fungal spores down here, they are perfectly clean! Do your 'versatile' shirts have any armpit stains I need to be concerned about?"

They do. I've never learned (or had the motivation to Google) how to get rid of the white deodorant stains under the arms. Sometimes I'm convinced that if I sweat a tiny bit in them again, the stains clear away or get sucked into the fabric or something. "Not...if you're better at doing laundry than I am."

"Oh my god. You dirty, stinky hypocrite!"

"The Narubim mentioned last night," Oliver begins, quieting everyone's chatter, "that we may experience some, ehhm, difficulties with the bridge we need to cross. They were there several days earlier and reported that it was splintered. One of the colossum may have stepped on it—happens occasionally, heh. It takes their village some time to make such repairs, but depending on the degree of damage we may still be able to cross unhindered. If not, detours—ehmm—may be inevitable."

The news brings an unexpected mix of emotions. Yes, I'm devastated that returning home will be delayed, but there's part of me that isn't ready to leave all of this behind. Not yet, anyway.

"You hear that, Lawrence?" Jupiter says. "Start practicing your pole-vaulting with that stick."

"On it!!" he shouts.

Sophia looks pleadingly at Jupiter.

After another hour of walking, we gradually hear rushing water in the distance.

"Wow, listen to it! It must be huge!" Jupiter says.

"She's a purrin'" Lawrence agrees, jumping up with an excited heel-click. He winces momentarily from last night's turin-riding injuries.

"If we aren't able to use the bridge," Sophia begins, "are there are places in the river where we can cross without it? Or does it run too fast?"

"In most places the current is too fast," Oliver says. "There may be some locations where we can wade safely, if this is the case. No way to tell, ehhm, without assessing the damage first." He points forward, directing our eyes toward a massive wooden structure.

The bridge is clearly fucked. The intended design of it resembles half of a ribcage: small sticks are tied together to comprise the walking center, with a series of twisting, arching vines curving up around it in a U-shape. Parts of the thirty-foot crossing seem to still be functional, but about halfway through the vines are snapped, leaving a chunk of the bridge missing. The other end seems to be hovering in the air with almost no structural support left; the stiffened, hardened materials simply remember the shape they had been held in for months or years.

As we approach the shattered bridge, our eyes glance down to the white foaming rapids thundering against the rocks below.

"I'm open to the idea of attempting a heroic leap," Lawrence says to Oliver, beginning to stretch out his calves, "but not sure if any of the others can manage. I could never leave Tim behind like that."

"Message received," Sophia says.

"Heh," Oliver chuckles. "Yes, going around certainly seems like the best solution. I feel compelled to mention that—based on the height of the water level and extent of the, ehhm, damage—this will likely extend our travel for another full day."

The group is silent, the weight of this message sinking in.

"That's okay, I guess." Sophia finally says. "There's really no other alternative, right? So long as we get out in one piece it should...Tim?"

"Lulu," is all I say. So much has happened in the last day—life threatening, reality-shattering events—that I had entirely forgotten about her. Guilt rips through my insides. "The family's dog," I explain to Jupiter. "They trusted me to watch their house and puppy while they're away, and we've been in here for...I don't know how long already." I imagine her alone in the house, starving and terrified.

Lawrence puts his arm around my shoulder and grips it tight. "It'll be alright, my dude. You said yourself that Lulu's been getting at the pantry and tearing through everything, right?"

My breath is caught in my throat, but I nod.

"So you'll get back and find the doggo with shredded food wrappers on the carpet, toilet water splashed around the bathroom, and a few turds on the ground. No harm done to anyone. She'll be lonely, sure, but we'll be back ASAP and give her an extra dose of playtime to make up for it. It may even be liberating for her to dump wherever she wants."

I shake my head and give an exasperated smile. "I guess."

"Also don't forget," Sophia adds, "you haven't been off screwing around. We went for a walk—maybe a little farther than we should have—but no one with a healthy mind could have predicted we would have stumbled into whatever the hell this is. Law is right, Lulu's going to be okay. We just have to worry about getting ourselves out safely, because we can't do anything for her if we don't survive. She'll be our first priority as soon as we're home."

I nod, looking down at the rapids again. Crashing water weaves around sparse, sheer rocks, masking an unknown depth. The idea of a heroic leap almost seems appealing, if it would cut travel time by an entire day. Still, I do agree with everything they're saying. A small trickling of self-hate drips into my mind, but for some reason it's not the bursting dam that it always is. Jupiter rubs her hand gently on my back, silently offering support.

"It'll probably be fine," I say.

Oliver isn't great with emotions. I can't tell if that's because he's lived mostly alone in a hole for thirty years, or if isolation from human emotions was part of the appeal in staying down here. He is kind, though, and seems to hesitate a polite number of seconds before speaking. "Do we...ehm...are we ready to continue?"

The group murmurs in agreement, looking anxiously at me.

"Ready," I say.

When we turn from the bridge, we see something we weren't ready for: a pack of beasts behind us...silently creeping forward.

CHAPTER 24

Barrel-sized, boar-like creatures close in on us. They have short, razor-sharp tusks protruding not just from their faces, but their entire bodies. Pin cushions with a lot of aggression. Thin barbs prickle out from their flared snouts as they stare us down.

"Oliver," I mutter from the side of my mouth. "Help."

"Hendrina are not typically in this region of the plains. Their natural habitat is further west..."

"Do they attack people?" I ask, glancing down and seeing a rock near my feet.

"Yes. Particularly with such, ehh, large numbers in their pack."

The hendrina snort viciously as more and more of them arrive from the nearby brush, making their total about fifteen. Lawrence is still holding his rock from before, poised and looking wildly at each animal to see which he should focus on. Oliver continues muttering absently to himself, "...makes no sense as to why they would be this far east given the time of year...always been able to avoid their territory patterns..." Jupiter looks blank—mind somewhere else entirely, for better or worse. Sophia is as freaked as I am, glancing back at the river behind us.

The creatures are forty feet from us, forming a semicircle that traps us against the river and broken bridge. They inch closer...and the ring tightens. My voice feels like it's on the verge of catching.

Still looking forward at the hendrina, trying not to rouse them further, I mutter "Heroic leap. We have to."

"Dude, yes," Lawrence says, without hesitation. "You all go first, and I'll clobber a couple if they get too close."

"Isn't there any..." Sophia whimpers, unable to finish. She's staring directly at the predators looming ahead.

"On three," I say, tapping Jupiter on the shoulder, hoping she can wake up from wherever the hell she is. "We all turn and go for it." I am furthest along on the bridge, meaning I get the privilege of leaping to my death first.

Sometimes in cartoons they open up a character's skull and reveal that there's a tiny man inside of their brain, controlling their movements with a series of buttons and levers. I desperately hope such a tiny man exists within me right now. The entirety of my body shakes, protesting against the stupid thing I am about to command it to do.

"One." My chest is hollow, breath trapped inside me.

"Two." The world is still. This can't be happening.

"Three—"

I pivot and sprint across the damaged front-half of the bridge. The wooden platforms clatter beneath me, stifling the chorus of commotion behind—my friends screaming, the squealing hendrina, our thundering footsteps. None of that matters, though; if I don't clear the bridge, we're all fucked. If the bridge breaks on me, we're fucked. If I slow down and block the others behind me...fucked. This logic somehow helps me understand that this is the right decision, even if it is impossible.

The shattered hole in the bridge is rapidly approaching. I have to time my spring-off perfectly so that I maximize distance, but not wait so long that I lose my footing or snap through a weak part at the edge of the bridge. The tiny man in my brain tells me to jump...

NOW!

I'm suspended in midair, momentarily weightless. Everything slows down, and I feel a surprising sense of relief. Life is out of my hands for these precious few seconds. I lean my weight so that my sneakers are in front of me...

And I connect! My foot stomps down—the broken bridge teeters at my sudden weight—and I quickly reach for the rib-cage railings to try steadying myself. I need to get off as soon as I can to make room and allow enough weight for—

—The bridge jolts again, a groan escaping from Sophia behind me. I continue forward, hearing her on my heels, breathless—

—Another jolt. The bridge cracks below, and my legs buckle momentarily at the sudden lurch. My final stride reaches the grass of the outer bank and I immediately dive to the side, clearing the way for the others. A painful stitch in my chest reminds me that it's over. I look back in time to see Jupiter land on the bridge...before it collapses.

Her foot goes through a slat in the bridge. Jupiter clutches madly for the ribcage walls, but the bridge loses all structural support and swings, crashing toward the cliff. Oliver is almost on land when it breaks, but he manages to clasp at the top of the hill and heave himself up. Jupiter, further down, claws herself up desperately as new planks snap under her touch. Sophia lays on her stomach at the edge of the hill, reaching to help pull her up. My eyes fall on Lawrence...who's still on the other end.

He watches all of it happen in front of him, just before his foot springs off from the other side. He has no choice: either get gored by a dozen boars at the end of the bridge...or jump. He makes his heroic leap into nothingness. Only air in front of him, Lawrence plummets twenty feet below into the rocky rapids. His arms flail at first, but quickly go limp by his sides to prepare for the fall. It doesn't look real. This...this isn't how it was supposed to go.

Tiny brain-man can fuck himself.

I scan the rapids to follow Lawrence's body—underwater and struggling in the current—and I slide down the edge of the cliff, legs first like in little league baseball. This side of the river isn't a sheer drop below; there's the slightest slope that slows my fall. Friction shaves my jeans and leg into mud and scrapes. If I can grab him the two of us might be able to climb back up the slope somehow. Everything went so wrong so fast that there's no time for me to consider nerves or regrets; I have a laser-focus on Lawrence because this is the only thing that matters.

The last thing I hear before crashing into the water is Sophia's shrill scream ringing across Inferis.

CHAPTER 25

The current is faster and more chaotic than I could have imagined. I crash hard—and am immediately swept under the surface. My body is tossed underwater like a sock in a washing machine. I rush forward endlessly, knowing I somehow have to find Lawrence. My body collides against mossy rocks and rotted branches—pinballing me into desperate disorientation. My head surfaces above water for half a second—a sudden gasp for air, looking frantically for him anywhere—then submerges again. I focus on limiting the number of blows I take to my body from the debris, sticking my arms out in front of me to shift myself away. Head above water. Even if I do find him, I don't know what I would try to do. That's a problem for future me. I'll find a way to...

There he is. His head briefly materializes above the water's surface, heading for what looks and sounds like a sudden falling of water.

More commonly known as a waterfall.

The rapids are still battering me, but I swim with the current to catch up with him. It's almost working, but not nearly fast enough.

"LAWRENCE!" I call, words half-gurgling. I still swim even though the waterfall is getting closer. I need to speed up in order to slow him down, but where the hell is he?! My arms ache and I feel a bruise already forming on my rib, but I wade faster, faster towards the edge. I finally see him again, far too late. He surfaces and I hear a loud gasp for breath.

"LAWRENCE!!"

He turns to me, shocked...and then disappears over the falls.

I couldn't stop myself from going down the falls even if I wanted to; the slick rocks around me just slide off my struggling limbs. The volume of the waterfall cranks up; a deafening roar and no more white water. Just a blue-green arc curving down. I hear the faintest, weakest scream as Lawrence plummets. I have just enough wits to remember to swim slightly to the left so that I don't land on him. My body feels a moment of weightlessness; sucked down the arc like a toilet bowl, and then spit out.

I shrilly scream, purposelessly. Whatever nerve I had coming down into the water is long gone. The fall is both too fast and impossibly long. I feel my naval drop and the wind rushing against my face. Please end. Please be okay. Please—

Uueegh.

I submerge, the weight of the falls hammering me down further. I sink incredibly deep; at least thirty feet down. I feel like a truck ran me over, but my brain reboots itself and my body is still able to swim. The shadow of a body floats above me, flailing awkwardly toward the surface. He's struggling hard, but then again he's much closer to the air than I am. Harder and harder I flap my arms and scissor my legs, emerging into a lighter and lighter shade of water as I near the surface. It's still too far. The dam that is my lungs is ready to burst. My chest is on fire—I'm flailing now too. The violet glow above me is an angelic light, a crowning beacon of renewed life only a few yards away. A few feet away. Closer...

Sudden relief—a choking gasp and heave of air. The violet sky feels like divinity. I see Lawrence gasping and doggedly swimming toward the shore on the left. The cliff is too steep to climb up, but there's a rocky ledge there for him to prop himself on.

"Law!!" I shout, wading toward him.

He turns, wide-eyed and shaken. "You followed me down?!"

"Of...course!" I say, finally clasping the rock ledge next to him. I throw my arm around him, giving him a weak hug. "In my head I was going to try and save you, but that quickly went to shit. Then I just decided, at the very least I'm not going to let you plummet to death all by yourself. You need company!"

"You complete lunatic!" he says, still shaken and surprisingly lost for words. "I...thanks, Tim."

"I've got you, dude. I think the others are probably safe somewhere across the bridge, but I didn't plan with them on where to meet. Maybe we should just stay here for a while and see if they show up?"

"Sounds good. And—ahh fuck, watch it."

My foot accidentally bumped into his leg, and a sudden wince of pain flashes on him.

"You okay?"

"My right leg is definitely broken; when I didn't make the bridge jump I landed on a rock. I still totally lucked out, all things considered." He exhales deeply, staring up at the violet flecked-sky as if to steel himself against the pain. "All of this shit is just too crazy to process."

"I know."

He sighs again, as if casually trying to catch his breath. "It's just one thing after another down here," he manages after a long silence. "I had this long talk with Sophia before we went to sleep and I know she's really struggling, too. Usually I know what to say to make her feel better and get her laughing again, you know? I want to tell her everything's going to be fine, even though it feels like a complete lie. And now my leg is completely fucked..."

In the three years I've known Lawrence, I've rarely seen him be anything more than the confident, silly boyfriend. I know he supports Soph when she's stressed, and occasionally I'll see glimpses of depth, but it's always gone in an instant. To be honest, I can't say that I've ever really tried to ask him about deeper issues like this. After a near-death experience, maybe some of his guard is down. Or maybe I finally have the nerve to try to reach out.

"How are you doing? With all of this, I mean."

"I'm alright," he manages. "In pain now, and obviously terrified. Also just...exhausted? I don't know. Sometimes I feel like I need to be positive for everyone all the time, and it's hard right now."

"Why do you put that on yourself? Always making everyone happy?"

He glances briefly at me but goes back to looking up at the violet sky. "I don't know, I just always have. When I was young and money was tight at home, I would do these silly voices that made my parents laugh, just so they didn't start shouting at each other. When guys at football practice would start getting under each other's skin and fighting, I'd make some stupid sex joke and everyone would just laugh. I love doing that stuff, don't get me wrong, but I kinda had to lean into it to keep the peace." More sighing; he can gladly take the air trapped in my chest if he runs out. "I feel like there's enough shitty and depressing stuff in the world, and if I don't keep pushing against it we'll all be swallowed up. So I try to keep everyone's spirits high; make everything some big joke, or find excitement in the little things like when you were a kid. But when it's less genuine I have to force it, and after a while it can feel really heavy to keep masking over everything. Sometimes I feel like I'm just boiling over, and there are some days where I...can't get out of bed..."

He stops suddenly. There's this look in Lawrence's eyes like he's finally waking up, startled and horrified by what he's sharing.

"Well," I begin, "I do the exact opposite, and I can't say that it helps either. I feel crappy, and then sit in it until it spirals into hating myself even more. Your shenanigans really do make me laugh and help my day, but it's not worth it if they're making you boil over. I know Sophia well, and for her it's always been the unknown that's most stressful. If she can sense that something's off with you but you hide behind a joke, that could be even harder for her. She might think you don't trust her, or that she might have done something to upset you—"

"Never," he says firmly. "She's never done anything wrong. Man, I can't explain how perfect she is for me. And I do trust her—more than anyone—but still there's sometimes this block. It's hard to tell her what's going on if I know it'll make things worse, and even harder to watch her be upset without trying to do something about it." His face looks immensely tired. The bright, sunshine-yellow jumpsuit dripping on him feels like a mockery. I brace myself to risk asking another question, wondering whether it'll be the one to close him off again.

"How do you deal with all of that pressure and stress if you don't open up to anyone?"

He lets out an exhausted laugh that melts into the roaring waterfall behind us. "Nothing, really. Maybe this?" he says, nudging his head up to the violet lights. "Things have been extra stressful lately with the med school process. I know I don't talk about it much, but I've seriously studied my ass off for the MTELs and polished up my applications. When things get bad, I've always been into looking up at the stars. Even since I was a little kid."

"Are you kidding?! I *love* looking at the sky! It just puts everything in perspective and helps me relax."

"It's the best!" he says. "I don't know any of the constellations or planets or anything, but it's just so cool."

"I spent an entire summer, I think when I was like twelve or thirteen, learning about all of them. I can totally show you sometime!"

"Oh my god, YES! How have we not talked about this before?!"

"I'm not great at sharing either," I say, laughing. "We'll work on it."

"HEEEEEYYY!!!"

The two of us look up the cliffs and see Sophia, Jupiter, and Oliver calling down to us.

"EYOOOO!" Lawrence yells back, smiling like his old self. I wonder how much of it he's forcing, or whether the talk helped at all.

"Are you two okay?" Sophia shouts.

"Leg's fucked, probably broken. Otherwise all good!"

"What do we do, Oliver?" I say.

"We should certainly not remain, ehhm, split up. Due to the severity of your injury, the height of the cliff, and the challenging terrain up here, I see few other alternatives: we should jump down with you and wade through the water together. The river will be quite calm now that the falls are, heh, behind us."

Sophia's face wholeheartedly disagrees.

"Is there a safe spot to go down?" Jupiter asks. She's already taking off her checkered shoes and tying them together to dangle around her neck.

"I think it's all clear," I shout, "but I'll go check. Gimme one sec." I kick off the cliff side and propel myself underwater. It's dark and murky, so I keep my arms extended from my sides and wave them around to see if they hit anything. I swirl in wide circles, not making contact with any obstacles. I feel my breath giving—until bright yellow lights suddenly illuminate from the depths of the water. A ring of nine yellow eyes open in unison, oval-shaped with sharp points at both edges. The eyes are patterned like flower petals, joining together in a central point and flaring outward. They blink—again, in unison—with giant pupils beading the center of them, and then shrink away in the depths, finally closing.

I dart up as quickly as I can while keeping my eyes fixed below.

"I appreciate the thorough search!" Sophia shouts down, not joking at all.

"All clear?" Jupiter asks.

"Oliver, it's not safe to come down!!" I gasp. "Come on, Lawrence! There's this giant monster thing with yellow eyes!"

Lawrence is quick to understand. He kicks off the cliff with his good leg and we both start swimming as fast as we can. I wish I took more swim lessons as a kid. My breaststroke probably looks like I'm drowning, but the two of us are able to speed fairly quickly down—

"TIM!!!"

"TIM!!! STOP!!!"

Sophia and Jupiter are both shouting down to us. I turn and whack Lawrence on the back, forcing him up in confusion.

"WHAT?!!"

Oliver trots across the cliff so that he's directly above us, out of breath. "That's just Edward! He...is a sillimus. Edward is quite harmless,

I assure you! In fact, sillimi, ehhm, give excellent massages with their tentacles...if you can train yourself to hold your breath for some time."

"...massages?" I say.

Lawrence hollers with laughter and starts rubbing my shoulders. "You do seem tense, buddy."

I hear Jupiter scream a wild "AYAYAYAYA" behind us as she cliff-dives directly over Edward.

CHAPTER 26

"**H**ell of a leap," I say to Jupiter, smiling. I make room for her to grab onto the rocky ledge next to me.

"Are you joking? You and Lawrence dominated me in style points." Her sopping wet hoodie hangs heavy on her waist, hood bobbing up limply near the surface.

"No one warned me it was this cold, what the hell!" Sophia props herself onto the ledge next to Lawrence, Sox hat in hand and teeth chattering. Before Lawrence can respond, she grabs his face tightly with her free hand and kisses him. She keeps kissing him—again and again on the lips, mouth, cheek—then flings her arms around his neck. "Are you okay?" she whispers, pulling her head back to read the expression on his face.

He smiles softly. "I'm good, babe." He kisses her back on the forehead and squeezes her close with a free arm.

"We thought you died," she begins, teeth still clattering, voice cracking. "All those rocks...the rapids..."

"I know," he says seriously. "But we're good. My leg is probably fractured, but the cold water helps reduce the pain and swelling. We'll figure the rest out once—"

A loud kerplunk. Oliver drops down from the cliff, splashing heavily in the water. We laugh, watching as our goggled guide surfaces his nose and begins paddling like a cartoon dog. He smiles a crooked, toothy grin. "There may be caves and, ehhm, unknown tunnels underneath the waterfall that we could further explore and map. If you are not in a hurry?"

"No," Sophia says. "Home. Out. Now."

"Understood," Oliver replies, and swims downstream.

The five of us slowly wade forward, fully shivering now that our adrenaline is wearing off. Jupiter is bobbing underwater to look for exotic fish, while Lawrence is busy chopping at the surface to try and splash Sophia. After some time, a shore emerges to our left.

"Not, ehhm, that one," Oliver says. He picks up a piece of driftwood floating near him, and throws it at a backpack-sized rock on the shoreline. The rock springs to life, unfolding into a gray, scaly beast. The creature catches the stick in its ring of sharp, triangular fangs, shaking its head and thrashing it side to side until it splinters and scatters to dust. The beast glares at us drifters, snarling its lumpy face and eyes toward us viciously. "Rogmarks are quite territorial, particularly during mating season. Incredibly useful, however, due to the egg sacks that they lay. When not fertilized, the sacks provide fresh water in protected skin pouches. These can be harvested and carried with relative ease in longer desert excursions."

"There are deserts here, too?" Jupiter asks, fascinated.

"Yes..." Oliver says, looking momentarily uncomfortable. "We...ehhm, may have to venture through portions of it. To get out."

The river is teeming with life. Moss on the rocky walls slowly, creepily wriggles its way up the wall with blue-green tendrils. Cute frogs somehow manage to stay perfectly still on the river's surface without being carried away by the current. When we pass by them they shoot their tongues out, causing a mild, stinging rash on our hands.

"Completely harmless, unless it gets in the eye!" Oliver says cheerily.

Coming from the only man wearing goggles. We splash water at them until they topple over. Red fish with spiky fins leap out of the water, and in midair tilt their bodies toward us and press their faces against our shoulders, faces, and hair.

"That's an act of war!" Lawrence shouts, swatting at the first one that "attacked" him.

"No!" Oliver interjects. "Kissing muckins are no threat to you! They, ehhm, rather enjoy the salt from the sweat on our bodies, and some say that their kiss has beneficial properties for the skin."

Sophia giggles as one leaps and smooches her nose. "Think of all the bogus skin-care remedies out there. If companies found these little guys they would make some sort of 'Neutrogena Fish Wash' to sell to everyone."

"That is precisely why Inferis is safeguarded against outside knowledge," Oliver says seriously. "There are far more beneficial resources and wildlife properties down here that would undoubtedly be mutilated, poached, and harvested into decimation should they ever be discovered."

"Like...some cure for cancer?" Lawrence asks.

"Maybe an alternative energy source, or a ton of oil?" I offer.

Oliver shrugs, turning his goggled face to us as he wades the calm stream. "We do not know, and that is a deliberate ignorance. My wife and I have guessed at some of the richness inhabiting Inferis, but the reality is that we do not trust the majority of those in the Above to exercise restraint at a frontier of such magnitude. Some maybe, but, ehhm, it only takes one, as they say." He eyes us with scrutiny.

I environmentally agree with everything Oliver says, but the questions still itch at me. What if all of the suffering endured by cancer patients could get eliminated by some stupid fern down here? Is it up to some hermit in a cave to decide whether humanity should benefit from this world? Lost in thought—spiraling with questions of whether a place can belong to anyone, and whether humanity has a warped relationship with nature—I see a slithering yellow eel moving by my leg. It sails swiftly downstream in a way that reminds me of a Chinese New Year dragon. Its curving, glowing body drifts away, trailing off to wherever it is meant to be. I sigh and smile. I don't have the moral answers to any of this. Maybe I'm not supposed to. In some deep, unknown part me, it makes me happy to leave this beautiful creature undisturbed by everything in the Above for the time being.

"Well, the secret is safe with us," I say.

"Agreed," Sophia adds. "If anyone asks, we got lost in a cave. We can say everything that happened to us before things started getting...weird."

"And no pictures!" Lawrence adds. "Although I do already miss my fuzzy riding companion. Our selfies could look hella fire."

Our group takes a moment of silence for the missed social media opportunity.

We pass by another rocky shore that appears to our left.

"Oliver, how's this one look?" I ask.

He hesitates briefly, still looking dubious at all of us. "It...will suffice."

CHAPTER 27

"Okay, hold on," Lawrence says. He's lying on the rocky shore leading to the Dead Wastes, his jaw clenched in pain. "I'm no doctor yet, but I'm very confident that my leg is fractured. I heard a crack, there's limited range of motion, I can't—" another harsh grimace as he shifts forward "—bear weight on it. We need to RICE it briefly. For that—"

"Haven't had rice, ehhm, in quite some time," Oliver mutters to himself. "I once used to frequent this establishment..."

Lawrence manages a pained smirk. "The RICE technique just means you rest, ice, compress, and elevate the injury to reduce pain and swelling. We'll probably have to build a splint after, if someone wants to help work on that."

"I can give that a shot," I say. "Just let me know what we need."

"Same," Jupiter adds, glancing at me. "I'll give him a hand, and Sophia and Oliver can stay with you now."

"And for team RICE," Sophia asks, nervously grabbing his hand. "What do you need from us?"

"It's pretty easy. We're already doing the 'rest' step," he says, trying to present himself lying down with the flair of a gameshow assistant. His smile quickly turns into another grimace; he notices our concern and gives up trying to lighten the mood. "As far as I know, there's no ice down here. You can just soak my jacket in the cool water of the river and wrap it around me." He moves to untie the dirty, neon-yellow jacket from his waist, but Sophia quickly moves to his side and does it for him, gently.

"No more doing everything yourself, okay?" she says. "Tell us what you need; we're here."

He nods. "Soak the jacket. And my t-shirt. Rotate the two of them so that you can swap them out with whichever is cooler. They'll heat up quickly against my skin."

Sophia eases the shirt over his head and then heads to the river.

"Oliver, the last step is that I need to elevate my leg above my heart. It might be most comfortable for me to just have a slope to rest against. Could you dig a hole in the gravel here for my body to rest down in, with a ramp for my leg to gradually go up? That way too much pressure isn't on the fractured area itself."

"Ehhm, yes. I will regularly seek feedback."

"Thanks, Olly. So for RICE team, we should be doing this for about twenty minutes. Then the splint team can work on getting me a semi-permanent brace, hopefully."

Sophia is already back with the wet jacket, glancing down at her wrist. "My watch still ticks; I'll keep time." She leans over him with his dripping jumpsuit, stretching and guiding the fabric around his leg like a heavy pizza dough. She does this incredibly carefully, letting the soaked jacket glide in the air until it's taut and ready to drape over him. I've never seen her so focused. Not tense, either; just precise and honed-in.

"Great," Lawrence says, still effortfully inhaling. "For team splint, one of you can grab a few pieces of thin, flat driftwood while the other finds some kind of cloth to bind it. We can use our shirts if we get desperate, but we might be able to use seaweed or something, too. I think I saw some in the river."

I glance over at the stream behind us, seeing a few odd pieces of driftwood around already.

"I, ehhm, can offer that there is ample seaweed down there for binding." Oliver shines a crooked, toothy smile at me. He hands me a sharp cutting stone from his hide pocket. "Must be careful down there, heh."

"Careful how? From what?" I look back toward the river, seeing no clear threats.

He bursts into a fit of manic wheezes, clutching at his chest.

"Seriously, what?" I repeat.

"AHHAHHAHAHA," Oliver cackles on.

Beads of sweat drip down Lawrence's forehead, transfixed in pain.

"Whatever," I say, stalking angrily to the stream.

"Not sure what he's up to," Jupiter says, jogging to catch up, "but I'll be nearby collecting driftwood if anything comes up. We can tag-team any river monsters that get you." She leans forward and plants a quick kiss on my cheek, walking away with a gentle glide of her fingers on my shoulder. My head follows her magnetically, the sensation of her touch still tingling on me.

"Careful not to miss any good sticks!" I call back, seeing some driftwood heading downstream.

"Ohhh no you don't!" she yells at a branch. She sprints toward the river and dives in head first—clothes and all—swimming frantically toward it. "You little devil!"

I strip down to my boxers, still clutching the sharp stone that Oliver handed me. I dive down into the river again, swimming to the long wisps of seaweed at the bottom. I reach out to one slimy strand with my left hand...and feel a sudden pressure as the seaweed wraps around my arm. I tense—desperately trying to yank myself free—but to no avail. My left foot drops down in an attempt to propel myself upward, but other strands of seaweed latch onto my leg. I close my eyes for a moment to relax my heartrate, to think. The only parts of me that are stuck were the ones that touched the seaweed. No more touching...only cuts.

I slowly, gingerly glide my right hand with the stone around the drifting seaweed, feeling eerily like I'm dodging laser beams. I maneuver past all of them, then quickly slice the taut seaweed clutching at my arm. It immediately relaxes to a normal, still plant. I quickly do the same for my left leg, then hurriedly swim up to catch my breath. I think about calling Jupiter for help, but decide against it. I submerge again, defiantly tempting the tendrils to lasso around me. For some of them I intentionally let my left arm get tangled again so that they tense, make them easier to cut. I slash at these fuckers hard, channeling the same mania I applied to cleanup Scott and Jeanette's basement. I get lost in a haze of aggression, at times forgetting to rise up for air simply because I'm hungry to slice a few more.

Sopping wet, I heave myself out of the river. Sophia is fitting driftwood around Lawrence's leg to see which fit more snugly in each spot. Both Soph and Jupiter are awkwardly hanging over the patient, holding the planks in place like a puzzle. I drop the green slaughter of seaweed in front of Oliver and he looks up, smiling wildly.

"It is, heh, exciting to see how much we enjoyed our assignment, ehh Tim?"

I don't quite understand the look in his eye, and I don't like it. I drop the cutting stone on the ground and join the others.

Lawrence continues orchestrating his haphazard splint. The planks are all different lengths and sizes, so it's a bit awkward. Some begin near his ankle and go up all the way up to his thigh, while shorter ones are piecemealed together.

"The important thing is for the larger sticks to cover the area near the fracture, to prevent it from moving."

Jupiter, Oliver, and I gently raise his bad leg in the air as Sophia carefully wraps the seaweed strips around. She works quickly but cautiously.

"Remember to keep it tight, but not cutting off circulation," Lawrence adds, sweating from the strain.

Sophia nods. She seems to have a real intuition for this...or maybe she just knows how to read the minute expressions on his face as she tightens. Within minutes, the splint looks surprisingly passable.

"Thanks a million, guys," Lawrence says, looking at all of us uncomfortably. "I...really appreciate it. Seriously."

I smile. "It's no problem at all, Law. You'd do the same for any of us."

"Yeah," Jupiter adds. "Also very cool seeing you work under composure like that. I believe I heard mentions of you going to medical school before, but found it extraordinarily challenging to imagine such a silly boy applying. I get it now."

I watch the corner of his mouth shiver to a smile, his eyes welling with emotion. He swallows, trying to shake it off. "One last thing. I really hate to hold up the group more, but I will need crutches or something. Hopping through Mordor on one foot will only slow us down."

"On it," Jupiter says, already mid-sprint toward the water. She dives back into the river looking for more driftwood.

Sophia and I stare at her, mouths open in surprise. Her clothes had just started to dry off.

CHAPTER 28

The Dead Wastes are misery.

Our water-logged shoes quickly dry out; the parched gravel soaks out the moisture from them like cat litter. Craters in the ground expel smoking, putrid vapors, giving us hoarse, throat-scraping coughs as we stumble along. Lawrence, who would normally outpace all of us, is working twice as hard to propel himself across the unsteady gravel with his makeshift crutches. The violet lights still faintly shine through the dust, but the floating lights seem significantly higher in the sky as if they, too, are repulsed by the landscape. Our vision stifles to a blur of about a hundred feet in any direction rather than the expansive panorama we saw before. The only landmarks to differentiate the terrain are the skeletal carcasses of exotic, oddly shaped creatures.

"Anyone else get the feeling—" Lawrence begins, panting from exertion, "that we're in some middle school field trip at a science museum?"

"They do look like..." hacking cough from Jupiter. "Fuck. They do look like dinosaurs. Especially the huge one up there."

A wide skeletal shape comes into view as we approach. Its face is triangular, with a split across the middle of the skull. There are beautifully curved horns that swoop behind its head and turn back toward the front, each branching into a series of smaller prongs. The whole carcass is weathered and cracking from the dry air; the harsh desert leeched out more life than it ever had to give. I reach my hand out, very hesitantly...

"Oh shit, Tim touched it!" Lawrence shouts. "What's it like? Do you suddenly feel yourself shapeshifting into an animal? Or perhaps you can see through its eyes from when it was alive?"

"Does he have an off switch?" Jupiter asks Sophia.

She smiles, simply relieved to have Lawrence back to his normal self for a moment.

"No powers," I say. I touched the rib bone that curved from the ground up above our heads...and an intense thrill came over me. A shiver coursing throughout my body. Life in the twenty-first century—for me at least—has always consisted of staring at a two-dimensional rectangle of light for sixteen hours a day. Homework, Instagram, reading, job applications, GPS, videogames, porn, text messages, Facetime, and hypochondriac Google searches at one in the morning. The two-dimensional screen is real, but there's an unmistakable hollowness to it that leaves me feeling like a passive observer to life rather than a participant. Touching this skeleton gives me a sensation unlike anything I've felt from a screen. This is real, grounded, ancient, and magnificent. And I share a world with it.

"Tim is in the shapeshifting process as we speak..." Lawrence whispers behind me.

"Everyone down!" Oliver whispers suddenly, dropping to the ground.

Yesterday we might have hesitated, but our survival instincts have attuned to the demands of Inferis. We drop in the clattering gravel, Lawrence toppling over backward with his good leg dangling in the air. The bones of the carcass are wide enough to almost entirely obscure us, but Oliver peeks above one section of it with his dusty goggles. I sit up to do the same...

"No," he mutters, a firm arm pressing me down. "Varsiik scavengers are nearby. We cannot let them see us, ehhm, under any circumstance. Each of you should bury yourselves under the gravel. Now."

I lay completely flat and use both arms to swipe piles of gravel onto myself. I struggle to stifle a cough as a puff of dust comes near my mouth. I have a lovely thought...how much of that dust is bone particle from centuries of carcasses crumbling in this wasteland? The others, including Oliver, bury themselves quickly as well.

"I saw a total of eight individuals," Oliver says, "but where there are some there may be many. Varsiik often conceal their numbers, and, ehhm, have other hunting parties within relatively short distances."

We lay still, entombed in gravel. Silent...

Voices emerge. At first they're mumbled, but then we hear an unknown language similar to that of the herdswomen. This dialect feels harsher, though; a hoarse bark to their words that seems to reflect, or possibly be the result of, the noxious fumes filling the air. The voices grow closer. Perhaps not heading directly toward us, but definitely too close for comfort. I feel naked. I would have shoved gravel up my ass if it concealed me more. Worse, the gravel on me is centimeters from my mouth, tickling my lungs with vapors and dust. The faintest scratch, begging and pleading with me to just...cough. I try taking deep breaths...but as my chest expands the gravel on me trickles off, revealing me further and creating a faint crackling sound.

The immediacy of the threat swallows me whole. Every pervasive thought floods into my brain—every outcome that will occur if I do cough, that might still happen if I don't. I try to relax my mind...and then I remember Jupiter. When we went off the bridge, everyone tensed except for her. She was elsewhere; her entire body and mind relaxed, despite the world insisting danger was in front of her. I always imagine untrue scenarios that are horrible...why not allow myself the respite of a happier delusion?

We're safely out of here, and I'm driving the two of us to the beach. After sunbathing and swimming, she insists on burying me in the sand. She sneaks a kiss on my exposed face, then cackles menacingly as she unburies and tickles my feet, watching me squirm to grab at her. As the sun fades, we remember that we passed a waterside tapas restaurant with silly drinks that she wants to try. We clink glasses over the gentle crashing of waves...

The Varsiik voices grow fainter, far away.

"Are we safe?" breathes Sophia.

"The primary threat has passed," Oliver replies. "But I will request that we stay buried for a few more minutes, and, ehhm, keep discussion to an absolute hush."

"Do you think there are more?" Sophia mutters.

"I believe....I..." Oliver trails off. Whatever attuned senses he has are lost on me. I try to peek out into the sky above, but don't see anything. Nothing...until I feel a slow rumbling in the ground beneath me.

"Is there an earthquake?" I ask.

The shaking intensifies. A narrow line of gravel raised slightly above the ground slithers its way toward us. An armored, scaly-brown missile shoots up from the ground. It emerges from the gravel trail and arcs over us, torpedoing downward. A shriek erupts from the airborne creature that pierces my skull like a migraine. Its mouth is as wide as the entire front of its face, stretching and revealing a long string of pointed teeth that protrude outward. The murky whites of its eyes seem to stare down through me and at nothing at all. It descends toward my face...but I'm still helplessly buried. I rush to unbury my arm and aim a weak side hook at it—but Oliver beats me to it. His walking stick hammers down with a loud clank against its armor, causing another piercing shriek. Hardly any scratch or damage was done to the beast, but the impact knocks it aside. It wriggles its body away from me, nuzzling its conical nose downward and disappearing into the gravel. A trail curves away from us, leading back to the Varsiik scavenger party.

"They're coming!" Sophia shouts, pointing to a group of people charging us.

"Ehhm, behind us too," Oliver says faintly.

I sit up and see that we're surrounded. Swarms of at least twenty ghastly pale men and women approach from every side, shouting "VAR! VAR!" in unison with a spitting, animalistic malice.

It doesn't take them long to tie us up, prodding us across the desert like cattle. Our calves are bound together with hide straps, rubbing our ankles raw and only allowing us to shuffle six inches at a time. Our arms are tied tightly behind our backs, shoulders screaming in protest. At first they make Lawrence walk too, but between his screams of agony, Sophia's desperate pleas, and Oliver's rapid attempts at translation, the Varsiik eventually give up. Instead, they wrap his entire body, with three of the Varsiik hoisting his mummified figure like a pig being carried off to a luau.

But the pain is nothing compared to the terror invoked by our captors. They are a mob of vicious, scabbed skeletons. Both the men and women are almost entirely naked, save for the hide wrappings around their genitals and the breasts of the women. Their skin is paler than moonlight, thinly draped over protruding ribs, shoulder blades, and a concave hollow where their stomach should be. Their skin is cracking from the noxious air, with patches of flesh missing and wretched scars that are poorly healed over. Not everyone believes that the eyes are the windows to the soul...but I am a firm believer that the deranged mania lighting up theirs is indicative of some unknown horror.

The Varsiik also seem to have a competition as to whose weapon can look most gruesome. They seem fairly primitive, made of some combination of bone, leather hide, and a dark, shimmering metal. Each, however, are designed uniquely to the wielder. One woman has a weapon that looks like a giant keyring, connecting three gorging blades with spikes pointing both out and inward. One man has two armguards extending from his wrists to his biceps that are lined with metal spikes. Another wields a massive, curved tusk that's been transformed into a scythe. It has a thin metal blade along its top and bottom, and a cracked human skull ornamenting the handle.

After being forced on for close to an hour, Sophia loses her balance and topples over. She falls hard on her shoulder—harder because she has no limbs to break her fall with. Most of the Varsiik continue walking, but the older gaunt behind Sophia kicks her hard near the kidneys as she squirms to regain her footing. She heaves an exhale, gasping for breath.

"Hey!!" I shout, shuffling faster against my restraints.

Lawrence hears Sophia groan, but sees nothing from his mummified posture. Twisting wildly to crane his neck down toward her, he thrashes about in the arms of his carriers. "You fuckin' shits, I'll kill you before..."

The men carrying Lawrence drop his body to the ground. I dive forward to try and break the fall, but as I lunge I feel a heavy blow hit the back of my head.

The world around me spins as I collapse to the ground. My vision fades and grows darker. I turn, seeing my friends struggling and screaming beside me. My eyes water...lips trembling into the heaviest smile. If I am dying, I am proud to have it be with them. They're all that matter. Sophia, Lawrence, Jupiter...even Oliver. What a wonderful life, to feel so much love.

In an attempt to stand, I drag my head back across the gravel—scraping horribly, but utterly numb to it—and see streaks of blood painted in a smear. I look at it and think, "Hey, that's me."

CHAPTER 29

Darkness.

I can't tell if I'm awake or alive. There's definitely someone crying.

"Mmmnnnhh." The uneven groan escapes my lungs when I shift my body. My head weighs two hundred pounds and is painfully throbbing. I'm not wearing my own clothes; I feel the weight of some thick, heavy hide material and nothing underneath. I wriggle my legs to the side—unbound, I notice—and my foot makes contact with a series of small upright bars.

Am I in a cage?

"Tim...?" A sobbing whisper.

"Mmnnnnh." Apparently I'm turning into Frankenstein's monster.

"Tim, we thought you were dead!! How do you feel?"

"Sophia," I manage. I take a deep breath before struggle to open my eyes. Still darkness. "Where are we?"

"Some sort of bone...palace, if that's possible," Sophia says, semi-hysterical. "Everything in the city is made with bones, but the building we're in is the size of a small skyscraper."

"Ehhm," I hear Oliver clear his throat. "In English, its name would be the 'the Transitory Citadel.'"

Big words are hard right now. "Where's Jupiter? And Lawrence?" I was probably supposed to ask those in a different order considering I've only known Jupiter for two days, but my head feels like scrambled eggs fed through a woodchipper.

"I'm here," Jupiter says from behind me. "And I'm okay."

"Lawrence is fine, too," Sophia adds. "He's been in and out of consciousness; I think he's just tired at this point. After..." her voice catches for a moment. "After they dropped him, it made the worst cracking sound I've ever heard. He blacked out almost immediately from the pain. When I turned to you, your head gushing with blood and the weapon that the skeleton freak was holding was... covered in it. You just dropped." She breaks into renewed sobbing, gasping and coughing as she struggles between the tears, snot, harsh air, and abuse. "We thought you were dead," she repeats. "We thought..."

"I'm okay," I say, hoarsely. I feel the back of my head; my hair is scabbed over and sticky, but I'm not bleeding anymore.

The darkness goes quiet again.

"Do I want to know what the..." I squint my eyes, struggling to scan my short-term memory. "...the Transitory Palace is? Are we in some sort of prison?"

Oliver clears his throat. "It is no prison, ehhm, although we are captives here. The Transitory Citadel is the place of worship for the Varsiik tribes, and we are here to participate in their oldest ritual. The Varsiik exist on the, ehhm, brink of life and death. That is their way. They occupy the world of the living, which is why they were able to capture our party, but they dedicate their lives to the undead realm. Their pride is in starving themselves to the point of near-death, and have, over generations, learned to thrive and function near-fully on such meager substance, heh. The closer they are to death, the closer, they believe, they are to connecting to His will and contributing to his cause."

"His...?" Lawrence asks, groggily.

"Good morning, Law," I mutter.

He laughs; I can't express how incredible it is to hear it in such a gloomy place.

"Finally decided to stop faking it, ehh Tim?"

I smile on the verge tears. "Says the guy who wanted a piggy-back ride through the desert. I bet your leg is fine."

"I can't with this," Sophia whines, somewhere between a laugh and more crying. "I love you idiots."

"Love you, too," Lawrence says. "Tim, how's your head? Do you have a concussion?"

I'm sure this was supposed to be a simple question, but it takes me several seconds to process and make sense of it. "Umm...remind me what concussion symptoms are again?"

"Loss of consciousness after the impact—which you had. Then there's headache, dizziness, confusion, concentration problems, feeling sluggish. There's a few related to light and movement, but given where we are those are less relevant."

After each one he lists, I mentally check off yes, yep, got it, yeah. "I have a concussion," I grunt.

"I figured," he replies. "The good thing is that, so long as there isn't any internal bleeding, there's nothing to do for concussions. They'll go away with time and rest, and if we can't rest now we can get it when we get out of here."

The fact that he still says "when" we get out is why Lawrence is so amazing. Maybe it's my head being clobbered or the weight of the situation that we're in, but suddenly I'm tearing up again. Hopelessness can feel so oppressive and permanent, and then one tiny word choice reminds me how fragile that negativity can be.

"Oliver," Lawrence continues, "what did you mean by 'he' and 'his cause'? Is it an actual person, or is that just how they refer to their god or something?"

Oliver cackles wildly. "The person most definitely exists, though I do not know him. In fact, heh, I believe you all were close to meeting him!"

We lay in darkness, puzzled and terrified. "You mean the thing we saw at the lake?" Jupiter asks. "With the chains and the blue torches?"

"Heh, you are nearing the truth. Agonault is his name, and while you did not see him directly, the chains you heard were likely the sound of one of his servants. Agonault has many of them residing under the—ehhm—lake. Yes, under. That is the Varsiik ritual. The bodies please him..." Oliver says, intensifying in excitement, in savagery. "They please him, so the Varsiik bless, drown, and sacrifice their captives into

139

the river, which ultimately feeds into that very lake. My wife and I, ehhm, do not know how Agonault does it. Preserves them. Brings them to the state that is neither living nor dead. We have seen his servants with our own eyes; their existence is all too real." His words ring in my head. All I can imagine is the lake as some kind of vast pickle jar; corpses floating and bobbing under the surface with glowing eyes, waiting to be summoned. "We also do not know what purpose they serve. Their numbers continue to grow, and he keeps them, ehhm, in hiding. A plot of utter wickedness occupies their existence."

"Why do the Varsiik serve him?" asks Jupiter. "What do they get in return for an outcome that leads in their deaths and his benefit?"

"Many people in the Above," Oliver begins, "do their god's will without ever having seen them or being assured of their existence. The Varsiik have seen the one that they serve—only a taste of his power, ehhm, but quite enough to convince them of Agonault's deism. Just or not, people will serve a god out of love, fear, awe...they fall in line behind those with power. I am not fully informed of their culture—and it has evolved over time, as his needs, ehhm, change—but I believe they are convinced that he will provide his faithful with a special seat by his side in the afterlife, should they aid in his bidding. The truth of this I cannot confirm. Heh."

We all fall silent again. Whatever storybook we've fallen into, it becomes overwhelmingly clear that we're intruding. The Narubim herdswomen, the Varsiik death-worshippers...entire tribes and cultures of people living for generations without the Above. I would feel more secure if I were dropped in the middle of a bustling street in Delhi, or jungle-dwelling people in the Congo. We would at least be akin in our shared experience of sun, sky, and ocean in the Above.

A loud clank. A series of grunting noises...a person out of breath.

A bright orange light pierces the darkness from a trap door in the floor. I stare in horror at the "cages" that contain us: every bar is made with human bones. All of us are wearing the same strange clothes:

something resembling oversized hide ponchos with ceremonial shapes rudimentarily painted on them. It isn't too different from what Oliver normally wears (although gratefully more modest). The outer walls around us are white pillars that form a massive teepee, all angled slightly inward to form a sealed point at the top. From everything Sophia said, these pillars might be bones as well...except they're as wide as a subway car and god knows how long. The floor is the same gleaming black stone of the Varsiik weapons and the stone altar, but its effect on a full floor is incredible; a mirage of swirling black and gray, creating an optical illusion if you stare long enough. As the torchlight moves closer, the flame joins the swirling colors and reflects across the room.

A woman emerges from the trapdoor ladder. Skeletal and pale like all the others, hunched over nearly sideways with bone jewelry ornamenting her wild, mad-scientist tufts of graying hair. She clutches a torch in her left hand, and in her other she cradles some sort of heavy clay pot that's strapped to her shoulder. She grunts, looking angrily at each of us as if our captivity were a nuisance for her. She props her torch in a stone sconce on the outer wall. More grunts from the woman, and suddenly my face and poncho are coated in a reddish powder with an acrid smell. What the fuck? The skeletal woman quickly dips her hand in the clay pot and throws a new handful on Lawrence.

"Timmy-Tim's not enjoying his original blend of seven herbs and spices," Lawrence says. I ignore the comment, violently spitting out the flecks that landed in my mouth.

Sophia's eyes closed too slowly, and she ends up squinting and blinking to get it out.

Jupiter stands there quietly. When the woman leans near, Jupiter quickly lunges for her wrist to snap it against the cage. The woman growls and screams, wrenching her arm free with a force beyond what her bony body should be capable. She quickly grips a stick leaning against the wall, and pokes aggressively at Jupiter until she's pinned at the back wall. Then Jupiter gets doused in powder.

"Worth a shot," she says, massaging her prodded shoulder and glaring at the woman.

Oliver closes his naked eyes (they must have taken his goggles from him), seals his mouth, pinches his nose shut, and waits patiently for his crop-dusting to take place. The woman throws one final handful straight in the air as she storms out, thundering quickly down the ladder she had come from. I can't say why, but she reminds me of a nurse with a horrible bedside manner.

"I'm just glad she forgot the torch," Sophia says. "I'm so sick of being stuck in all of these dark caves."

I nod, but none of us seem to feel like talking. We've been trapped for almost two days, now fully caged behind these vile bars. We're being prepared for death. There's the smallest part of me that wishes I had already died; the anticipation and unknown while waiting for this ritual sacrifice is unbearable. I look over to the others. Whether lost in thought or just lost, everyone's eyes are downcast, staring at the hypnotic swirls on the floor.

The pervasive thoughts shift in time, though. I'm confused at how relatively unpanicked I am. I spend my whole life stressed, but now as a seasoned death-row inmate I feel freer than I did when I was working in a climate-controlled cubicle at Finway's. In part, it might be that the abstract fears of life—getting to work on time, having a cavity, milk spoiling in the fridge, staining my favorite shirt—are so abundant and so unrelenting when things are going okay for me. Down here, there is exactly one fear—the death of me and my friends—that clears away all the other silly noise. There's also some part of me that feels more confident in dealing with these real and abstract fears. Every step of the way I've doubted whether I could handle what's happening to us...and I'm still here. We all are. How many times can I call it luck before I learn that I'm capable of more than I thought?

CHAPTER 30

Prison breaks are a thing, right? This cage just feels so...rickety. I grab the bones on the floor of the cage, trying to see them as a material rather than a former human being. I tuck my hands under a curved nook in one of them, shaking. It's firm, but also somewhat flexible. The bones are held together with thick straps of scaly leather hide, crossed in X's at the joints between cross-bars. A thick, glue-like coating covers and seals the X's.

"Anyone have some kind of knife?" I ask. "Or see anything sharp around the room?"

"Frisk me and find out," Lawrence says, winking. Sophia gives him a look, and he quickly revises his answer to "No, I don't."

Jupiter shakes her head.

"Oliver?" I ask.

Oliver is sitting in his cage, looking absently at the floor and muttering something inaudibly. I clear my throat and ask again, startling him back to us. "Ehhm, I had a knife on my person previously, but they searched our belongings prior to our incarceration. It was in my pocket, there." He tilts his head to the back corner of the room behind the trapdoor, where our filthy clothes and belongings are piled together.

"Keep looking around the room for other things," I say to the group. "These strips on the cages look really thick. So does the coating over them."

The gaps in the bars are about three inches wide; just barely too narrow for my foot to fit through. If I want to move, I need to get my feet underneath the bones and fully planted on the floor. After thinking for a moment, I crouch in my cage—dizzy...forgot about the concussion—and turn so that my feet are perpendicular to the bones beneath me. I grab the bones on the floor with both hands, then slowly rise on my tiptoes while I lift the cage. My angled feet provide a narrower obstacle to fit between the bars...and eventually the bones go just above both of my heels. I breathe a sigh of relief, lowering both feet down and flat against the cold stone floor. Now comes the hard part.

"Eyo!!" Lawrence shouts, seeing me shuffling my cage forward a few inches.

"Shh," Sophia hisses at him.

I lift the top of the cage with my arms so that bottom is hiked up to my calves. I rotate my feet so they're facing the length of the cage, allowing them to move up and down the bones. It's more awkward than I imagined as the bones chafe, rub, and scrape against my skin with every small step I advance.

"Keep looking for sharp stuff!" I whisper back, shimmying myself to our pile of belongings. I stop over the closed trapdoor, pausing to listen and hearing nothing. I stretch my arms through the bones, rummaging in the remains of our clothes and bags. A scraping sound—I turn to see Sophia, Jupiter, and Oliver managing to shuffle in their cages as well. They spread out across the room looking very strange: four warbling bone cages teetering in slow, silent steps. I continue sifting through the clothes pile in front of me, eventually making it to Oliver's semi-disgusting leather romper. I dig through every pocket...but don't feel the knife. They must have taken it.

I glance up, seeing Lawrence wildly, silently waving me toward him. Jupiter is gripping the torch from the wall, and raises the flame to the epoxy and leather bindings at the corner of her cage. It takes a moment for anything to happen, but soon the epoxy melts off and the leather strap burns away. We all silently cheer, and I crab walk over as quickly as I can. One by one Jupiter melts the corners of our cages, and we're all able to pry them open and slip out!

I quietly make my way back to our pile of clothes, handing them out while the group turns away from each other to get dressed with what limited modesty we have left.

"Oliver," I say, "Will there be people all over the citadel? And outside of it too?"

He straps his goggles back on, blinking his eyes rapidly. "The Varsiik are not a densely populated people, but the Transitory Citadel is in the, ehhm, center of their village. In daily life they have a combination of community dwellers as well as, ehhm, scouting parties wandering about the Dead Wastes. Unless there is a major hunt or they are at war, in which case they all go into the desert."

I walk around the room, examining the massive bone pillars leaning against each other to form walls. There are a few crawlspaces where the bones meet, in addition to a few gaps that overlook the world outside. I wedge myself in and look out at the expanse of the Dead Wastes. It's amazing. We're incredibly high in the air...hundreds of feet, maybe. A billowing haze of toxic air drifts across the gravel ground, and the ever-present violet lights float above. Far in the distance is a tangled, gnarled forest, and directly below are scuttling humans the size of ants, busying themselves with the day-to-day of their lives. These are our captors...but from this distance there's no telling anyone apart.

Jupiter comes crouching toward me in the crawlspace. "Enjoying the views?"

"Yeah, it's incredible up here," I say. "Want me to move so you can see better?"

I feel her lips, soft but cracked from the harsh landscape, press against my cheek. "No. I came here for privacy. There's a severe lack of it among the other inmates."

I turn her smirking cheek, kissing her on the lips. Her hand lays across my chest, but quickly drips down my stomach...my waist. I stiffen in my jeans as she grabs by my zipper in a rush of euphoria. I struggle to keep my eyes open, mouth hanging stupidly as I exhale in her caressing. This can't be happening now, can it? My body feels broken and beaten, and somehow this simple hunger is all it craves. I want to look out at the world and have this beautiful woman's tongue down my throat, all while my dizzy head struggles to hold up its own weight. I want to escape from a bone city with my friends, then eat the juiciest, bloodiest steak and collapse into sleep for twenty-four hours. I want to tear at Jupiter's clothes until they're shredded to nothing...

"Apologies for the tease," Jupiter says, pulling back with a flushed face. "Unfortunately, now still isn't the time, considering we might die and everyone is four feet away. I just needed a taste to hold me over." Her smirk is back, but there's also a savage hunger in the expression as well; it's easy to recognize when I feel the same way. My heart is racing. My body and mind are struggling to realign themselves to the present reality.

"Any ideas for getting us out, Tim?" It's Sophia, whispering from inside the cage room. I hear the laugh in her voice.

CHAPTER 31

Everyone is facing me and waiting for instructions. I feel like I should want to puke, but I'm surprisingly calm.

"Okay. Get all of your gross leather ponchos, coats, sweatshirts, and belts, then tie them together. We're making a rope."

"Aye, boss!" Lawrence says, taking off his sweatshirt while hopping on his one good leg.

"You're sure it'll be able to hold us?" Sophia asks.

"I share similar, ehhm, concerns," Oliver adds.

"It probably wouldn't safely hold us, but that's okay. It just needs to look like it could."

Sophia's face brightens with understanding. "You want to pretend that we escaped down it so the Varsiik run out to look for us, and then we can just walk out?"

"Very cool," Jupiter says, nodding.

I sigh. It sounds worse than it did in my head. "Happy to accept other ideas, but I don't know how pressed we are for time. Maybe that lady will come back and sprinkle us again or something." I was hoping they would pick the plan apart or at least improve it, but somehow everyone seems to accept it without question. "There should be enough crawlspace under the bone walls for us to hide. I'm thinking we should just wait for the coast to be clear at ground level, drop the rope down, then wait to sneak out once they've run into the Dead Wastes looking for us."

More nods. Seriously guys?!

We collectively tie every spare bit of clothing we can find, plus some of the hide strips that sealed our cages. It looks cartoonishly hodgepodge, but hopefully the Varsiik take it more seriously. I'm shaking my head at this monstrosity when Jupiter pokes my chest, hard.

"That is my favorite sweatshirt of all time. Do you understand that? I've had it for nearly four years, it fits me exactly how I like, and it is perfectly cozy and soft."

I try to look concerned, stifling a smile. "If we ever get out of here, I promise I'll buy you a new one. Exactly how you want. Custom fitted, if need be."

She smirks, tracing her finger across my chest threateningly.

"Guys," Sophia mutters, glancing outside. "I think all of the people are gone from down below. A big wave of them left and I don't see any others coming out."

Time to drop this sucker.

Oliver ties the rope to the nearest stone sconce on the wall. I stand with the giant ball of fabric in my arms while the others crouch in position under the crawlspace.

"Ready, Rapunzel?" Lawrence calls out.

"Ready," I say, exhaling and dropping the fabric. I watch hypnotized as it falls...falls...satisfyingly unraveling the different colors of fabrics that cascade down. When it ends—slightly short of the ground, but convincing enough—the rope flaps like a whip, swinging. I look down, anxiously watching...waiting. Surely someone would see the multicolored pendulum and call out. We're lucky that the palace walls are big enough to hide most of it. Far in the distance I see hunting parties wandering the Dead Wastes, but time passes and the rope's momentum slows down to a stop. One minute...two minutes. No one comes.

"Alright," I say, crawling and joining the others. "Now we wait for all hell to break loose below, or for someone to come in and see we've disappeared."

It's awkward and tight for sure, especially with Lawrence's broken leg stretched out fully. At least his makeshift cast held up. I squeeze next to Jupiter and Oliver, all of us shoulder to shoulder as we wait for my shoddy plan to unravel.

The extended silence shatters in an instant by the squealing trap door. More grunting, this time likely male. Sounds of confusion. Then screaming. Multiple voices shouting. Thundering footsteps up the trapdoor ladder. The five of us look at each other in our dark corner, eyes wide as the shouting becomes more aggressive in their spitting, harsh language. A loud clatter and cracking sound—someone being thrown into the bone cages, howling in pain. I'm the closest one to the opening, and out of the corner of my eye I see the shape of someone bending down to follow the path of the makeshift rope. The man spits in anger and storms off—out of sight again. More shuffling footsteps, then they stomp down the ladder with wild cries. The trapdoor squeaks shut.

"Oh my god," Sophia exhales. "That went well though, right?"

"I think so," I say. "Oliver I forgot to ask: can you make out what they're saying?"

"I am able to understand passably. The nuances of their colloquialisms escape me at times, but what they said here was, errm, basic commands. What you all likely could have guessed. 'You—heh—idiot, what happened?' 'They're gone!' 'I can see they're gone, go find them!' And so on. I missed the last portion of what was said, but I presume it was some sort of order to assist the search."

The Varsiik fury from this room spreads like a virus outside. Shouting, screaming, pointing specks down below are gathering together. More and more appear, but slowly they all run out into the Wastes.

"We ready to bounce?" Lawrence asks. "I mean, they won't be out looking for us forever."

"Yeah..." I say. My plan feels dumber by the second. Sure, we've gotten them away from us here, but they're bound to close in on us somewhere in the Wastes.

We shimmy out of the crawlspace. I walk over to Oliver's cage—the one that must have had someone thrown against it, by its broken appearance—and grab one of the bones. "Might come in handy," I say. The others follow suit, although Sophia looks particularly uncomfortable wielding part of a human skeleton.

"I already got my bashin' sticks!" Lawrence says, waving his crutches around like an air-traffic controller.

We creep to the trapdoor. I have absolutely no clue what to expect below, having been brain mush on the way in. The leather handle on the trapdoor lid is waiting for someone to reach out and pull it open, but I'm certain it'll squeak like it did for the others. Jupiter sees my hesitation and nods. She grabs it and slowly...

Stops. We hear the unmistakable sound of ladder climbing beneath us. I quickly wave everyone behind the trapdoor—there's no time to get five of us to any decent hiding place. Lawrence somehow manages to stay silent, even with makeshift crutches. We crouch low, directly behind the hinge of the trapdoor. The hatch opens, and I stare as a shaved, skeletal head bobs up the ladder. He fully enters the room, walking toward where the cages are. Everyone's eyes go wide; whenever he's done, he'll turn and see us all standing in plain sight.

I swallow. Before my mind can begin to panic, I feel my body moving itself toward him. He's standing in the back of the room, inspecting the rope we "used" to get down. A part of me thinks he's figured it out. Creeping on the toes of my shoes, I've managed to get two steps away from him, staring. Practically breathing down his neck. Strapped across his back is a brutal weapon, just like all the other Varsiik. His is a wide, thin black blade with jagged, saw-like teeth running up the side of it. I see caked blood dried at the bottom of it...and my reflection on the glimmering black metal. I don't know why I smile at the sight of it. I also don't know why it takes me ten minutes to pick out a carton of eggs. I spend so long agonizing over every choice; imagining all of the paths that could go wrong rather than handling the one that I'm on.

Somehow, raising the large bone above my shoulders takes no time at all. Inferis allows my instincts to kick in, to clear the fog. This man can't know we're here. They hunted us. Bashed my skull in and broke Lawrence. Trapped us in cages and left all of my friends cowering in the corner, all to sacrifice us to some psychotic magician?

Not going to happen.

The skeletal man turns to look back—fear striking his eyes the moment he sees me. That's never happened before, and I don't pause to think of how satisfying it feels. I send the bone down hard, crashing it into the man's skull. He almost dodges—but the wide, curved end clips him. He dizzily collapses to the ground, laying still. I exhale, closing my eyes for just a moment before turning back to the group.

"I don't know if we have any more cloth or rope left, but do we want to tie him up in case—"

A savage scream from the ground and a searing, stabbing pain in my calf. I collapse with a loud groan—teeth clenched—to see the skeletal man wild-eyed and clutching a small black knife stained red. Before I hit the ground he begins thrusting the dagger again. I shift my hands in defense, trying to grapple his arm. I almost shudder at the boniness of him—how horribly, grotesquely thin the Varsiik are—and get sliced in the process. I land my body weight onto him, still holding onto the bony arm. I hear a slight crack as my out of shape, fast-food-eating body collapses hard on his rib. I expect him to keel over in agony, but he shows no reaction. A surprising strength is still trying to wrestle my arms away from his and take another slash at me. We're at a deadlock. Both straining every muscle in our body. Veins bulging. Sweat beading down as hate and will—

The others join. I don't see who it is, maybe Lawrence and Jupiter. All the force of my grapple becomes light as air. They pin his arms back and I'm freed from him. The savagery is still in his eyes, tinged now with the slightest fear as he sees he's grossly outnumbered. He starts to shout. I don't know what he says, but I end it quickly. My fist connects with his sharp, angular cheekbones.

Objective reality would tell me my hand hurts, but I feel nothing but the need to clobber him again. I hit him in the same spot, and he lets out a squelched scream. My knuckles might be broken. Again and again I connect. My bones shatter against his shattered bones. His face rolls over sideways with his tongue lolling out slightly. His gaze is blurred and lifeless. I add my left fist too—awkward, but much fresher. However dead he is isn't dead enough. If I turn around again, he'll just get up and stab me. This time he wouldn't just get my calf. I was lucky the first time; stupid and lucky. I continue raining blows down. I should have finished it, finished him. It would've been the same outcome, but a lot less messy for everyone involved.

My punches slow to a halt at the limpness beneath them. My Varsiik enemy is reduced to a lifeless sack of flesh and bone; one that resembles a scrawny chicken cutlet on my kitchen counter far more than any human being. My hands are violently trembling and dripping with a mixture of our blood. I turn to the others, staring at me. Sophia is worried. She's always worried.

Lawrence clears his throat, trying to sound calm. Maybe to calm me. "Hey, Timmy. You...you okay, man?"

I look down, stunned at the volume of blood staining my hands and pant legs. My mind wanders back to Lulu, happily panting with her bloody muzzle clenched down on a squirrel. Such an unbelievable concoction of hormones coursing through her...and through me, now. Overflowing with pride, satisfaction, hate, relief, anxiety. Primal adrenaline. Humans keep developing complex and convoluted rituals to establish a mimicry of the most natural, universally rich feelings. Grown men dedicating their lives to elaborate ball sports...Wall Street investors risking billions...bored wives racking up credit card debt from online shopping...

All of them chasing the feeling of chasing a squirrel.

The sensation makes me smirk, just like Lulu. I see Jupiter and Oliver with a similar untethered fire in their eyes.

I grab the same knife that pierced me and use it to cut a long strip of cloth off the bottom of my shirt. I quickly tie it several times around my bleeding calf.

"Yeah, I'm okay."

CHAPTER 32

"Take two?" Lawrence asks, still glancing uncomfortably at me.

We're gathered behind the trapdoor again, this time with ears hovering above to listen for signs of life. Quiet. Jupiter lifts the handle and cracks it open. I peek through...again, nothing.

"Okay, I'll go down first and wave the next person down. Lawrence, do you think you can make it alright with one leg?"

"Yeah, I should manage," he says. "Just take down my crutches so I have em.'"

I descend the ladder quickly and quietly, then wave the others down, arriving one by one: crutches, Jupiter, Lawrence, Sophia, and Oliver.

"Anyone else get Hansel and Gretel vibes?" Sophia asks, looking around the strange room.

"Definitely," I say. We're in some kind of mystic storage room. Structural pillars stand between shelves of clay pots, like the one the woman brought up. Racks of ceremonial adornments, staves, weapons, and headdresses line the walls. In the center stands a hulking stone cauldron, filled with swirling indigo and pink tides of liquid. Whatever ceremony they had planned for us was going to be quite the spectacle.

Oliver closely observes the clay pots, occasionally sniffing and rubbing the various powders between his fingers. "I am not familiar with all of these, but I believe, ehhm, many of them to be incredibly valuable. My wife could use these in her alchemical experiments."

Jupiter studies the pots herself, and finds an ornate stone vial on the far left that she squints at. She smirks up at us. "Housewarming present for Mrs. Oliver?"

"Ooh, that's sweet!" Sophia says. "I'll hold it in my bag if you want."

"Girl pockets are the worst," Jupiter says, gratefully handing it over.

When we're done poking around, we gather by a downward ramp. Still quiet. I take my first step down and immediately tense; I feel the ramp wobbling beneath me.

"What's going on..."

"Ahh, the ehhm, webbing." Oliver says.

I try to patiently wait for clarification that doesn't come. "What webbing?"

"Sometimes used for construction purposes in Inferis," Oliver adds. "A few of the larger woodland insects create webbing that can be harvested and transported, if one coats the adhesive outer layer with some form of—ehhm—dust or powder. Very flexible and abundantly strong."

"It held when we went up, Tim," Sophia says. "It was scary, but definitely strong."

"This is stronger than any steel, pound for pound," Oliver adds.

I continue jiggling my legs a bit, trying to get a feel for the rocking, bouncing motions. As each new person steps on behind me, I feel it strain underfoot like a taut guitar string ready to snap. I readjust my stance each time, warbling both from the pressure and everyone's uneasy motions. Neither side of the webbed, arched bridge has railings or walls. I tell myself not to look down...but when I do I'm not disappointed. This place really is like a palace. The webbed bridge we descend is not the only one, but rather one strand in a series of intertwining bridges. They remind me of a DNA sequence; a weaving spiral shape of double helix illuminated and silhouetted by torches along the walls. Each bridge swoops and descends to various circular platforms, some against the walls and others connecting several bridges in the floor. From the ceiling hang gnarled tree branches that drip below, the tip of each bearing a small flame like a decadent chandelier.

It's easy to forget the need for urgency and stealth as all of us gawk helplessly at its magnificence; this place rivals the scale and artistry of the Pantheon. We reach the first circular platform against the wall and find a mural, created through intricate paint and burning techniques. It portrays scenes of mythical animals (although they likely are real, down in Inferis) and gruesome rituals. I approach slowly, tracing my finger along the rough textures of the carvings and smooth coloring spread across it. My finger stops at a depiction of a large head, staring straight at me and floating above a crowd of bowing and cowering skeletal onlookers. The longer I look at the eyes, the more magnetic it is.

Jupiter hooks her arm into mine, grabbing my hand and smiling. She leads us both down the ramp again, toward the center of the floor. Here a large circular platform meets, joining all of the archways winding down and up. This platform is made of web as well, but has deliberate, patterned holes in it like an Afghan blanket. The floor isn't coated with the same gray dust, but rather a multicolored spectrum of color. Light bursts through the holes, taking the chromatic interweaving and creating infinite shades in between. The patterned web forms the image of a large skull.

"This place is incredible," Sophia says.

"Far better, ehhm, than legend ever described," Oliver responds, looking equally enamored. It's exciting to explore this place with Oliver for his first time as well; I suppose non-Varsiik only get to tour here if they're on death's door. My arms are still interlinked with Jupiter's, her face glowing with awe and carefree glee in the torchlight. She's like a kid at Disneyworld; this is a place and an existence more magical than she had ever dared imagine. A part of me wants to abandon all caution and sprint through every nook and cranny of this place, desperate to see every intrigue.

As we make it down to the ground floor, my eyes are drawn to a massive chain hooked to the wall. I stop dead when I see what it's suspending in the center of the room: a gargantuan skull, far larger than an entire elephant. Its eye sockets alone are taller than I am. Its yellowing bone has cavernous flames spilling out of its broken jaw, nose, and eye cavities. The skull serves as a chandelier for the ground floor of the citadel, emblazoning the shimmering black stone floor and ritual altar. The altar, I notice, looks almost identical to the one that we'd seen back at the lake: the same black shimmering stone, with a thin, circular disk of purple gemstone. Next to the altar, we also see...a small boy.

The four-year-old boy has a pale face and light brown hair. He's laying belly-first on the ground, with a pile of small rocks lined up neatly on the dark stone floor. He grabs the pebble at the front of the line, bouncing it up and down against it like a horse. Maybe like one of those turin that Lawrence rode.

"Mak...mak...mak" he chimes quietly to himself, then swoops the stone in a big arc and crashes it down onto the others, giggling.

I smile at the sight, hoping in the back of my head that this cute kid isn't the one who derails our entire plan.

"Aww," Sophia says with a smiling, pouty face. "I just wanna squeeeze him!"

"You go give him a big hug while the rest of us run to safety," I say.

"Well, if creepy skeletal kids are anything like my little brothers," Lawrence says, "anything loud or shiny should keep him entertained for a few hours. That way we don't need a sacrificial hug. Tonka trucks would be ideal, but if the dork's playing with rocks the bar is pretty low."

"So..." I say, trying to think.

"It's not hard, dude, trust me," Lawrence says. "Anyone want to hustle back to the storeroom and grab me one of those clay pots?"

"Fine," Jupiter says, trotting back up. In a minute she returns with one, about the size of a softball.

"Perfect, thank you!" Lawrence says, grabbing hold of it. Without warning, he torques his body and throws, sending the pot sailing across the citadel. It flies through one of the gaps in the bone walls, disappearing just outside of the palace.

"What the fuck?" Sophia mouths to him.

The clay shatters loudly outside, and we watch the child startle up like a prairie dog. He gets up and runs, bare feet pattering clumsily against the stone floor. His little arms propel him forward until he disappears outside.

"Move it, people!" Lawrence calls out, heaving his weight down the last web arch.

We follow, occasionally stealing glances as we spiral around different angles of the looming, hanging skull. Still no kid. We bolt past the altar and toward the thin, triangular opening of the citadel. I pause at the ornately carved and decorated frame around the door. No sounds outside. I glance out at the gray, deserted village of lean-to's crafted from stick, stone, bone, and hide. It is mostly small hovels, with a handful of larger ones that have a bit more decoration. A sea of the gravel and decay lies beyond.

"Alright, coast is—"

The boy re-emerges right in front of us. His hands and feet are covered in the brown powder that was in the clay pot, probably from playing in it. We see him and he sees us. No one moves. A blank stare from his small, beady brown eyes.

Lawrence crouches down on his one good leg, coming eye-eye-to-eye with him.

The boy doesn't move.

Lawrence uses the palms of his hands to spread the sides of his mouth out like a fish, his eyes scrunching and slanting in the process.

The boy giggles, and replies by using his fingers to droop the bottom of his eyes down while sticking out his tongue.

Lawrence, in counter, stands up on his leg and hops in a 360-degree rotation, arms up with hands drooping down like a kangaroo.

Another giggle. But now it's serious! The boy holds no punches. Crouching on his hands and feet, he starts hopping like a frog around the floor. "Bap! Bap! Bap!" he shouts, circling and jumping around us and then out deeper into the room. He goes farther off, seemingly forgetting that we had ever been there.

Lawrence chuckles and tilts his head toward the door, gesturing our freedom to leave.

CHAPTER 33

"We are aspiring to go, ehhm, that way," Oliver says. He points beyond the haze of the Dead Wastes to the vague outline of a forest. "It is the most direct route out of here and is likely the least guarded. And, heh, my beautiful wife and I live there. We have many allies there who can offer us protection, should we advance there safely."

"Any ideas for how to get there quickly with Lawrence on crutches?" I ask.

"Those," Oliver says, indicating a pair of tethered gray...things. If I squint, I might have thought they were camels. On closer inspection, their lizard features start to show through: scales, long and forked tongues, eyes looking in different directions. They lazily traipse about on their webbed feet, sniffing at the corners of the Citadel like bored pets.

"We're going to ride them?" I ask.

"We would stand out quite clearly if we rode on them. I was envisioning that we walk between the tenori, to provide, ehhm, camouflage. Typically, tenori are used to carry fallen carcasses back to camp. A party of hunched walkers in the Wastes would not be abnormal, if the village presumes a kill has been found."

As we listen to Oliver, a few straggling individuals pop out of a lean-to. They're fully encompassed in their own day-to-day lives, but it's enough of a wake-up call to hurry us toward the tenori. They sniff their fill of us, with one daring enough to lick its red tongue on the back of Sophia's neck. I watch her freeze at the sensation, horrified.

"We don't have to worry about them eating us, right?" Sophia asks.

"Heh!" Oliver responds, ever-helpful. He untethers them from a nearby stand, holding the cords that are looped loosely around their spiky necks. "I will ask everyone to remove their shoes and socks, and to, ehhm, roll up your pants as well. Our legs will be visible underneath the tenori. While you are all darker than the Varsiik people, it will certainly blend more effectively than blues and..." he glances at Lawrence's abomination of a yellow jumpsuit.

"Message received!" he says, rolling up his pants and stringing his shoes so they dangle over the back of his neck. We take gravel and rub it on our bare legs, hoping the dust will camouflage our varying levels of dark skin.

Oliver guides the tenori forward with us sandwiched tightly in the middle. Each step is one closer to freedom, to getting the hell home. Words cannot describe how desperate I am for rest and health, especially now that the adrenaline and anxiety are subsiding. After an hour of walking, my body gradually remembers all of the misery I've put it through: the fights, the injuries, the dizzying desert. My thighs and calves scream in protest at every step, while dull aches course through my wrists and hands even when they're at rest. My head has a constant throbbing in the back, and I'm struggling to decide whether my vision is blurring or the Dead Waste haziness is just getting to me. Usually my physical self is hardly inconvenienced at all; I spend most of my life as a soft vessel whose job it is to take my cushy brain cells where they command. Today, and possibly more often than I realize, my world is inescapably corporeal.

Gravel grinds and sinks under my bare feet, each step new yet exactly the same. The passage of time is a mystery. Endless waves of bone dust, of carcasses, of...

"Oliver, is that a giant hole in the ground?"

"Ehhm, yes," he replies.

To my right, a crater the size of half a football field sinks deep into the ground. I squint my eyes, peering through the haze of dust. Several more come into view as we advance; a gray, Mars minefield of wasteland.

We steer the unflustered tenori just to the right of the nearest crater. The top walls of it are slanted in with gravel, but just below is a hard, black stone. Giant spirals are carved into the rock like they were made by some gargantuan drill bit. Piles of tools and equipment lay near its side: rope ladders, pickaxes, some kind of pulley mechanism.

"Who made all this?" I ask.

"Tunneler worms," Oliver replies. "Impressive, aren't they?"

"Imagine seeing one..." Jupiter says, staring into the crater.

"You have already, heh. Do you remember the small, tunneling creature that came for us when we were first captured? That was, ehhm, an infantile tunneler. At that stage they can be domesticated to hunt, but as they mature they become increasingly less docile and, ehhm, less cooperative to the Varsiik. So they are released from 'official' service. They remain symbiotic with the Varsiik, however, as they mature. They burrow naturally, which allow the Varsiik to spelunk and mine precious metals and stones with easier accessibility."

"What are they mining?" I ask. "That black metal we saw on some of the Varsiik weapons?"

"Yes. That is also the same material—although refined differently—used to make the stone altars that you witnessed as well."

"Can you tell us anything more about those altars?" Sophia asks. "Why were we hypnotized like that?"

Oliver glances at us thoughtfully. "That, ehhm, requires a more involved response, of which I might only be able to postulate. Agonault, who dwells at the lake near to where I found you, uses the altar as a means of control, and, ehhm...security. Within that stone is a very precise gneissic banding; that is, the dark and light lines, swirls, and features that you see in the stone. Additionally, I believe he has carved them in such a way as to provide auxiliary patterns and textures to its surface. These patterns create some form of, ehhm, trancelike-effect on the mind when harmonized with the surrounding torchlight. I cannot explain all of its physical components, but I can confirm its consistency. Elly and I have dared venture quite close and risked its effects, to learn what we may. One of us stood at the altar while the other pulled them back with a rope. Heh." Oliver's goggled eyes gaze upward, reminiscing about his romantic evenings of playful mind-control.

"I obviously don't know shit about the altar," Lawrence begins, hesitantly, "but I have heard of the term 'absence seizures' in a few rare medical cases. They make people go totally limp and space out for several seconds, sometimes minutes, like we were. They usually occur in kids or people with epilepsy, and are generally thought to be caused by abnormal brain activity. There can be a lot of environmental triggers for them like bright and flickering lights, smoke, changes in climate, smells...but I've never heard of them being induced in four young healthy adults."

"That is incredibly helpful to know," Oliver says. His mind is still clearly adrift, head poised upward. "I do not believe that there is a purely scientific explanation, ehhm, for the phenomenon about which we are speaking; Agonault's powers of influence are quite strong. However, it may be that this altar aids him in his work—softening the minds of victims, thereby easing his ability to mold and meld them to his will. The altar found at the Transitory Citadel was likely made by his original and most devout followers, ehhm, per his request. After it was made, it paved the path for him to cultivate Varsiik devotion indiscriminately. From the knowledge of his power alone, all would willingly serve. But he is not one to take chances on fealty, heh."

I stare down at the cavernous black tunnels, imagining myself hypnotized by this endless precious stone. Oliver notices me, incorrectly guessing my thoughts. "Yes, I see it in your eyes as well. Imagine...the cartographic ventures that are ripe for the taking in those treacherous labyrinths, uuhh." The guttural sound that escapes Oliver's mouth is grossly passionate. This fucker really loves his maps.

My eyes trace the rope, descending deeper into the tunnel's darkness until it is completely lost. I kick a small rock down and hear nothing. Twenty seconds of silence pass until the faintest clattering echo reverberates back up. Inferis has already taken us so far down into the depths of the Earth...I can't fathom how treacherous it could be to go any deeper.

Is there ever a rock bottom?

CHAPTER 34

B ack in middle school Sophia always seemed to have her life together; she was the rarest blend of confident and kind. But as I spent more time with her, I noticed she would get the nervous habit of absently stretching, twisting, and contorting her elastic hair ties around her wrist. It took me a while to get the guts to mention it to her, but I was curious to see if she was aware of it.

When I finally spoke up, she suddenly grabbed me by the shoulders and yelled "I KNOW! Pinky promise me you'll flick me every time I do it. This ends today!"

I laughed, and we spent the rest of that study period test-flicking her to gauge the appropriate strength for helping her kick the habit. After a few months of guilt-ridden flicking and companionship, she had conquered it!

Until today. Haggard, bruised, dirty, and anxious, Sophia marches herself through the Dead Wastes. She protectively keeps her left hand on Lawrence's shoulder as he crutches his way across the sinking gravel, and as she does, her eyes never stop darting every which way. Meanwhile, the fingers on her right hand are surrounded by a hair tie as they expand and close—expand and close—again and again like a flower blossoming. Those bright, lost memories of our friendship make me smile. I proceed to flick her in the ear.

"Heeey! What..." Sophia turns in annoyance, but her poor ear gradually remembers the sting.

"Was I...?"

"Yes," I say. "We'll get out soon, Soph, I promise. Everyone's going to be okay."

Her face grows taut; the skin stiffening between the bridge of her nose and eyes to prevent tears. "We can talk more about everything, too," she says. "Process things. I think we could all use that." She gently rubs my shoulder, spreading the tears to me as well. After what I did to the Varsiik guy in the citadel a few hours ago, I've caught Sophia glancing at me nervously. I don't know why I'm not freaking out about it; I know I should be. More importantly, though, I don't want any of what's happened down here to get between us.

Lawrence isn't faring much better down here. He's just as strong and stubborn as Soph is, but there's been a noticeable decline in shouting and sex jokes since his fall off the bridge (and I'm confident it wasn't just the effect of my heart-to-heart). He's visibly in pain from not only the leg injury, but also the constant aching of his wrists and armpits from the makeshift crutches digging into him. Occasionally, the quietest grunt escapes him. I wish we could carry him somehow, or have the tenori drag him like the carcasses they're used to carrying. I mull over the idea in silence, failing to come up with a good solution.

Unlike the others, Jupiter seems to be coming to life more than ever in Inferis. Her strides are longer, her posture better. She isn't the jaded, eye-rolling cashier at a gas station convenience store, nor is she the prisoner to a home-life that is sucking the life out of her. For possibly the first time in her existence, she is surrounded by excitement and beauty and is unrestrained to bask in it. All of us are lucky to bear witness to her unveiling.

"Tell me something I don't know about you," I say.

"Oooh!" Jupiter announces. "This is stressful; I empathize with your earlier squirming. My favorite color is yellow. My favorite food is extraordinarily spicy curry. My favorite movie growing up—and possibly still is, I recently re-watched it and it stands the test of time—is the first *Jackass* movie."

"Wow," is all I say.

"That had better not be a tone of judgement I hear."

"Maybe about the whole 'yellow' thing. But it's just weird; I watched the *Jackass* movie on Monday, a few days before we started all of this. I hadn't seen it for a decade before that, at least."

"Monday?!" she blurts. "That's when I watched it too! I was up really late taking care of my mom. It must have been two in the morning."

I smile, puzzling out when exactly I watched it. "I...watched it when I couldn't sleep. I must have started it at three in the morning at the latest...maybe earlier. That's so strange to think; we were watching it together."

"Yes, the cosmos are very strange, indeed, Tim, but right now I need you to focus. What is your favorite skit from the movie? This is my all-time favorite film and I've seen every nut-shot at least twenty times." Nut-shots...now it makes sense!

I take a moment to think, eyes drifting far across the Wastes. The others in the group are silently struggling forward, but somehow Jupiter is sustaining enough life for the both of us. Pain can hardly be real, if it can be so easily intensified or assuaged by the genre of my thoughts and mental state.

"I have to go with the toy car up the ass," I say. "Alone it's great, but the German doctor begging him not to tell anybody was perfect."

"That is a very commendable choice. Mine has changed a few times, but I'm personally a fan of the airhorn in the middle of golf swings. So many snobby rich white dudes foiled during their dad games. Plus, it has the added vengeance layer of one disgruntled golfer throwing a club at them."

I grin stupidly from her analysis.

"When I was younger," she continues, "I had actually filmed a few stunts of myself, because of them. It was nothing special; things like rolling down steep hills in shopping carts, or trampolining myself into a kiddie pool."

"God I'm thirsty," I moan thoughtlessly. "Sorry—that's really cool though! What other stunts did you try?"

Jupiter ignores me, glancing at the rest of our wilting party members. "Oliver, are we near any water sources?"

He dazedly looks behind us, resting his weight on his walking stick. "Such a task would be, ehhm, quite improbable. It would take weeks; far longer than it will be for us to simply evacuate the Wastes."

Lawrence stops with the others, but teeters like he's on the verge of collapsing.

"Oliver?" Sophia asks, pointing a weak finger toward the horizon. I can barely make it out, but a small, moving silhouette patters off in the dust and disappears. "Is that one of the markeet that we saw earlier? Didn't you say they could find water in a desert."

His eyes widen, and he hurriedly wipes at his dusty goggles. "Ahh, there you have it. I could greatly use a pair of eyes like yours, heh. Most valuable."

I nudge her with my elbow. "Saving our ass, as always."

"Well someone has to!" she replies, smiling and nudging me back.

Oliver follows the markeet trail, a faint glimmer of hope rising in the group. It doesn't take long for us to spot the beast in the distance, this time surrounded by friends. A pack of four of them huddle in a circle around a small area, noses close together. Oliver doesn't slow his pace in the slightest, still stiffly walking across the gravel. We're only thirty feet away now. I expect the markeet to bolt at the sight of us, or growl in attack. One of them momentarily glances back at us; its sunken eyes peer from matted brown fur flecked with gray dust. He looks as weary as we do, then turns his nose forward again, head low.

We're right behind them now, and still Oliver continues. He wedges himself right between the markeet, like someone trying to inch their way through a crowded bar to order a drink. He dips his head down to the ground with them. The four of us raise our eyebrows and laugh, following his lead. I find a gap among the furry, dusty animals, trying my hardest not to touch them. Clearly they aren't too dangerous, but I don't want to push my luck. Their patches of fur are rough like straw on the sides of my arms. One of them takes a break from drinking—tongue out, heavily panting and dripping with water—and glances at me with a yawn.

There's no shot in hell we would've been able to find this on our own. The markeet (as well as Oliver) are ravenously licking from a gray puddle the size of a dinner plate. It's color perfectly resembles the surrounding area, with flecks of gravel also floating in it. The water seems as pure as a 3-year-old coffee filter, yet still they lap it up desperately. Some instinct, some innate need to survive pushes them regardless of the hardships that come their way.

And Jupiter is right there with them. Across the puddle, I see her smiling face look up at me, eyebrows raised. "Tongue-tied?"

I laugh, and we both lower our heads. I go with a sucking-slurp instead of the tongue technique. It tastes like I'm drinking gravel, only slightly wetter. I half-gag as tiny sediments and a filmy grayness drains into me.

"Oliver," Lawrence asks, face contorted from the taste, "you sure this water's safe to drink, buddy? Or that our stomachs will process it if we're new here?"

"Heh, yes. Certainly not pleasant to drink, but I am convinced that it is far more nutritionally rich in healthy minerals than standard drinking water in the Above. No way to test, however, ehhm."

"And you haven't gotten sick from it before?" Lawrence prods.

Oliver ignores him, tongue lapping with focus.

"What do you think tastes better," I ask Jupiter, who's taking a pause as she clutches her stomach in disgust, "desert water or whatever the hell we drank with the herdswomen in that tent?"

"Tough to say," she smirks. "The tent drink had the added benefit of making us nice n' tipsy. We're more desperate now, though. And in arguably better company." She stares at a markeet two inches from her face, who is absently drooling into the puddle that all of us are drinking from.

Whistles wetted, we say goodbye to the markeet pack and stumble our way through the Dead Wastes again. While it was nice to stop for a rest, my body revolts even more at having to start back up again. I can't say how far we go or how long it takes; over time, I feel dizzier and more tired than ever. I've never been more acutely aware of the weight of my spinal cord, dragging the core of me into the center of the ground. The dried blood matted into my hair feels like mulch crystalized in a hard winter frost. My filthy rags are stiff with dirt but loose with wear, dripping off my body like a melting Dalí clock. My stomach has a hollowness and a sickness to it that feels comforting, even if it isn't helping. I don't want to slow anyone down, though, and I certainly don't want us getting ambushed again. The task feels a lot more manageable when I remind myself I only need to walk forward. Walk forward.

I walk forward without noticing everyone's excited shouts, or the large forest looming ahead. I only stir back to reality when I see a river. No...not just a river. A sea monster coming out of a river.

The tenori suddenly rear. We stop in our tracks, watching helplessly.

Oliver offers a wide, toothy smile and runs forward to the sea monster. "How are you, ehhm, my honeysweet?"

CHAPTER 35

O liver embraces the camouflaged being. Her entire face and hair are a disfigurement of natural materials—speckles of gravel, globs of clay, twigs haphazardly woven into wild curls of graying brunette hair. Oliver sees past it all, kissing her warmly and grabbing awkwardly at her waist. As the kiss goes on and on, his hands pawing to the rhythm of his asthmatic moan, I struggle to decide whether I'd rather be locked in a bone cage right now.

In the distraction of Oliver's wife, I failed to notice the other camouflaged figures. They seem to spring out of the ground itself; embedded in the riverbank, under boulders, behind driftwood. They are archers, not making a single sound as their bows are pulled taut, aimed directly at us. They stare with black, beady pupils, awaiting orders. The lovers disengage, seeing the tension on our faces.

"I am uncertain as to how much intelligence you have received on these travelers, Elly, but—ehhm—these are the Above visitors that stumbled here accidentally. They had intended to turn back until they were chased further into Inferis by servants of Agonault. Tim, Sophia, Lawrence, and Jupiter are their names. Good people," Oliver adds, smiling through his dusty goggles.

The woman does not react. Her steady, wild eyes gaze deeply into our own, one at a time.

"We come bearing gifts!" Lawrence says. He gestures his hand toward Sophia with a flourish, offering a cheesy smile.

"Oh right!" Sophia says, digging through her bag and eventually holding out the stone vial. "We have no idea what it is, but it looks beautiful and Oliver said you might be able to use it. Any help that you could provide in getting us out safely would be sincerely appreciated."

The woman leans her camouflaged face over the gift and aggressively sniffs at Sophia's hand, all while retaining her gaze on us. "If this is what I believe it to be..." she says, shifting back without touching the vial, "then this is unfathomably generous of you. I have only seen it once before." Her voice is velvet. Soft and warm, yet deep and powerful like all of Inferis.

Sophia smiles in embarrassment, but Lawrence grins even wider. "Eyy, happy to help! Oliver's been a champ since we got lost; it's the least we could do!"

"Please," the woman says, waving her hand down. The fifteen archers surrounding us— several of whom were hidden so well I had not spotted them at all—lower their bows and stand at rank beside Oliver's wife. "I am Eleanor. These guards are the Murasi people. Together we will provide you with protection and assistance, as my husband has vouched for your character. Come...it is not safe here."

We follow Eleanor, Oliver, and the Murasi archers across the shallow stream, grateful to be putting the Dead Wastes behind us. I look back only once, glimpsing the two tenori that Oliver had released before our crossing. They glance at each other confusedly before slowly shuffling their way back in the direction of the citadel. I hope they're happy there.

Oliver and Eleanor walk in front, but I manage to catch pieces of updates that the two of them share: dangers in the northeastern quadrant of somewhere, rumors of something being revived. In my attempted eavesdropping, I again fail to notice key elements about the archers beside us: they have tails! Long, hairy ones! Listening to gossip is infinitely less interesting. The camouflaged Murasi use the stream to wipe themselves clean of gravel and muck, and the transformation is shocking. I don't know the distinction between a fur coat and a really goddamn hairy dude, but this feels somewhere in the middle. Their faces, backs, shoulders, chests, and legs are covered in thick, black hair with pale skin gleaming underneath. Their feet are short, very wide, and curved down with long, talon-like nails at the end. They seem shorter in stature than us, but maybe only because of their incredibly broad shoulders and hunched posture.

As one of the Murasi cleans himself, a thin, furry tail curls up and then cracks like a whip to shake off the water. The tail curls and bends...and then pokes me gently in the rib. I recoil at the sudden motion, and the Murasi who it belongs to laughs heartily. "Khazerim" he says, pointing to himself.

"Tim," I say, pointing to myself.

The tail pokes me again and he repeats "Teem" thickly, grinning and walking on.

After crossing the stream and a short stretch of field, the group approaches a vast forest. I expect us to wait or regroup before we enter, but Oliver and Eleanor continue on as though we were passing through the front gate of their house. Everything in the forest is made of vines and roots. I know this because, within seconds, my shoe gets caught in one and I proceed to wipe out.

"Tim, are you okay?" Sophia asks, grabbing me by the hand and heaving me up with a groan of exertion.

"Yeah, all good," I say, rubbing my knee that landed particularly hard. Sophia still seems oddly concerned. "I'm fine," I repeat.

"I'm just worried!" she explains. "I don't know how your head is feeling, but Lawrence said you could be more prone to dizzying spells if we don't take it easy."

"Yeah," Lawrence says breathlessly, still crutching his way across the uneven forest. "Just keep us posted, alright Tim? I'm sure one of these hulking monkey men can carry you if we need; we don't want you passing out and hitting your head on something."

I'm used to a Sophia lecture, not a Lawrence one. I rub my hand absently against the back of my head, still feeling the scabbed blood across it.

Vines and roots tangle across the entirety of the forest floor. Some are sleek and shimmering wet with dew while others are coated in a prickling purple-gray fuzz. Even the trees look like vines; gnarled and twisted among each other, some twirling like corkscrews or bending at the trunk like boomerangs. Despite the angles, they are still wide, fully-grown trees too big for anyone to wrap their arms around. The tops of them aren't covered in leaves, but rather inverted cones of fungal funnels that emit spores. I glance up at them—dizzy again. The violet jellyfish from the skies occasionally touch down against the funnels, brushing against them like bees pollinating. But the forest has far more illumination than their quiet violet. Yellow lights drift and speckle the dense air like fireflies, and rich green glows emanate from boulder-sized mushrooms. Every shade of red, purple, blue, and white berries drip from vines tangled on trees and bushes. It's like walking through the center of a Christmas tree. I've watched enough survival shows on the Discovery channel (thank you Bear Grylls) to know not to eat strange berries, but I'm only now realizing how ravenously hungry I am. These dangling berries are literally oozing with a glistening juice.

"So will this forest get us back on track to leave?" Sophia asks our guides, carefully helping Lawrence navigate his crutches.

"This will lead to the Northern Passage, in time," Eleanor responds in her deep, whisper of a voice. "Your original road would have been faster, but troublesome news has plagued us on all fronts as of late. The forest is far safer, at least in the Southern region, than traveling on the open plains. We will first find respite at our home. There we will treat your wounds, resupply, and determine the next path that should be taken, both for your safety in returning home and for the pressing matters of Inferis."

"What's been happening?" I ask. "More stuff related to Agonault?"

A moment of pause; I see Eleanor give a momentary glare at Oliver. "Yes," she speaks. "This is not the place to discuss such matters openly, however."

"Everyone's so secretive all of a sudden," Lawrence whines.

Jupiter, Sophia and I laugh. The Murasi guards surrounding us chuckle, too, although we can't tell if they understand what he said. That only makes us laugh harder.

We walk on a few more paces, glancing around at the trees and wildlife nearby. Sophia turns to ask the Murasi, "Do you all live in the forest with Oliver and..."

When she looks back, they're all gone. Vanished into thin air. "Did you guys see where...?"

"No," Jupiter says, looking impressed.

"How did we not even hear them leaving, though?" Sophia asks. "Maybe they're patrolling the area or something?"

"I don't know," I say. Weariness weighs me down. My mind spins with the suspicion—possibly paranoia—that Oliver and Eleanor are luring us into the forest intentionally. Or maybe that the Murasi archers are double-crossing them?

"Hang in there," Jupiter mumbles to me. She puts her arm around my shoulder and rubs gently. Even glancing over at her feels like work; my head is so heavy that it's weighing down my eyelids. The two of us walk together under the lights, stumbling among the terrain.

An animal the size of a small deer bolts ahead of us. I point vaguely at it trotting along—crash. An arrow comes straight down through the beast, felling it in complete silence. Within seconds, the trees bounce and shake under the weight of the Murasi archers as they descend. Many of them go down headfirst with large, hairy hands clenched on the bark itself, while others swing down acrobatically with a soft drop. The first one to reach the carcass pulls out the arrow stuck into its neck, then hoists the animal's body over its shoulder with ease.

I feel a fuzzy poke on the back of my arm and jerk in surprise.

"Missed us, yes?" Khazerim says.

I smile. "Very impressive. How did you get away from us so quietly?"

"Practice," Khazerim responds, springing back up without a sound to his movements. Within a breath, he's up the tree and leaping from one vine to the next, hurling his body weight with more grace than an Olympic gymnast.

"Look at you, making friends," Jupiter whispers to me.

Oliver and Eleanor trail back, waiting for us to catch up. "Almost home!" Oliver announces. "I can finally present you with my maps and records of Inferis. Especially, ehhm, my most recent work!" He's fully transformed into a kid showing off his refrigerator drawings, and it's adorable.

"You can," Eleanor adds, looking at me, "but only after we have tended to their injuries first, and rested well. The maps will certainly aid our planning discussions."

We stay close to them for the remaining walk, which is fortunate because things begin to get...blurry. My head is pounding, but Jupiter keeps her arm on me and guides us forward. I don't have the words or emotional capacity to tell her how much this means to me. At one point I try to, but she quickly shushes me.

"It's okay, Tim, I know. We're almost there."

"...almost home?"

She gives me a strange look that I can't understand. "Almost in a nice warm place for us to sleep. That's it, just a few more steps. Lower your head here for a minute; the ceiling is a bit low."

I follow her instructions with whatever remaining command I have over my faculties. Before I can process where we are or how we got here, we're all standing inside of a shelter. No, more than just a shelter...it's like being in the residence of a garden gnome. Everything is small. The oddly shaped wooden table is a foot off the ground, with no chairs around it. The structure of the home is made entirely of vines, but they are interwoven and overgrown so tightly that every square inch of the hut is cozily sealed and protected from the elements. A small pit with a circle of charred rocks is in the center of the dwelling, with a dangling rope above it that controls a latch for chimney smoke. A narrow dirt staircase circles around the back of the hut, leading underground. An inordinate number of things dangle from thin vines tied to the ceiling: dried meats, colored roots, berries, a striped leather hide. The smells are pungent and overwhelming; mixtures of familiar spices, floral oddities, and harsh chemicals entertain a belligerent coexistence.

I feel light-headed. The Keebler Elf home begins spinning. I quickly spot a heap of furs tucked in a corner of the hut. I collapse down onto it.

"Is it okay if I just..."

CHAPTER 36

I forget where I am. Soft furs surround and warm me. Before I can open my eyes, I realize that my body is pressed against someone else's. I don't know why my first thought is that it's Oliver. I'm ready to fling myself away when I hear him and Eleanor muttering something farther away. Grogginess and sleep take over again. I hear her soft breathing, her chest expanding and releasing. I see her arms wrapped around my stomach, black fingernails holding me. I feel safe, for the first time in...years. I'm on the verge of drifting back asleep...

"How are you feeling?" she whispers behind me.

"Okay," I say, nestling closer into her. "Tired."

"Tell me something I don't know about you," says the whisper.

"Unnhh," I moan. I love the prompt; the groan simply escapes me. I rest my hand across hers, our fingers clasping. "Umm, I've only had two girlfriends. One long-term one broke up with me because she said I was too bored." I shake my head, grogginess taking over. "I mean boring. The second cheated on me."

I feel the soft hand tighten its grasp in mine. "I'm very sorry to hear that," she mutters. "Relationships are..." she trails off, thinking.

"The worst," I finish.

A millisecond of a pause, the slightest relaxing of her hand in mine. Is she...disappointed? I'm so used to saying and thinking this, but I'm not sure whether I believe it anymore.

"Well, you've got me beat. I've never had a serious boyfriend."

"How is that possible?" I say, almost irritated at the unreasonableness of the universe. Jupiter cackles in my ear and I smile. I know that she starts talking; I hear her as if she's far away and underwater, her warmth washing over me. My eyes close again. I'll have to...remember to ask her again...

Back to consciousness, alone but still lying on the furs. I feel more rested than I can remember. I scratch my shoulder, glancing around the strange hut and trying to piece together my memories. The others are murmuring quietly at the table, pointing at piles of thick parchment. I lift my heavy head up—still nursing a headache, but not the searing pain it had been before—and the others perk up at the sight of me.

"Eyyy, Sleeping Beauty!" Lawrence announces.

I sit up, my arms propping myself up like an easel. "How long have I been out?"

"Something like fourteen hours," Sophia says. "You needed it," she adds quickly, seeing my reaction.

"Yeah, you looked awful, my dude," Lawrence says. "And getting rest is super important for concussions."

"Umm..." I say, trying to focus my thoughts. Brain still scrambled; software updates underway.

"Welcome to our home, Tim," Eleanor says. Her rich voice is warm to the touch. I don't recognize her with the camouflage washed off and Oliver's tongue not down her throat. She has long, gray frizzled hair down to her waist, loosely tied together by several loops of twine. It looks like a giant furry caterpillar sucking onto the back of her head. Her face looks rough, cracked, weathered, worn. It suits her well, I think; the soft smile on her face accentuates the wrinkles near her dark brown eyes, which have an edge to them that reveals how she's managed to live in such a savage world for so long. She's wearing a thick, moss-like fur fashioned into a dress, cinched at the waist with a leather strip tied loosely. She's showing much less thigh than her husband.

Meanwhile, Oliver is so excited that his eyes seem ready to burst through his goggles. "Tim! I believe there is, ehhm, some time to view my map room, before Elly has arrangements prepared for dinner! If you are still interested, heh."

"That would be awesome, yeah!"

Oliver's fists ball up in excitement, his breathing ragged. We laugh and follow him to the narrow dirt staircase. As it spirals down, we have to duck our heads to avoid the ceiling. The walls of the staircase are rich, dark-brown dirt and stone. Every few feet there's a recess carved in the wall that houses a luminescent yellow fungus which brightens our path. The growth itself emits a pale light, in addition to teeming flecks of floating neon particles spreading up and down the staircase. Sophia waves her hand through them, and they billow and float away like dust near a sunlit window.

When we reach the landing, we emerge into a dank, cluttered cell of a room that barely fits the five of us. It is filled to the brim with strange papers that are oddly shaped, colored, and strewn about. Stacks of them are layered on top of uneven shelves constructed from vines. These vines seem impossibly straight and regimented for a living, growing thing, and they cover all four walls. In the center is a wooden table that's overwhelmed by messy stacks of parchment and an odd assortment of metal and bone instruments. The only ones I recognize are the protractor and compass from my sophomore-year geometry class. The perimeter of the room is neatly lined with the luminescent fungi, resembling a tarmac landing strip at night.

Jupiter's hands are already lifting some of the papers in the room.

"How did you do all of this, Oliver?"

His toothy grin is so wide that it looks painful. "I...well, thank you, very kindly. Heh. I was quite determined to document as much as possible in Inferis—geographically, yes, in addition to species classifications, plant alchemical properties, migration patterns, ehhm—which of course require systematic approaches and sustainable documentation materials. Crafting paper was far more straightforward than I had initially considered," he continues on, grabbing a stack of uneven, multicolored papers. "The combination of water and, ehhm, either sawdust or plant fibers can typically create parchment, if mixed and poured in the square mold you see on that shelf. I frequently add coloring from various plant dyes, to...to the mixture in order to distinguish different classification pursuits. Ehhmm—"

Oliver's usual practice of throat-clearing, in his manic excitement, turns into hacking coughs. His eyes water, and I take the opportunity to pore through some of the parchment myself. Many of them are dusty and dirt-stained. I lift the corner of one pile and see that the bottom-most sheet is dated June 6, 1984. The second is February 8, 1985. I flick through them like a deck of cards, but quickly notice the entire dating system change. Shortly after 1986, days and years are replaced by phrases like "Dormant 694, Teal" and "Harvest 781, Violet." I stare at the papers, vaguely aware that Oliver is still gasping for breath in a corner while Sophia awkwardly pats his back and asks, "You're sure you don't need water or something?" I slowly begin to piece together the system after sifting through the stack more closely. The number continues to gradually go up by one, as if it's some kind of year. The words "Harvest," "Dormant," and "Growth" are the only three options for that section, making me believe they're the cyclical seasons in Inferis' weather. And the most recent eight papers in the stack are all "Violet." It's possible that the floating jellyfish change colors every few years, marking something like a decade.

The documents I'm holding are anatomical drawings of creatures and wildlife. Unsurprisingly, they're incredibly detailed; each animal is drawn from multiple angles and with measurements providing their scale. I flick through each of them, thinking this library alone would be worth trillions of dollars to scientists. Brief descriptions in the top-right corner offer bulleted facts for each, the first one describing the following:

Typhicus Grondulundus (Gronds)

- *Average Lifespan: 80+ years??*
- *Strong maternal protection; heavy aggression*
- *Small (RTS) dwellings; cavernous alcoves*
- *Teeth shavings herbal remedy; arthritic joints*

While I'm reading, I feel the strangest furry sensation against my leg. I recoil as a hedgehog-like rodent waddles between my legs. My fight response is so heightened that I step quickly away, ready to tell everyone to run. Instead, the little guy merely peeks his pointed nose up to me curiously, then waddles his backside against my legs again. I laugh to myself as he nuzzles his way under the table.

Oliver, who has mostly composed himself at this point, watches the encounter. "That's Bumbrick, heh. He assists in eating insects that like to nibble at my parchment. Invaluable for certain, but he is rather moody; Bumbrick can make an unfortunate mess of my records if he feels, ehhm, slighted in some manner."

Lawrence already looks like he's losing interest in the library; he's glancing around aimlessly like a kid who's been dragged to a stuffy museum. Jupiter, however, looks like she could spend a lifetime here. I shuffle closer to her, watching her eyes glued to the same stack of pale blue papers she started with.

"Find anything cool?" I ask.

She looks up at me, smiling. Her fingers peel through the pages, showing a huge series of maps in different scales. "All of it. The entire catalogue of work he's done on this is unbelievable. It makes this place so real, like looking at a globe and seeing all of the countries you could visit someday."

"That's cool," I say, thinking of everything she told me about having to stay home with her mother.

"Hey, don't go feeling sorry for anyone," she retorts, reading my thoughts. "I can't guilt-free travel now, but a day will come when I'll tear up the world. Outliving my mom won't be a problem. And until then," she says, flicking through the maps again, "Inferis has been an adventure that people would pay a lifetime to have. If Oliver doesn't sell postcards down here, he certainly could."

The smells wafting down to us signal that food is prepared. After days of nothing to eat and endless exertion, we're all starving beyond comprehension. Lawrence leads the way, hopping up the stone steps on his one good leg. I come up last, relishing the warmth and the aromas greeting me from the blazing fire. Upon reentering, however, I feel a strange shift in energy. Sophia, Lawrence, and Jupiter look back at me, fear in their eyes.

Eleanor is busying herself in the kitchen. Behind her...is the bloody, severed leg of a pale and hairy human man. There's another one beside her that's shorn, cleaned, and simmering in a pan with vegetables. I step next to Jupiter, closer to the doorway of the small hut. Eleanor turns and greets me with another warm smile.

"Hungry?" she asks.

"I...I think Tim's still too shaken up to eat," Sophia says. "Food might make him sick right now. Isn't that right, Tim?"

Eleanor continues smiling. "Trust me when I say that I understand the trials of the wounded, particularly those at the hands of the Varsiik. Tim is beyond famished...all of you are," she says, glancing around at the group, her calmness and warmth radiating off her like a sauna.

I tense suddenly, feeling the presence of two people behind me. They're Murasi guards who just entered. I'm forced further into the room—involuntarily closer to the table—to make space for them. Strange but delicious spices fill the air. My head spins and I start to feel a little woozy again—I rest my hand on the hard wooden table to stabilize myself.

"I..." before I can get any words out, Eleanor has already lowered a large, flat slate rock in front of me. She does the same for the others, as well as two slates for the Murasi who sit at the end, chatting casually. I sit down at the table with Jupiter next to me.

The meat is staring up at me. No, there are no indicators of it being human anymore; it is deliciously dark brown with charred bits on the outside, dripping with fat and grease that seep their way into a small pile of pale roots. My mouth is salivating. I close my eyes to steel myself, but that only intensifies the wafting scent below me—the violent pang in my hollowed stomach. The reptilian part of my brain runs on overdrive. I want to gorge myself; I'm so famished and it looks unbearably satisfying. I want...

"Unfortunately, there have been delays in our plan to guide you out of Inferis," Eleanor says, walking slowly around the table. She stops behind me, her soft hands resting on my shoulders and massaging into them. My mind and body melt like butter under her touch. "Several immediate dangers are stirring on the borders of this very forest. It is advantageous that Oliver has returned in time to aid with them, for alone we may have perished at the gravity of this threat. Even still, we may. We must leave as soon as we are able, to gather our forces and address Agonault before the damages are irreversible to Inferis. But first...we need to regain our precious strength." Her hand slowly traces along my back as she speaks in her deep, soothing voice. I feel spellbound, although this is nothing like the circle of torches that put us in a trance. It feels as if...she's awakening something in me. Some unknown, dormant part of myself, deep within.

Oliver has already sunk his crooked teeth into the meat. No knives, no forks. He paws at it with his bare hands, his dirt-rimmed fingernails dripping with fat. His mouth tears viciously, anchoring it against the tug of his head as he rips sideways. It should disgust me.

"Lawrence..." I mouth silently across the table, a sudden, desperate thought coming to mind. "Any more jerky?"

He squints his eyes for a moment, trying to understand. Then I watch his face sink as he does. "The Varsiik took it. We can try to find...something..." he whispers.

"How much longer will we be stuck down here, Oliver?" Jupiter asks.

He looks up for half an instant, glancing to Eleanor like a dog looking up at his master. Then he resumes ravenously eating. He spits a small bone out of his mouth, missing the slate table.

"It may depend," Eleanor says calmly, "on how severe the threat is that we face. It may delay us by only two days...or this may very well cost our lives. One cannot know."

I have a vague awareness of the threat of death, and a full awareness of having gone two days without eating. Jupiter bumps my shoulder softly with hers, echoing my thoughts back to me. "We can't go much longer without food, especially you. Not if we're ever going to get out of here in one piece."

Sophia and Lawrence look at her in shock. Jupiter stretches her hand out to mine, looking down at her slate. A deep, measured exhale escapes her lips. I close my eyes, and the smell is overwhelming again. I reach my hand toward Jupiter's. Our fingers interlock, the metal of her rings pressing against my skin. We squeeze each other tightly. I pick up the meat with my free hand, and so does she. I raise my arm up...trembling slightly...

This shit better taste like chicken.

CHAPTER 37

I take a deep, delicious inhale of the forest air as we march forward. I smile at everything: the floral smells rushing to meet me, the critters rustling through the brush, the light bugs cascading playfully around us. The world is breathtakingly beautiful in a way that the zombie version of me didn't get to appreciate when we stumbled here yesterday. With a full meal in our bellies (that we try not to think about) and plenty of sleep, the four of us happily trail through the forest behind Eleanor, Oliver, and the Murasi.

"I think I've finally got it this time," Lawrence says.

"At this point I trust you even less," Sophia retorts, rolling her eyes.

Lawrence crutches himself sideways to appeal to us. "I can totally remember the full plan, step-by-step! Tim you believe me, don't you?"

I laugh. "I have no idea, dude; I was asleep when you all went over this."

"He's got no shot," Jupiter whispers.

"I've given up trying to understand, Law," Sophia says. "They only explained it to us once, and it was confusing. Don't even worry about it."

"Not worried!' Lawrences says, "I'm just the war-master general of our group, and I would like to be recognized as such. Do I have the floor?"

Jupiter breaks a twig off a warped tree and hands it to Lawrence. "You have the talking-stick, war-master."

He nods importantly. "Alrighty! So the lake wizard dude Agonault is being a little shit. The ultimate worry is that he's building some sort of undead zombie army to do *something*—we don't know what yet—and he's been expanding his enterprise to get dead stuff from more places than just his lake vacation hideaway. The forest that we're currently in has started getting spooky lately. We're talkin' dead birds and animals everywhere, rotting plant life, monkey-archer friends going mysteriously missing, and dead zombie things wandering amuck. For those of us familiar with the film franchise *Halloweentown*, the parallels are numerous."

We all nod our heads, remembering the Disney original classic.

"The Murasi archer dudes keep reporting weird activity centered around a location farther up, which is close to the safest exit from Inferis. Eleanor, Oliver and the gang have to go there now to try and stop Agonault, because the evil stuff keeps spreading and they need to put a halt to it ASAP. As a result, we're getting sucked into accompanying them. It's the quickest way for them to save the day, and for us to get back to a world with hot showers."

"Unnhh," Sophia groans, wistfully imagining the joy of being clean again.

Lawrence tilts his head up, painfully racking his brain for the remaining details. "It was too dangerous for scouts to visit the source of the decay, so we don't really know what's going on in there. When we show up, it'll just be a lot of quick-thinkin' and hip-shootin'." This is, of course, accompanied by his use of finger guns. "That's all I've got. I miss anything?"

Sophia erupts into applause. I can't tell whether he nailed it or she's just really good at being supportive. Either way I pat him on the back. "That's actually really helpful, Law. Thanks."

Our war-master general beams with pride.

As we walk to our uncertain doom by the hands the "lake wizard dude," I'm not all that bothered. We've had our lives threatened dozens of times already; I just can't muster the angst for another one right now. My relaxed attitude might also be the result of Eleanor's mending ability. Before we left, she applied a yellow, bubbling salve on my head that is taped down with a tree-bark bandage. In addition to cultivating a sexy mummified look, the salve also gives me a delightful head buzz that's making the forest really pop.

There's a commotion of breaking twigs and stomping ahead.

A familiar squealing.

Our party stops, hushed. A small hendrina bursts into the open forest, running wild and slashing its tusks in the air. It crashes itself into the trunk of a c-shaped tree with a shriek, then bounces off and runs further down the forest.

"What's wrong with it, Oliver?" Sophia whispers. "Does it have rabies or something?"

"Ehhm, no. Adolescent hendrina are growing into their tusks, which can be exceptionally uncomfortable for them. It eases the discomfort to scratch. Simply stay out of their trail, heh."

We all watch it bounce across the vegetation like a squealing pinball, leaving a wreckage as it disappears. Eleanor nods for us to continue when the commotion dies down. As we pass the tree, I notice the slashing in the bark is far worse than it seemed. Deep gorges penetrate the trunk, and a thick, red sap leaks out of its wounds. I feel bad for the beautiful, curved tree until I notice a small swarm of pin-sized insects already crawling toward the gash. I stoop closer and see them hungrily feeding from the sap, as if they had been long in waiting for the wild hendrina to storm the forest exactly as it had.

I reach for Jupiter's hand, holding her back a few paces from the others. She looks at me, her face veiled in the green and yellow glows of the forest.

"Last night...it was really nice having you there next to me."

"It was my pleasure," she says, smiling. "I didn't have many other options, anyway; Lawrence and Sophia took the far end of the furs and you were hogging the rest. I hope that was okay."

"Definitely okay," I say. "But next time stay a while. Preferably after I wake up and am done hallucinating."

Jupiter squeezes my hand a little bit tighter. "How about next time you don't sleep for twenty years? I'm a busy woman; I've got moves to make." She whispers this last phrase, her lips hovering inches from mine. I pull her toward me into a kiss. Her body presses against me and her soft hand reaches up to my cheek. My arm wraps around the small of her back, sliding beneath her dirty white tank top and feeling the softness of her. I will never tire of being this close to her. Our faces cross like fencers dueling; lips locking one way and then shifting again for more...

"Tim?! Jupiter?" Sophia's voice echoes from far ahead, out of sight along with the rest of the group.

The two of us—still holding one another—look toward the voice and then back at each other, laughing.

"To be continued?" she asks.

"Absolutely. Whenever you want to, just heave me into a bush and we'll do it." My face immediately reddens at the poor choice of words.

"Oh, we will?" she says, raising her eyebrows.

"Not what I meant!" I say, trailing after her as she runs to rejoin the group.

"Just be careful where you poke that thing..." she says, tapping her hand playfully on the front of my jeans. "Oliver might have goggles, but the rest of us could lose an eye."

We stomp back to the group out of breath. "Everything alright?" Sophia asks.

I came prepared. "Yeah—sorry—I just got a little dizzy for a sec and Jupiter wanted me to slow down. I'm doing better now, though."

"Okay," Sophia says. Her face looks worried, but I do my best to avoid her glance.

Things in the forest gradually begin to feel...different. It's nothing particular at first; just the vague sensation that the ecosystem around us is not how it should be. Streams become marshes. Plants become both darker and paler; a grayscale of what was once a carnival of chromatic experience. The mushrooms that were emitting a bright green glow dispel a gray, sickly dust. The trees are withered like old asparagus; they have cracks in their bark, and parts of them are leaking a white, snotty sap that doesn't entice a single insect.

Everyone intuits the need to be watchful.

I shuffle up quickly to Eleanor's side. "Are we close to him?" I whisper.

Without turning to me, she speaks in her deep tenor. "We are. We have some time still before arriving at the heart of the destruction, but its grasp has already begun to take hold here."

Oliver offers a sad nod. "The rate of disease and death that has spread has been, errm, nearly exponential, and Agonault plans to continue this indefinitely. But what he has failed to understand is that his aims are unsustainable; death is finite, limited by the existence of life. If he does destroy all of Inferis for dominion over death, it will blaze a wildfire that will eventually burn itself out and leave no fuel remaining for himself or anyone else. When he finally grasps this, ehhm, it may be too late to reverse the effects."

A rustling sound. Several Murasi archers climb deftly down the trees and stand at attention in front of Eleanor and Oliver. There are no poking tails or laughs from Khazerim now; he's out of breath and reporting to his commander in broken English with a thick, unknown accent.

"Movement ahayd. Thowsand paces foward. De hart of the dayth."

"How close can you safely stand guard around the perimeter?" Eleanor responds. "We are all at risk and must proceed with great caution; your warriors included."

"We circle areea. Closing een. Seegnal if see anytheeng."

Eleanor nods. She presses her lips together to create a realistic insect chirp, just like those we heard earlier in the forest. More rustling, unseen, in the trees above us.

"Sayfty for outsyders?" Khazerim asks, pointing to us.

Eleanor considers for a moment, then turns to face us. "We believe, for your protection, that it will be safest for you to accompany the Murasi to their canopy camouflage. Oliver and I have business on the ground level, but the tree line should offer some additional cover from the foes we will be facing."

The four of us look at each other, silently. I finally manage to clear my throat. "Do I want to know how we're getting up there?"

"You will be escorted," Eleanor says.

Khazerim finally grins again, tail curling up.

"Wait, are you—"

In an instant Khazerim is behind me and I feel a strong grip around my waist.

It's his fucking legs.

Thick, hairy, trunk-like legs wrap tightly around me. He leaps, and my elevator ascends. It's a shockingly smooth glide; his massive, flexible arms cascade like water up a nearby vine. Up, up, up—snap. The vine breaks—a sudden tug on my navel as my weight momentarily free-falls—then the quickest shift to the right as he clasps another vine and we shoot up again. The forest breezes by. I'm speechless as I fly into the canopy, thrust into a growing panorama of trees. In my ascension, the striking difference in forest decay is even more apparent; death on my left, life on my right...as far as the eye can see.

At the top, Khazerim gently lowers me onto a large mat of woven vines. Through its gaps, I see what's below: a terrifying seventy-foot drop to the forest floor. The vine platform is a walkway without railings, connecting each tree to one another. The vines are chaotically clustered—uneven, crooked, things sticking out. For a moment I think it's shoddy craftsmonkeyship...until I realize that these imperfections are intentional. Looking across to different portions, I can barely tell that a walkway is there at all; the unevenness allows it to perfectly camouflage with the rest of the vines in the forest canopy.

"You lyke?" Khazerim says, smiling and nodding.

I try my best to smile back—the lack of railings is a little spooky, but I suppose the Murasi need them as much as I need training wheels on a bike. That doesn't make looking down any easier.

I watch in renewed awe as my friends slowly pop up into their own trees, each on a different section of the walkway. Jupiter's eyes are wide with excitement and wonder. Lawrence raises both crutches in the air in triumph. Poor Sophia looks...well, probably a lot like I did. Her arms are splayed out for balance, and I watch gratefully as her escort stays with her for a moment to ensure she doesn't fall. Jupiter immediately begins crossing the vine bridges and Lawrence and I follow her example, laughing as we converge around Sophia's tree to spare her the motion. We're able to grab a few nearby branches to stand comfortably on the walkway.

"Everyone okay?" Sophia asks, trying to sound calm.

"Yeppers!" Lawrence says.

"Same," I say. "Not sure what we're supposed to do up here, though." I look down at Oliver, Eleanor, and several Murasi on the forest floor, walking ahead. "Should we follow them from up here?"

"Follow," Khazerim says from behind, "but bee kwa-eet. Wee protect if fall."

"Lovely," Sophia says.

Thankfully, we don't have far to go. Jupiter leads our group, teasing me about how slow I am. The distractions certainly help. Even after being up here for fifteen minutes, Sophia's weary heart hasn't gotten used to the notion that it might splat at any second. Lawrence considers the choreography of an aerial acrobatics routine with crutches. Poor Khazerim is stuck babysitting the four of us.

Our spirits slowly sink as the forest grows darker. Before things looked weepy and spooky, but soon the area becomes utterly decimated. A black and gray that chill the soul. All life—including insects, critters, and plants—have either died or vacated the area entirely. The archers make silent commands to one another, until finally Khazerim's flat, hairy hand stretches out to bar our way. He turns himself sideways, nostrils flaring. Our breathing seems harsh in the silence. We stand completely still on the vines, which makes it much easier for me to imagine myself plummeting to the ground. I glance down instinctively, noticing...something down below.

A bent figure in a coarse brown robe.

CHAPTER 38

The hooded figure stands near a small black pond, his posture as gnarled and twisted as the dying trees. Eleanor and Oliver emerge in the clearing, ten feet from it. Eleanor looks up toward us and waves an arm, then jabs two fingers in the direction of the figure. Two whooshes of air breathe by my ear as arrows fly down. As soon as they make contact with the robe, it collapses to the floor in a flat puddle, entirely hollow underneath. Nothing but a scarecrow, keeping watch over this black pool.

Eleanor and Oliver peer into the still water. At first I'm puzzled as to why they're so fixated, but soon I am as well. It...isn't right. It's so black that it doesn't have any sheen or light reflecting from it; it swallows all nearby brightness like a black hole in space.

The pond suddenly reaches—no! A hand grasps!

A dark, murky arm shoots from the water and grips at Oliver's leg. His body tenses and he struggles violently—cursing and muttering—trying to tug his weight away. As he does, the body connected to the arm surfaces.

From this height it's difficult to see clearly...besides the fact that its face has no shape. It resembles a round, clay splotch without eye sockets or slits for nostrils. Its only feature is a dangling jaw that rapidly snaps shut as it pulls itself toward Oliver. Arrows rain down around us—some go for the head, but many are aimed directly at the arm that is inches from Oliver's leg. None miss their mark, yet still the arm clutches with an inhuman will. It does not flinch or falter at the dozen arrows piercing through it. Oliver shouts louder as its talons tear deeper into him.

The archers adjust. Silent still, more arrows pierce through the arm in a straight line together, severing the wrist from its undead hand entirely. Oliver breaks free as the one-handed monstrosity claws its way out of the black pool, advancing unrelentingly. Its broken hand is still wrapped tightly around Oliver's ankle, writhing on his skin. Oliver grabs his wooden staff and clubs the hand off him with a crack. He spits on the twitching hand, cursing at it and backing toward Eleanor. I only now realize how little Eleanor reacted or offered to help. She still stares at the black pool, her eyes somehow penetrating something beneath the darkness.

The undead body suddenly stops crawling, as if its battery fell out. More silence—

shattered by the radiant, booming voice of a man.

"Welcome!" he says. "I am so very pleased to see that all of you are here!" I look in every direction, helpless; the voice seems to be coming from everywhere at once. It has the charm of a car salesman, the juiciness of an apple with a razor blade in it. "I mean you no harm," it continues, "although I understand with utmost clarity that you have prepared for war when arriving on my doorstep. Please," he implores. "Leave me in peace. All I seek is the solitude of this forest. Is that so much for an aging man to ask?"

For a moment, the deep, pained sincerity in his voice has me charmed. Maybe Oliver and Eleanor made a mistake?

At the far end of the pond, I see another hunched, brown cloak appear. Within seconds, it, too, is shot down, melting like the first.

Eleanor speaks. "You are not welcome in these lands. You have plagued all that you touch, and are destroying Inferis for all who occupy—"

"You do not understand what you interrupt," the voice replies, no longer frail at all.

A single, large bubble materializes on the surface of the black pond...then bursts. Then another. A series of them erupt—boiling over. From the bubbling blackness emerges another hand, its arm extending and clawing into the earth. Then a second, and many more after. Bodies pour out of the water—not slow and menacingly like the first, but with desperate, hastened grasping. The gray, faceless forms grapple and fight with one another to race out. When they reach land, they bolt. It's not an army but a swarm—scattering in all directions—chaotically flinging their limbs on all fours, heads waggling limply in circular motions.

From our tree canopy it all seems unreal...until the first Murasi archer falls. We stand uselessly while he runs in front of Eleanor and Oliver, ushering them back to safety, and is trampled by the first wave. The bodies pour over him thoughtlessly, except a few that remain to gouge at his flesh and tear at him with their dangling jaws. The screaming—the helpless shrieking unlike anything I've ever heard—is stifled only when one of them bites into the Murasi's throat, gnawing until a hole is gored through his neck and into the dirt.

And then they climb.

They claw their way up the trees like giant pale spiders, scaling the bark almost as fast as the archers had. Sophia lets out a piercing scream as one approaches directly beneath her. The surrounding archers shoot at the monster but it continues with all speed; a dozen arrows protrude from its formless face like a dart board. Up close I see that it's not a solid body, but rather a patchwork of flesh clusters melted together; different shades of withered, lifeless gray peeling off from one another like scabs—

I'm grabbed from behind and hurled off the vines. Screaming, I turn to see that it's Khazerim. He grips a few vines and swings us down...swooping low to the ground and rising back up. I look wildly around, finally able to spot Jupiter, Sophia, and Lawrence in the equally capable hands of the Murasi. They're being carried off across the forest in all different directions, farther away from me and Khazerim.

No time to care or panic. We're fleeing from reanimated corpses and swinging toward more. A heavy breeze whips back my hair as we swoop. The black pond pours across the earth, shooting up in its center and spreading across the ground like lava flow. More and more bodies emerge from it, patched together from all of the life that has ever died across its reach. The vine walkways above us are already swarming.

Khazerim grabs another vine to pivot our direction, but once our weight shifts, we realize that the spidered corpses have already infested this vine, climbing down toward us. Khazerim drops—my weight jolts at the naval, still stuck between the muscular grip of his legs—and he clasps desperately with his tail and both arms. Khazerim exhales heavily from exertion but thunders on across the forest.

The monsters outpace us. The bodies are infinite. They sprint and climb below, above, and around us. The black sludge ceaselessly spews and spreads; its radius coats the entire forest floor in a darkness only penetrated by the birthing of its undead spawn.

We need to try something else.

CHAPTER 39

"Turn around!" I shout, craning my head to face Khazerim. "Turn back toward the center of the pond!"

He looks at me with furled eyebrows. "Crayzee?"

"No! It will just keep coming if we don't do something; we need to help Oliver and Eleanor or it will catch us."

A longer glance, likely trying to determine whether I am, in fact, "crayzee." I wish I had the answer, friend. He grunts, then grabs another vine and holds our weight on it until the pendulum swings...and shifts backward.

Two horrifying things come into view. The first is Eleanor, who is entirely tangled in vines. They're wrapped around her wrists, ankles, and neck—her body hovering in the air and spread in the shape of an X, like she's being displayed on a whipping post. She seems to be struggling in their grip, writhing and concentrating with all the strength she can muster. Her eyes are closed. She makes deliberate exhales of breath as if mastering herself against some great pain. Gray, lifeless forms race to reach her across all access points at her limbs. They are close...until the vines begin moving. They grow like a time-lapse, spreading from her as the source and curling out like snakes. She's controlling them. They weave their way around the undead, constricting them in place. Others continue clawing up, but more vines meet and trap them like flies in her ever-expanding web.

The second thing I notice is that Sophia is alone. She's screaming, holding herself thirty feet above the ground on a single vine, arms shaking. Below her lies the body of the archer that was carrying her. He's stacked on top of a pile of crushed gray forms, with several others surrounding him. His guttural cries echo across the forest madness as the undead claw into his flesh. Whether accidentally or deliberately, the holes they tear into him avoid vital organs to elongate his agony. Blood sprays out of him, dying the gray bodies with splotches of red.

Sophia and I both watch, helplessly. She lets out another scream as more undead drip their way down her vine, advancing toward her as she does her best to shimmy away. I point at her and Khazerim uses his remaining strength to fling us there.

"Sophia!" I shout. We are a five-second swing away from her. She's desperately shimmying down her vine, reaching out an arm to me. Just as the bodies close in around her, I extend my hand and grab hold of her. Khazerim strengthens his grip on me and I wrap myself around Sophia as tightly as I can. The three of us clutch at one another, swinging to safety with every effort we have.

"You okay?!" I yell over the chaos.

"Yeah!" she manages, still shaken but coming to herself. "What are we going to do?"

"I don't know!" I say. "But they're popping out faster than we can even get away. We need to stop it at the source somehow. Khazerim! Keep circling the center of the pond, if you can!"

Somehow, he does. His teeth are clenched with a sheer will to survive. On and on he swings, grabbing vines while barely avoiding the undead closing in around us. They're so numerous now that they fall from the treetops like rain. I have nothing. No plan. Again and again we circle. Something has to—

"Fuck it," Sophia says, freeing one hand and digging in her backpack. She pulls out the black vial that Jupiter had nabbed from the citadel.

"Do we even know what that thing does?!" I shout.

"No!" she yells, frazzled. "No fucking clue, but whatever's going on down there is magic shit, and this is magic shit, and....and I don't know! What other options can you think of?!"

I can't say the logic is inspiring, but we have nothing else. Before I have time to respond, Sophia grips the vial and chucks it directly into the center of the geyser.

Nothing happens.

We wait, staring desperately. In some fantasy, I had imagined it might cause—

BANG!

We almost fall out of Khazerim's grip from the sudden force. The geyser at the center of the pond explodes like a pipe bomb, and a black bubble bursts from where the vial landed. Soon, however, the geyser continues as normal. Sophia slumps a bit in my arms. It failed.

There is something strange about the aftermath of the explosion. A large stump stands to the left of the geyser. After Sophia's Hail Mary toss, black ooze had shot out toward the stump...but it's stain formed a small, perfectly shaped dome rather than coating the log.

"What is that?" I ask Sophia.

"Tim, I need you to stop asking me questions. I have zero answers and I need an aspirin!"

"Fair," I say, still staring at the stump and the black dome. We make another loop around the pond, swinging above the anomaly. My suspicions are confirmed when I see Eleanor's vines shoot in mid-air toward the dome like homing missiles. The vines crash into the it but are stopped in their tracks. Eleanor's face is red, her knuckles white, her teeth clenching; she stares with the intensity of a woman in labor. The first vine breaks through, piercing the dome like a cracking egg. Underneath...a man is revealed.

He's wearing a brown robe that's identical to the phantom ones that had melted before. He has long, black-and-white spiked hair on the sides of his head like horns. Under normal circumstances he might have looked regal and confident like the booming voice had suggested. Now, however, his features contort into the same intense, fiery expression as Eleanor; his nose is flared, staring at the intruding vines. His arms wave in the direction of the geyser, ebbing and flowing like an ocean tide. As the vines claw their way further in, the man's motions shift. His arms no longer wave; in an instant the geyser stops bubbling over and the black pool stills. He stretches his arms straight up, and as he does the dome rebuilds itself. His protective shell is made of the same gray, dead patches that form the swarming creatures. It scabs itself over once more, and the vines that had pierced through are sliced off as the shell re-seals. The geyser resumes its bubbling, and the pool spreads once more.

A labyrinth of vines wriggle through the black pond, and one emerges with a sharp stone. Eleanor focuses her control back to the dome, carving the stone into it. Again the vines wedge themselves into the dome, prying at the edges and cracking it. Agonault is revealed once more, but the walls surrounding him crumble more quickly. He raises his arms—stopping the geyser entirely—and the walls slowly rebuild themselves. A few stray vines are able to wrap around his body, but still his arms remain above his head, fingers clawing up like vicious forks of lightning. Eleanor and Agonault are in a bitter deadlock, straining forcefully against the might of one another.

Agonault lets out a bellowing roar that echoes through the forest. The protective dome slowly evolves. Patches of gray skin meld together before our eyes, forming the foundation of a great castle. Pillars rise, walls erect, swirling engravings carve into ornate archways; it becomes a palace of extravagance molded from death itself. I recognize its structure as the same stone-carved fortress that we had seen across the lake when we first entered Inferis. Soon Eleanor and Agonault are entirely engulfed in its rising fortifications, leaving us blind to—

"Aggghhh!"

A gray, lifeless form drops from a tree onto Khazerim. He is slammed down, releasing me and Sophia from his grip as the three of us plummet. I try to grab a vine, arms straining. The skin of my hands shreds and burns from the sudden friction of the textured bark. I get a good grip—jolt again. Sophia grabs my right leg on her way down and I am desperately supporting the weight of both of us. She's screaming. I'm screaming. She finally manages to shift her weight onto the vine below me, pulling it to her chest. The strain in my arms is desperately relieved, but they're still barely hanging on.

"You safe?" I say, looking down at Sophia. Below her Khazerim has managed to stay his fall, but he still can't rid himself from the leeching undead clinging to him.

"Above you!" Sophia screams. Another gray creature sprints down the vine toward us. My instinct is to panic and climb away, but there's no time and there's nowhere to run with Sophia below me. I manage to slow my breathing, realizing what has to be done. My body sways gently in the air as I brace myself...

The undead being rams itself into me—wildly grappling, grabbing, tearing—in a flurry of assault. Exhaustion kicks in from the swinging, the day, the concussion...and if I'm being honest, my pathetic lack of upper arm strength. I can manage nothing more than to endure with a feverish, adrenaline-rich grip, but it's essential that I do just that. As soon as I'm dead and fall, this creature will plunge down after Sophia and Khazerim. I can buy them time, at least. Its rancid claws shred my back while its arms bludgeon me.

Still, I hold on.

Its weight flounders against me, its skin an abhorrent blend of smooth, wet, and slimy. It heaves at my shoulders and pulls me down, tearing into my hands.

Still, I hold on.

My arms shake under the strain. The pain amplifies to a point where it can no longer be registered. My brain relocates to a space where there is no pain. There are no vines, no trees, no zombies, no me. My body locks in place and knows to hold that position ceaselessly, but mentally I've dissociated entirely. This is only as real as I allow it to be, and I choose to fixate on the nothingness of my consciousness. My mind is a white room, with endless white corridors leading on into eternity...

My hands slide down further. My mind might be far away, but physical limitations are still quite real. I glance to the black forest floor—the gaping void that I will soon collapse into—and am surprised to see Sophia. She's already made it to the tail end of the vine, swinging fast with momentum. The castle is still there, but vines have torn gaping holes through it and exposed Eleanor and Agonault to the world again. Sophia is directly above them. Her legs are sticking straight out, shoes poised to connect with the back of Agonault's head as he fiercely fights off Eleanor. Sophia arcs her foot back...and swings it, landing the kick!

Agonault's body keels over—a rag doll gone limp and crumpling—and Eleanor's vines use this opportunity to overpower him. They slither onto him, into him. They pour into his mouth, his nostrils, his eye sockets—gagging and gurgling in his throat. His limp arm reaches up one last time before he is swallowed whole by the overgrowth.

I feel a weightless sensation. The monster grappling on me jumps off in apparent terror; his slimy figure slips from my shoulders. With one final effort, I hold on just tight enough for my body to slide down the vine rather than drop. My vision spins and blurs as I go down...down...

The last thing I see is a herd of turin rampaging through the trees, stomping on the bodies of the undead. Lawrence and Jupiter are riding one of them, shouting war-cries in a foreign tongue.

I fall to the ground.

CHAPTER 40

Dying is hairier than I imagined.

No...that's just Khazerim. He has me slung over his furry shoulders, bobbing up and down with each step. My body feels like an old chew toy. I shift my head, struggling to open my eyes.

"No," Khazerim says quietly. "Rest."

"Mgeehhhh," I respond.

I hear everyone around me. Lawrence is on his crutches chatting excitedly with Oliver. Sophia is hobbling a bit, but still sounds cheerful. Jupiter has her arm around Sophia, offering some support and listening. Eleanor...

"Where's Eleanor?" I ask.

"Tim!!" Sophia shouts, hurrying over to me.

"How are you?" Jupiter asks.

Lawrence sobers himself for a moment, perhaps noticing the exhaustion on my face. "Let's let him rest a bit, gang," he says. "We'll swarm him as soon as he's had a better chance to sleep. You aren't supposed to free fall fifteen feet off a vine when you're already concussed..."

"We'll get you home real soon, Tim," Sophia says, her voice filled with tears.

Oliver comes to me as well. "Eleanor is, ehhm, safe. She has returned home and is resting. As you should be. We have resumed our final trek to the Northern Passage, to take you all home." He flashes his toothy smile. I try to ask him more, dying to understand all that we had witnessed, but the smallest shift in weight induces a searing pain across my chest. My limp hand reaches to touch my stomach, and I feel several jagged strips of blood scabbing over with an ointment smeared onto it.

"Are you okay?" I ask Khazerim.

He smiles down at me kindly. "Eye am. All tyred. Luckee to leeve. Four Murasi die tooday."

My eyes close, imagining the horrible screaming faces. It feels like it was only a moment ago...my last conscious memories. "I'm so sorry, Khazerim" If I had more energy I would have worried about saying the right thing. A lifetime ago I would have lost months of sleep over it. Instead, I say the first sincere thing that comes to mind. "Thank you for carrying me, friend."

He smiles again, teary-eyed, and holds me tight against his chest. "Rest."

Snapshots of sounds and sights rouse me...then I pass out again.

Dark forest gradually gives way to the luminous pink, green, and yellow lights of healthy growth. There's beauty in the air again. The soft graze of Jupiter's hand on my leg. Whispers from her and Khazerim—his chest bellowing and vibrating against my ear with the deep tones of his voice. Insects peeeooiii to one another from across the trail. A twig breaks. Lawrence trips and tries to play it off like he bent down to look at a dinosaur fossil. Making camp. I start to feel somewhat better, but not well enough to get bullied into building another fence. I play dead to avoid labor, but as I do I actually fall asleep again.

I open my eyes when everyone settles. We're at the edge of the forest, overlooking the wonderous Great Plains. It feels like relief, like we're home already. Far, far across the violet sky I see a gray blur of dust from the Dead Wastes. I imagine the bridge that we had so horribly failed at crossing. The herdswomen, the lake and the chains...the bats that had swooped down and cut us off at the start of all of this. I grin at the thought of a few bats scaring me. All of that is behind us. Ahead—maybe a few hours' march away—is the Northern Passage and our way out. And to the right...there is more. In the distance I spot it again: a monstrous, stony being, striding into the beyond of this world. It lumbers into the backdrop of a mountain range, disappearing in the hills and chasms.

CHRIS DELUDE

Jupiter lowers herself to the ground, lying beside me on the green-white grass. She curls her hand in mine and says nothing. We're silent for some time, listening to the insect chirps.

"How did the herdswomen find us in the forest?" I ask. "Back at the fight."

She glances to me, smiling. No, certainly not the same woman I met behind the counter of Sheridan's Gas Station.

"I called them," she says. "When we were in their camp a few days ago, they taught me how to do a whistling sound with my hands." She pauses and cups one hand in a tube, pressing it against her cracked lips. Her second hand cups precisely behind it, and she mimics blowing. "It took several tries to get it right, but once I had it, I knew it would be easy to replicate. They use it to signal predators across the Plains. I figured..."

"That's incredible, Jupiter. You're the coolest person I've ever met."

She smiles and leans over me, gently caressing the side of my hair. I smile back, delighted to be so close to her. She lowers herself down for a kiss, and I sigh from the warmth, comfort, and delight of it all. I could kiss her for an eternity...

"I thought laughter was the best medicine?" Lawrence says. He plops himself down on the ground with an "oof," and Sophia sits next to him.

"Lawrence told us all not to talk to you until you're fully rested," Sophia says, "and you know I normally wouldn't disturb your business—"

"*Business*," Lawrence emphasizes, wiggling his eyebrows.

"—but we haven't seen you since everything happened. How are you? Is everything bandaged okay?"

"Fine," I say, smiling.

Sophia's eyes are still filled with concern, looking over me as if assessing every rend, hole, scratch, and bruise. I slowly prop my arms

206

against the ground, and painfully—oh dear, this is bad—bring myself halfway up. Jupiter's hand gently presses me back down to the ground.

"No you don't," she says. "I'll only kiss you if you stay immobile. I'm weird like that."

"Unfortunately, I believe you," I say. "By the way...Sophia did you, like, save the day and kick that wizard dude in the face?"

"Oh my god you saw that?!" she says, blushing. "I don't know what came over me! I just...I saw you getting attacked and I could barely hold on anymore, and I saw him below looking the other way. I just went for it! I expected for it to be totally pathetic, but it landed!"

"Wait a second!" Lawrence cuts in. "You mean to tell me you were some freakin' action hero, and I had to learn about it from Tim?! Why didn't you tell usss baaabbbe?"

Sophia smiles, looking down. "I don't know. There was a lot going on, and I was so worried about you both getting hurt. I didn't want to make it all about me!"

Lawrence wraps her in his arms and squeezes. "But it *is* all about you! How many of us can say they've kicked an evil wizard in the face?"

"Eleanor did most of it!" Sophia argues. "I just distracted him for a half-second. Seriously, it was nothing."

"It wasn't nothing," I confirm with Lawrence.

"Obviously, Tim!" Lawrences says, almost agitated. "She's a hero. Babe, I'm buying you pizza as soon as we get home. And garlic knots! Heroes deserve garlic knots! We're raising you up on the pedestal that you belong on—that you've always belonged on. Deal with it."

Sophia doesn't know how to respond. Jupiter walks up to her, giving her a small side-hug. "Just accept the fact that you're a total girl boss. Your boyfriend wants to celebrate you, and you deserve to let him."

"I'd be dead without her," I add. "That kick was gnarly and just in time; that's what finally chased the gray thing off me."

"God, I wish I could have seen it!!" Lawrence moans. "Life needs an instant-replay feature for when your girl does cool shit."

Sophia blushes harder, leaning into Lawrence.

"Speaking of which," I say, "Lawrence, did you ride the turin into victory?"

Lawrence flashes me the cheesiest smile. "I sure did, Timmy-Tim!! I even remembered to duck when my fuzzy buddy ran underneath a tree branch!"

"He also gave some really helpful pointers for getting on," Jupiter admits.

"And," Lawrence continues, "Jupiter and I managed to save Oliver so that the three of us could kick ass together!" Lawrence sees Oliver on the other side of camp and interrupts an important-looking discussion with three herdswomen. "Hey Olly! We were pretty unstoppable back there, ehh?"

Oliver pardons himself, and Lawrence nudges him playfully in the side.

"We used our ninja skills and showed 'em whassup!"

Oliver chuckles. "We, ehhm, played our small part in the affair, for certain."

"Yeeeeah," Lawrence says, chopping both arms through the air

"Oliver," I begin, uncertain of the phrasing. "Is Eleanor...magic? I mean, some of the things I saw her and Agonault do were incredible."

Oliver smiles proudly. "Elly is a remarkable woman. Whether one would call it magic, ehhm, is entirely up to you."

"I was thinking of the shelves in the map room of your house, and the bridges above the forest. Those were all her, too, right?"

Oliver takes off his fogging goggles, rubbing them with his dirty finger before re-hitching them back on his face. "That is correct. From my own experience, I understand that Eleanor—in mind, body, and spirit, ehhm—connects to the natural world in a way that most of humanity could not fathom. She speaks it and breathes it like it is family and kinship with her. In return, it listens and responds, just as nature responds to the rest of nature. Plants grow when they receive nutrients and water over time, but are those the only elements that aid their blossoming? And what is time, if plants can grow—ehhm—at different rates over that time?" His crooked smile emerges again, looking over us curiously. "All beings are capable of more than they seem. Including the forest that Elly can connect with, and Elly herself. Including all of us, as well, heh. I have a love for nature and a passion for learning, classifying, and exploring all that it has shown us. In a way, quite possibly, because it allows me to better understand and grow closer to Elly."

"Hah!" Lawrence shouts. "Grow. I get it."

Sophia ignores him. "That's really beautiful, Oliver."

"Thank you," he says. "And thank you for your assistance with all that has happened today, ehhm. Dark times were upon us, and fate or some force beyond our understanding has brought you here to aid us in a moment of need. The death pools can be overgrown by new life now that we have preserved so much of the forest. We can begin to restore order."

"Our pleasure, my man!" Lawrence says.

"Yeah, thank you for everything," Jupiter says.

Still dizzy, still in pain, I lay down to rest for a while. My head drifts with the hum of everyone else's voices: planning the next steps in our journey, recounting the incredible events of last night, discussing the future of Inferis. It's beautiful how invested we've all become in this place. In our own way, I think each of us will be grateful to have come down here. Things may go back to normal in the Above and all of this might fade into some feverish memory, but for a few days we got to experience true nature...in all her beauty, complexity, and raw existence. Whatever masks we've been wearing over a lifetime, Inferis gave us the opportunity to glimpse ourselves without them.

Tonight, I fall deeply, happily asleep entwined in the arms of Jupiter. And tomorrow we go home.

CHAPTER 41

"**A**RRRREEEE we ready to rumble?!?!" Lawrence yells, pointing his crutches out from his mouth like a megaphone.

No response; we're still not a morning group.

Every part of me is in pain, but on the verge of the finish line I manage to force myself up. I glance around the camp, noticing that Khazerim is gone already. I sigh, wishing I got to say goodbye to him. Hopefully life in Inferis slows down a bit; I'd like to imagine him laughing and poking people with his tail again.

We begin our final trek across the Great Plains. The walk to the northern cave entrance goes slowly but incredibly smoothly, with nothing but wildlife and scenery to enjoy. We see a pack of markeet run far in the distance, pass glittering flies buzzing around a bush with berries on it, and spy a large, skeletal bird of prey swooping down toward a bend in the river. I glance again to the mountain range on our right, where the giant had crossed last night.

"Oliver," I say, catching up with him. "What's over that way?"

"Ermm, a great many things. The colossum reside in the mountains so I do not frequent the region. They are quite peaceful in nature, mind you; but even if humans mean peace to ants, they are still apt to do collateral damage, heh. Beyond the mountains there are recesses and pits of magma, from which is the source of heat in much of Inferis. Strange forests exist past the hills, which Eleanor and I only risk going in with significant preparation. And then...there is what lies beyond."

"You mean, you haven't explored all of Inferis?"

He shines a crooked smile. "Have you explored all of the Above?"

I laugh, thinking how little I've seen in the world despite vaguely "knowing" the names of a few countries and exotic animals.

"I do hope to at some point," Oliver continues. "Explore it all, that is. Great wonders are everywhere, ehhm, and so long as I can venture safely and make it back home to Elly, I intend to. These expeditions will be on hold for some time now, though. Work to be done on the home front."

"Speaking of which," I say, "we were in too much of a rush for me to see your maps as much as I'd like to. I...I'll definitely need to take care of some things in the Above for a while. On my own home front. But maybe afterward I could come down again and visit? If you still want to show me?"

Sophia overhears, her jaw silently dropping.

Oliver, however, smiles so wide that he has to readjust his shifting goggles. "Yes, that would be quite wonderful! I have felt horrible that you were so pressed for time, and that your visit, ehhm, has been so hectic. You and your friends are always welcome to rendezvous with us at any time. If you arrive, we will find you; Inferis has eyes and ears everywhere, heh."

"Cool. And maybe we can sketch out some new maps, too," I say, nodding my head over to the mountains in the distance.

"Nothing would please me more!"

After a few hours of walking across the crunching green-white grass, our path leads to a slab of rock wall. A giant crack rends through the middle of the stone, and Oliver guides us directly into it. The walls narrow and lower around us until there's hardly enough room to pass through in single file. The ground becomes oddly familiar; the vegetation gradually grows sparser, leaving rocky paths ascending upward.

"I didn't miss being in these dark, cramped tunnels," Sophia says. Without the violet lights above we can hardly see a thing. Oliver keeps going steadily, but the rest of us are left to feel and fumble our way through the enveloping darkness.

"Yeah, and I think my phone died a few days ago," Jupiter adds.

"Same," Sophia replies.

"Mine perished in our river ride," Lawrence moans, struggling with his crutches in the tight space.

I smile to myself, digging into my pocket. I hear the familiar crinkle of the plastic Ziplock bag, and wait for the Apple icon to glow and startup. After careful preservation, my battery is still at a gentleman's seventy-eight percent. I turn the flashlight on and the cave illuminates, revealing a damp rock jutting down near our heads. Good timing.

"How the hell?!" Lawrence shouts.

"Tim went in the river with Lawrence," Jupiter says. "How is his still working?"

"Oh my god," Sophia says, looking back at me and laughing. "It was your plastic phone diaper, wasn't it?"

I laugh too, waving the baggy in the air. "I get that I'm generally too neurotic, but I stand by this! You never know when a friend is going to plummet down a waterfall and you'll have to chase after him."

"This is why we keep Timmy around!" Lawrence sings from the front.

Pleased at reclaiming her vision, Sophia glances ahead through the narrow tunnel. "Any idea how long until we make it out, Oliver?"

"I estimate within an hour or two, variant on our pace and if we run into any, ehhm, disruptions."

"Any particular disruptions coming to mind?" I ask.

"Yeah, like swamp wizards?" Lawrence says.

Oliver snorts. "Heh. That is quite unknown to me. I presume it would be evident to all of you, at this point; it is a rarity in Inferis for things to go without disruption. Part of the allure."

Oliver has unbelievable comedic timing. A low rumbling vibrates the surrounding rock. "Hmmph," he says. "Grond habitats are typically, ehhm, much farther south and west of here. It was the case with the hendrina as well. A great deal of displacement has been occurring as of late, likely due to the workings of Agonault."

Sophia looks at me questioningly, but I just shrug. For some reason the name does sound familiar, though.

"What is a grond?" Sophia finally asks.

"Oh. It's—ermm—I am not always good at describing things, Elly has said. It is, ehhm, large. Their young have black fur, and it gradually fades to white with age. They prefer habitats with enclosed holes for protecting their young. The rumbling we have just heard would confirm my suspicions that this one has recently begun occupying the space."

"Do we have to worry about them stomping our faces?" Lawrence asks.

"I should hope not," Oliver responds.

The rumbling continues. As we approach, the entire cave feels like it's buckling. An occasional snort or roar reverberates along the walls. The air is dry and coated in thick rock dust, scratching at my throat.

Oliver turns to us, whispering. "I will advance forward to determine the grond's position and disposition. Depending on how docile it is, our large numbers may be enough to frighten it so we may simply walk past. Oh, and...ehhm, please turn that light off. It may have unpredictable effects on the creature's behavior."

I do as instructed, leaving the four of us in silence and darkness once more. A pebble clatters on Oliver's exit. Another rumble...followed by the loudest roar I've ever heard. The deep bellow dislodges several stones from the ceiling that shatter to the ground.

Among the noise, Oliver's voice re-emerges. "That is the largest grond I have ever seen! Quite remarkable, really! I will have to tell Elly all about it; she will, ehhm, be upset to have missed—"

"—Can we get past it?" I interrupt.

"Oh, that I do not know. For now, the grond is in quite a 'state,' as some might say. The only safe course to consider is to wait for it to tire out. That may take hours or days, and even then we still may not be safe to walk through. Not without enraging it, heh. But we have no other options."

"Is there anything that could put it in a better mood?" Lawrence asks. "I tempt Soph with snacks when she's hangry and it seems to do the trick."

"Are you comparing me to a giant furry cave animal?" Sophia says, eyeing him in the dark.

No response.

"A food offering could be effective," Oliver admits, "but unfortunately, we are far too aligned with the grond's diet for it to completely ignore us, heh. You may risk resuming your flashlight again," he adds, sitting on the ground. "The grond resides around several corners, and I do not believe it will be visible from here."

We sit next to Oliver. And wait.

CHAPTER 42

Hours pass in silence. Lawrence and Sophia doze off for a short while, propping themselves up against the cavern walls and leaning their heavy heads against each other. Jupiter sits behind me, wrapping her arms around my shoulders. I press my hand against the clasped fingers that rest on my chest. Life isn't so bad.

To come this far and get trampled at the finish line seems very plausible; Inferis has given me a crash course on the best laid plans being derailed. While that particular outcome would be unfortunate, I'm struggling to decide whether this entire adventure should be categorized as a massive unlucky or lucky streak. Despite a few manageable injuries, we've made it through so much—

A puppy yips.

It is the most confusing, cutest sound imaginable. Everyone bolts upright, including Oliver. It yips again, and small, scratching claws can be heard pawing across the rocks not so far off.

A strange voice.

"Hey! Hey buddy!"

A small glimmer of light shows around the corner and then dims away. Oliver and I stand up. I creep around the corner, heart pounding with fear, excitement, anticipation. Because that voice almost sounds like...

The light inside reveals the strangest scene I've ever seen.

It's Lulu!

Sweet, beautiful Lulu the pup is jumping on top of and licking a 30-foot tall, white-furry beast standing on two legs. It doesn't seem like a monster at all. In fact, it's smiling and tickling its thick, calloused fingers delicately against Lulu's brown fur. Lulu can't help herself—she is so excited and overjoyed with the attention that she runs in circles across the beast's chest, jumping and yipping and playing with the behemoth hand that dangles over her head. Shining the flashlight on her...is Bobby the plumber. His long, tangled black hair is disheveled and filled with dirt clods, as are his faded jeans and the leather tool bag strapped across his shoulders.

"What are you...?" I mutter.

"Tim?" he says.

"How did you get here?" I ask.

"I went to the house to fix your water heater. 'Friday at 3:00 PM,' we agreed."

I smirk; even in this ridiculous circumstance, his deep voice is even-keeled and down-to-business.

"I rang the bell, but no one answered. I was about to leave when I heard frantic clawing inside. I glanced through the side windows by the door and saw your pup freaking out. There was dog poop all over the floors and trash littered everywhere. I thought someone might have had a medical emergency or something. I tried opening the door and it worked. I was about to call for the police and look for you when the pup jumped on me and tried running toward the basement again. I followed; dogs are much smarter than people give them credit for." He glances up, smiling at the sight of Lulu prancing on top of the grond. "I was expecting to find a body, but instead I find a hole covered by a tarp that was shredded through. The pup dove right in, and I felt responsible for her given the situation. So, I followed," Bobby says, and points back to a tunnel behind him. He sounds like he's describing light traffic on his way to the post office.

"This, ehhm, seems like an advantageous place to part ways, then" Oliver says. "I presume you will want your animal companion with you? If so, go to your exit and call her, while I will remain on this side."

The finality of this statement sinks in.

"Oliver..." Sophia says, "how can we ever thank you for what you've done? We would have been dead a thousand times over if it weren't for you." She wraps her arms around him, hugging the awkward man, goggles, leather and all.

"Umm, ehh, the pleasure was mine," he fumbles, smiling. "You all have been of tremendous assistance. Getting to know you has been a treat for Elly and myself. Truly."

"You're the man, Olly," Lawrence says, hugging and patting him on the back.

"Stay weird, dude," Jupiter says. He's confused by this one, but takes her smile as a sign that it was still a compliment.

"I'll visit as soon as I can," I say, giving him a hug. "Just let me know if there's anything from the Above that you miss, and I can bring it down for you."

His eyes light up, growing wide and wild. "I...ehhm, have thought about Reese's peanut butter cups for many...many years. Do they still make those? I have so few cravings from that world, but..."

"I'll haul down an entire pallet for you," I say, grinning.

He doesn't respond, aside from an odd, grunting throat clear.

All of us tourists creep into the exiting tunnel, gathering as far toward safety as we can.

"Get inside and be ready to run," I say. "I'll call Lulu and then we'll be right behind you." They nod, taking their positions. I clear my throat nervously; whatever this grond's temper is like, I don't want to find out. "Here Lulu!! C'mere!"

Her head snaps to attention, tiny puppy-tongue panting and joyous. She briefly glances back at her giant fuzz mama, then bolts off the grond's chest to me. Her paws overshoot me, and she has to skid to a stop as I scratch behind her furry ears. She looks up, tail whipping wildly. I expected a frantic getaway run as we take away the yeti's tiny puppy, but the grond looks at me calmly in a way that suggests "if that beautiful fluff-ball trusts you, I trust you."

One last wave to Oliver...and we head back home.

"I told you!" Lawrence passionately announces. "I told you my yeti-senses were tingling before! No one listens!!"

CHAPTER 43

The dark, winding tunnels are narrow as hell. We pass through in single-file, with Bobby the plumber guiding in front. Lulu is thrilled by the presence of so many friends; we do our best to watch our footing as the puppy weaves her brown and white body between our legs. The floor steepens drastically, and the damp, cool rock walls begin to dry and warm up. Stone floors and walls give way to dirt.

"Watch your step," I hear Bobby say.

Pale phone light is met with the glowing radiance from above...

I feel like I'm being birthed out of the tarp flap and into the modern world. Everything is exactly as I had left it; the boxes stacked in the corner, the busted water heater. The fact that a dank, dark basement can feel so bright amazes us all. The iridescent bulb that I had replaced glows above, and to the right a small window reveals the burning radiance of daylight. My head throbs and aches the second I glance at it.

Oh right...the concussion.

"We are HOOOOOME!" Lawrence shouts, bad leg dangling in the air. The neon yellow jumpsuit is now almost entirely caked with gray and brown, stretched and torn to its limits. The rest of us look just as terrible. Sophia's formerly mom-on-vacation vibe is long gone, unless the vacation ended with the family getting mauled by a bear. Her Red Sox hat is lost somewhere deep in Inferis, and she has a jagged, scabbed gash on the side of her cheek. Her eyes water at the sight of modern plumbing. Jupiter is...well, she's still gorgeous. Filthy, but—

Lulu jumps up onto me, again and again, tiny paws pressing up against my gross Smith's shirt. I smile, imagining her inner dialogue.

"Hey! Missed you! Hungry? You left me so I'm kinda spooked, but missed you! Hungry?"

I take the hint. "Let's head upstairs, guys," I say. "Get some food in Lulu and get you all...going I guess."

My brain barely functions enough to put the sentence together. The group follows me up the staircase, except for Bobby; the dusty plumber pulls out his bag of tools and begins working on the water heater. Seeing a yeti was a mere detour to his craft.

"You...all right down here, Bobby?" I ask.

"Yeah. The part you ordered came in, so I just have to do a quick install then you should be set."

"Great...thanks. I'll just go and take care of Lulu real quick."

No response. Never in my life have I given a 500% tip to someone, but I think today's the day.

The four of us trudge doggedly upstairs—Lulu dashing ahead to remind us exactly where the food is kept, in case we forgot.

"Welcome home, Timmy-Tim!" Lawrence says, laughing among the carnage. One small puppy was able to overthrow an entire house. The reek of wet shit hits first and hits hard. White stuffing from something, my guess is a couch, is strewn about like tumbleweeds. Several boxes from the food pantry are shredded, their contents spread and mixed in a deliciously messy heap of honey nut cheerios, flour, bread crumbs, and a pre-made pizza crust. Several of Jeanette's expensive-looking shoes are mangled and left discarded wherever Lulu had pleased. The culprit at hand doesn't deny what she's done. In fact, she's currently spinning in circles, tongue flapping around the mess.

"We'll stay to help," Sophia says, looking horrified.

"No, it's fine," I say laughing. "You've all been stuck here way too long as it is. Lawrence needs to get his leg checked and call the med school to try and explain...well, explain something and get yourself another interview. Try charging your phone upstairs and see if it works with the water damage. If not, I can grab my laptop for you."

Lawrence looks horrified, remembering the reason why he came here in the first place. "Fuuuuck, I'm on it!" He uses his makeshift driftwood and seaweed crutches—now looking incredibly out of place in Jeanette and Scott's designer home—to take himself upstairs.

"Soph, your mom will literally kill you if you don't call her, like, now."

"Fair," she says, smiling and rolling her eyes. She follows Lawrence upstairs.

"Jupiter..." I say, grabbing the curve of her waist and kissing her on the cheek. "You've missed a lot of work. And your mom."

She sighs. "Your plumber said it was Friday, right?"

I look at my phone, which now miraculously has service again. A lot of spam emails, and a missed call from Jeanette (just last night, luckily).

"Yeah, it's Friday. We left Tuesday."

"Not good," she says, wincing. "Well, it's been a pleasure. Hopefully the house hasn't burned down and I still have a job."

"If you show up to work now and tell them you were lost in the woods, they would reasonably believe you."

She cackles, looking down at herself. "Not a bad idea, Tim."

I grab her hand, helpless to be helpful in any way.

"I'm sorry," she says. "It was a hell of a time while it lasted." Before I can respond, she kisses my cheek and walks away. I hear the front door open and quickly shut behind her. Lulu trots away as well, heading upstairs toward the commotion of Lawrence yelling. I shuffle behind her.

"I am a telepathic genius!!" he shouts.

My eyes are sagging and my body feels like it's about to collapse, but I smile nonetheless. When I enter the bedroom, I see the two of them are huddled by the nightstand, Sophia reading his laptop over his shoulder.

"Why are you telepathic now?" I ask.

"Dude!" Lawrence says, looking up, almost shaking. "I didn't say anything, but the whole time we were down there—except when we were dying and stuff—I was thinking 'well, maybe they might last-minute reschedule the interview or something?' And they fucking did! A bunch of the interviewers went out for dinner the day before and got food poisoning, so all of their scheduled interviews got backed up. Pun intended! They postponed mine 'til next week!"

"That's insane!" I say, clambering over the suitcases and giving him a clap on the back. "If you can't get into med school with telepathy, you're just not trying hard enough."

"Uugggh, yes!" Lawrence yells, hugging Sophia tightly.

"I know, love," she says, kissing his forehead. His eyes are welling with emotion, overcome by relief and fate.

I decide to slip out to give them privacy. I trot downstairs, thinking that now is as good a time to call back Jeanette as any. Of course she picks up within half a ring.

"Hello? Tim, hi, how is everything?"

"Good," I reply.

"Great, yes, I was just getting worried when I hadn't heard anything from you. Are you okay? You sound a little..."

I laugh into the receiver; I'm sure I don't sound nearly as healthy or eager as I had when we first met. An idea comes to mind, though.

"I know," I begin, "I got hit pretty hard the past few days by a cold, maybe the flu. I slept through most of the day yesterday so I missed your call. Everything here is great, though. Lulu might have scratched at a few things when I was sleeping yesterday, but nothing to report otherwise."

"Oh dear, I'm so sorry!" Jeanette says. She talks in one long-winded breath about everything I can find in the medicine cabinet and who to call if anything gets worse. She's tightly wound, but she really does care.

After a few more updates about the basement and their trip, we end the call. I shuffle back upstairs to check on Lawrence and Sophia, and I'm surprised to see that they're already packed to leave. Suddenly I feel terribly alone for the first time in days. It isn't just the loss of them, but everyone.

It must show, because Sophia immediately pulls me into a hug. "You haven't lost her, Tim. You know where she works; just get her number and spend whatever time you can together before this family comes home."

I nod my head. Maybe not convincingly.

"She clearly likes you," Sophia goes on. "She's just busy and has some life-cleaning she needs to do first. Make the effort and it'll work. I've never seen you as alive as when you were with her." Somehow, this makes it hurt more.

Lawrence, Sophia, and I painstakingly hobble across Jeanette's Autumn-adorned porch and toward their car. Sophia looks down at Lawrence limping, shaking her head.

"Are you going to drive and pretend your leg isn't a problem?" she says, half-joking.

I see Lawrence briefly glance at me, then look to the pavement. "Actually...my leg is killing me. It hurt the whole time down there, but now that the adrenaline's worn off I'm really not doing too hot. Could...you take me to the nearest clinic? If you're not too tired or anything?"

Sophia tries not to look surprised. "Of course, love. We can go right now." She guides Lawrence into the car, a gentle hand rubbing his back. Sophia helps him with the makeshift-crutches and adjusts his seat back to create more room. Before ducking gingerly in the car, Lawrence looks back at me, smiling sincerely.

"You're the best of us, Timmy-Tim."

I limp back inside, closing the door behind me. Lulu and I watch from the window as they drive off into the beautiful Autumn afternoon, down the long, winding path. Alone again.

"Tim, the boiler is fixed."

I turn, startled. I had forgotten Bobby was still down there. He had arguably rescued us from certain demise, and yet his quiet resolution to provide affordable plumbing service had overshadowed it all. I'm about to thank him profusely when he continues on, speaking hesitantly for the first time since I've met him.

"I have a few two-by-fours in the back of my pickup, and some cement. This isn't your house...but it may be wise for us to take care of that hole before the owners return. We don't need any more accidents. I assume you going down there was an accident?"

The question wasn't meant to be pointed, but an unease creeps over the both of us.

"Total accident," I say, thinking of the cave we had stumbled into, deep in the woods. Oliver had referred to this being the "Northern Passage," which was meaningless to us at the time. Who cares which way the compass is pointing when we need to get out? But you don't bother distinguishing an exit unless there are multiple. We carelessly stumbled through two...but how many other roads lead to Inferis? How many basements or casual hikes are a slip away from that deep abyss? They could be in other states—other countries, even—leading to regions of Inferis that even Oliver hasn't explored.

"I think that's a great idea, Bobby. Let's fill it now, if you have the time. I'll help."

He nods. "I have another appointment after this, but I can cancel. This is more important. I don't know how far in you delved, but it's best that it never happens again. Some secrets are best buried. Buried and forgotten." He averts his eyes as he says this, but a pained expression lies on his face. For a fleeting moment I think to ask him: have you been there before? To Inferis? However desperate I am to know, it's clear that he wants to forget. Bobby whistles and Lulu comes running to him.

"Come on, you two. Let's grab the materials."

We work in silence. The floorboards are replaced. The hole is filled.

CHAPTER 44

I dedicate my remaining strength to cleaning the house and playing with Lulu to make up for the neglect. The puppy-induced turmoil is shockingly easy to fix; picking up trash, poop scooping, Febreezing, vacuuming, and mopping does most of it. There are a few scratches on the pantry door and only one couch cushion is ripped. I find Jeanette's sewing kit in the closet and do my best to replace the stuffing and stitch it back together. I leave all of the windows open for good measure. A cool, fall breeze wafts in; that perfect, smoky smell of a neighbor burning leaves. I've noticed these things peripherally before, but today it feels like my senses are at the forefront of my existence.

As I finish the final inspection, my stress and adrenaline are drained to empty. My body screams. The ointment that Eleanor and Oliver had applied worked wonders, but I still have six gashes on my chest, shoulders, and back that are several inches long and fairly deep. One particularly jagged cut is still bleeding. I strip off my filthy clothes—mere rags at this point, caked in grime and tearing at the seams—and shower, the water blissful and painful all at once. My body is littered with bruises and scabs, each one a passport stamp from our time in Inferis. My mind continues to wander lazily. I turn the water off, dry myself, and dig through Scott and Jeanette's medicine cabinet to find antiseptic, gauze, bandages, and painkillers.

I pull on a clean pair of boxer shorts, the comfort of which almost makes me weep. I make my way back to the designer living room and splay myself lazily across the couch. Every motion hurts. My arms reach slowly, achingly toward the foot of the couch. I grab a thick, fuzzy blanket. Pull it toward me. Stretch it out. Unfold. Drape it across me. The windows are still open; another breeze tickles its way inside and across my face. My back softens into the cushions.

My laziness is contagious. Lulu sits next to me on the floor, while I absently scratch behind her ear with my drooping hand. This is far too much separation, she decides, and quickly gets on the couch by my feet, curling in a ball. I close my eyes momentarily, until I feel more wriggling. Still too far apart. Her body nuzzles up into the wedge between my body and the back of the couch. Her nose points up toward me, eyes slowly drooping shut in unison with mine.

A thousand moments and a thousand memories wash over me like a tide. The remainder of the day gradually dims as the sunlight fades against the living room. A scarlet haze softens to a violet glow, not so different from the one I had grown used to seeing below. A dim twilight settles in the room, lit by the quiet light of a near full moon and a few neon-green dots on the ceiling's smoke detector. I see a few stars in the distance...and I feel no need to escape to them. Not anymore. They can rest easy with me and Lulu tonight. Time passes in a slow blur. Nothing happens, and nothing needs to happen. I am so grateful for all of it; every second. This blanket is the softest and warmest thing I have ever felt.

EPILOGUE

"Fancy seeing you here," I say, leaning against the counter. She smirks, closing her register after her last customer of the evening. The ringing bell signals their exit. "If you're here to look at eggs for an hour, I'm afraid we're closing soon. Sir," she adds, raising her eyebrows."

"No shopping for me today," I say. "I just came by to see you."

"How lovely," she says, genuinely pleased. "How is Lawrence's leg?"

"I got a text from him and Soph the day after we all got back. It's broken in three places, but no surgery needed at least. We're hoping the giant cast gives him some sympathy votes for his med school interviews, too. Any major fallout from going missing for a few days?"

Jupiter cackles, taking her nametag off her black polo and flicking a switch to turn off the glowing "Open" on the window. "Almost none at all. I showed up the day of, just as you suggested, and I looked so terrible that I barely had to explain what happened. They insisted that I take another day off, actually. My mom hardly knew what day it was or that I had been missing," she says, rolling her eyes. "Aside from her being somewhat behind on meals and cleaning, no significant change. Things are...back to normal."

"How back to normal?" I ask.

She looks at me shrewdly and shrugs. "It all looks and feels the same to me. What happened was all just a strange dream. A vacation from it all."

"Right. And I am leaving in a few weeks to go back home, anyway." She nods.

"Oh yeah," I continue, "we're still on for our shopping trip this Tuesday, though, right? I do owe you a new sweatshirt. And I bet Sommers is picturesque in the snow, we should probably make plans next month too, right?" I try keeping a straight face, but I rarely get the opportunity to catch Jupiter off guard.

"But you're leaving...?"

"Right," I say, "but the invention of the automobile is really doing wonders for modern transportation. So I can go home as I choose, and then hang out with you whenever you'd like. It'd be two hours each way, and we can meet in the middle sometimes. If...you're interested."

She pretends to glare at me through her heavy mascara. "And what gives you the impression that I would want to spend my one day off with you, Timothy?"

"Whether you'd enjoy it I can't say. I could just Venmo you for the sweatshirt I threw off the bone tower, but then there'd be far less opportunity for you to tease me about it. All I know is that I would really like to get to know you better."

Her face reddens. "You're sure you'd want to keep commuting up here so often? Seriously, with work and my mom, I wouldn't be able to put in as much effort."

"I know, and with where you're at right now I don't expect you to. Don't take this the wrong way..." I begin, finally getting nervous myself. "I was actually thinking about moving here."

"Here...?" she says. "Why?"

I sigh, thinking about how big of a step it is. "A lot of reasons. Weill Cornell is Lawrence's top medical school choice, and he's too weird to admit it but his scores and resumé are unbelievable; I know he'll get in. Sophia's planning to move with him wherever he goes, and they're my closest friends. So if they're nearby and you're nearby, it just makes sense. I don't know...I just keep focusing my life around a vague career ambition, even though that's never brought me an ounce of joy or purpose. Being around beauty and people I care about might be the answer I've been looking for. I can find a paycheck anywhere, so long as it allows me to prioritize what matters."

"Well, you have a lot of thinking to do," she says after a brief pause. It's impossible to read her expression, but that won't stop me from trying. "Until then, it's great to see you while I still can. Help me close up so we can get the hell out?"

"I'd love to," I say. "What do you need me to do?"

"Your first task is to stay there and not break anything while I count out the register. And no funny business; we're on the clock."

"Absolutely," I say, leaning across the counter to kiss Jupiter.

Did you love *Inferis*? Then you should read *The Scholar's Sanctum* by Chris Delude!

Cleo Thompson might lose everything after his PhD advisor threatens to cut his scholarship. Desperate for dissertation results, Cleo discovers not only a budding romance with a young faculty member, but a new source that could save him. Underneath his university library, he finds a hidden tunnel to an occult academy known as the Sanctum. Surrounded by the dangerous, knowledge-obsessed scholars in this surreal gothic landscape, Cleo is forced to confront what he's willing to sacrifice for a single book. Unfortunately, the Sanctum does not welcome outsiders.

The Scholar's Sanctum is a story of obsession, self-discovery...and survival.

About the Author

Chris Delude is a public health researcher, administrator, and advocate. In his free time, he is the author of the novels *The Scholar's Sanctum* and *Inferis*. Chris lives in Boston, Massachusetts with his brilliant wife, Margaret.

For more information about his writing and future project announcements, visit: www.chrisdelude.com

www.ingramcontent.com/pod-product-compliance
Lightning Source LLC
Chambersburg PA
CBHW031951240626
47153CB00003B/946